BURIED SECRETS

ROD MCKEOUGH

BALBOA.
PRESS

A DIVISION OF HAY HOUSE

Balboa Press books may be ordered through booksellers or by contacting:

Balboa Press
A Division of Hay House
1663 Liberty Drive
Bloomington, IN 47403
www.balboapress.com.au
1-(877) 407-4847

ISBN: 978-1-4525-0977-8 (sc)
ISBN: 978-1-4525-0978-5 (e)

Printed in the United States of America

Balboa Press rev. date: 04/09/2013

CONTENTS

PROLOGUE

G uy studied the newspaper clipping in his hand. The headline
"Human remains found in mine shaft." was indelibly etched in
his memory. A feeling of sadness and melancholy overwhelmed him
and he blinked away tears, as he ripped the clipping into tiny pieces.
Exasperated, he tossed them out the window of the car, before opening
the door and stepping out.

He placed his hands in the pockets of his trousers and stood in
reverent silence, as he looked into the sunlit valley below. Nestled in
the centre of the valley was Roxborough, the small township of his
youth. A river, its contours smooth and brown like a sunning snake,
twisted its way past the town.

Though it was now bathed in sunshine, his memories of Roxborough
were at once clouded in a mask of intrigue and death. He was returning
to his home town, struggling with grief over the sudden death of a dear
childhood friend, who had been a close ally during his teenage years. He
choked back a sob and brushed away the tears trickling down his cheek.

His train of thought was interrupted by another car door
slamming nearby. Thirty seconds later he was joined by a woman.
Reassuringly, she took his hand and rested her head on his shoulder.
Together they surveyed the scene below. Although twenty years had
passed, the memory of that summer of '64 remained undimmed. As a
teenager, barely sixteen-years-old, he had met the girl of his dreams.
Unfortunately his relationship with her had ultimately led to a tragic
death and a murder trial.

It was the summer that had changed his life forever.

CHAPTER 1

THE SUMMER OF 1964

A hot sun in a clear blue cloudless sky greeted me as I left my father's grocery store in Roxborough and wandered down the main street. Summers were usually hot and this was no exception. A heat haze shimmered above the roadway and the pavement was like a bed of hot coals. I could feel the heat rising up through my feet as I walked, prompting me to quicken my stride. There was silence—broken neither by any soft breeze to rustle the papers scattered in the gutter, nor the rumble of cars passing by. Apart from a few vehicles parked in the street and two or three people walking aimlessly by, the main street was deserted.

It was a typical Saturday afternoon and as was the custom, I was meeting my friends at the local cafeteria in the central square to discuss plans for the weekend. As I entered the café, I could hear the music from the jukebox above the incessant chatter of teenage voices. Tired ceiling fans, which had worked too hard on many searing summer days, had already lost their battle to circulate cool air in a room packed with teenagers and a few adults. I stood in the doorway, looking from right to left for a familiar body or voice.

"Guy!"

I spun in the direction of the sound and spotted my friends in the back corner of the room. They waved to me as I grabbed a Coke and moved in and out of the tables and towards them. We were all sixteen and lived in the same street.

I sat next to Ivan, grinning inwardly at the infinite care he must have taken with his appearance: not one blond hair out of place, even his sandals were polished. I sipped on the Coke.

"Geez it's hot!" I remarked, wiping the perspiration from my forehead.

"Yeah!" he replied, as he finished downing a milkshake. He carefully wiped his mouth with the back of his hand.

"How come you never look hot? I'm sweating like a pig and you . . . well you . . . not a sign!" I remarked.

"Dunno! The heat doesn't really affect me much," he answered nonchalantly.

"I saw your dad loading the trailer. Goin' somewhere?"

"Yeah! We're going away for a holiday. Dad has four weeks off work," Ivan grinned.

Ivan's dad, a Hungarian immigrant, worked at the local sawmills.

"When ya going?" I asked, as I leaned back in my chair, and placed the icy cold bottle against my forehead.

"Next week."

"Then why is he loading the trailer now? He's got plenty of time."

"Dad likes to be prepared. He'll load most of the gear now. The rest he'll load the day before we leave."

"My dad would wait till the last moment and then he'd get angry at everyone because he had to rush it or he'd forgotten something," I said.

"What about you, Georgie? Goin' away?" I asked my friend, sitting opposite.

"Huh?" he grunted.

Georgie Henderson had an intellectual disability and sometimes it took him a while to understand what you were saying.

"Are you going away for a holiday or staying here?" I repeated.

"My dad can't afford a holiday so I'm staying in Roxborough," he answered, running his hand through his thick, dark curly hair.

Georgie then proceeded to pick at the multitude of pimples that blemished his face. All this time, his restless, inquisitive eyes moved constantly—at once observing everything, yet comprehending little. Sometimes, it was difficult to grab and retain his attention.

"Looks like you and me, Guy!" He grinned.

I muttered, "Good to know Georgie."

I wasn't being petulant or sarcastic about spending my holidays with Georgie. In fact he was good company. I was simply frustrated because Ivan was leaving Roxborough for four weeks and I was, I had to concede, just a little jealous. I wasn't looking forward to spending another vacation at home.

At the end of the table sat the pin-up boy of our group, Billy Jenkins. He had his back turned to us as he chatted to some of his football mates. He was easily recognised as an unabashed fan of Elvis with his long, slick, black hair complemented by the mandatory blue jeans and jacket he wore like a uniform.

"How ya goin' Billy?" I asked loudly, to get his attention.

He did not reply at first, but eventually turned around, to acknowledge my presence.

"Fine! How's it goin' Harmon?" he answered with a grin.

"Hot!" I replied.

"Yeah! Too hot! I need another drink."

Like most city-bred boys, Billy moved in a manner that was different from his country peers. He carried himself across the room with a blatant swagger, exuding an air of confidence. As I watched him, I remembered when he arrived in town with his father, Jim Jenkins, the local policeman. I had helped Billy settle into the house opposite mine. He had confided in me about his mother deserting him at an early age. I didn't ask why, but assumed it was because his father transformed into an abusive, loud, foul-mouthed man when he drank—and he was a man who certainly liked a drink.

On many nights, I heard him arguing loudly with his father. Sometimes I heard Billy cry out in pain and I guessed he'd been hit. My suspicions were vindicated when I saw him with welts and bruising on his face following an argument with his father. Billy always proffered a viable excuse, so I chose to ignore both the rumours that were generated by some townsfolk and the physical evidence of his injuries. I didn't envy his life—no mother and an abusive father.

"Watcha doin?"

A thump on my arm followed this greeting, heralding the arrival of the last of our group, Samantha Bennett.

Without looking up and turning around I remarked, "Well! We were just saying how quiet it was without Sam. Then you turned up!"

I grinned, expecting another thump but instead I got an angry retort.

"Okay! I know when I'm not wanted. I'll go. See ya!"

As she turned to go I grabbed her arm and hastily apologised, realising she was angry.

"I was only joking. Sit down, silly!" I said, motioning to the chair beside me.

Sam pouted and remained standing. "Only if you say 'I'm a great big girl'."

Both Ivan and Georgie giggled as I blushed. "No way!" I exclaimed.

She pulled away from my grip. I quickly mumbled, "Okay! I'm a great big girl."

"Sorry! I can't hear you."

She was goading me—and it worked. Without thinking, I shouted, "I'm a great big girl."

Everyone in the room automatically stared in my direction. I could feel the blood rushing to my face as I rested my head on the table. I tried to cover my embarrassment by hiding in the crook of one arm. Ivan, Georgie and Sam laughed hysterically and soon everyone else joined in.

Sam sat alongside me, grabbed my Coke and took a swig. She enjoyed teasing me and I tolerated her antics because she was my best friend, even though she was a girl. Back then it was unusual for a sixteen-year-old boy to have a girl as a best friend but I had grown up with Sam. From an early age she had followed me around. We had done many things together and I found it difficult to imagine not having her around, even though she could be a pest at times. She took off her cap and ruffled her honey blonde hair.

She grinned and winked. "Well, You should know by now that no-one messes with Sam. Isn't that right Georgie?"

A huge smile crossed Georgie's face as he agreed, "Yep! No-one messes with Sam."

Sam lived in the same street as the rest of us. She was a tomboy. Her father had wanted his first child to be a boy and had even picked out the name—Sam. When she was born, Sam became Samantha. She spent more time with us than with girls her own age. To look at her, you'd think she was a boy—jeans, shirt hanging out untidily and a baseball cap tucked firmly on her head hiding her hair.

Spare time in Roxborough allowed teenagers a raft of pursuits. We 'hung out' with friends, played sport and rode our motor bikes on the dirt roads and tracks on the outskirts of town. Sometimes we went hunting. Most teenagers had access to a gun and the forest areas were perfect for hunting. Many sixteen-year-old boys occupied their spare time by pursuing the local girls but Ivan, Georgie and I were rather self-conscious and shy. As a result, girls were off limits for us three, at least for the time being.

Billy Jenkins had already logged plenty of experiences with the opposite sex and compensated for our inexperience with his ever-present eagerness to regale us with his many escapades with girls from the city as well as local girls.

I looked around at the others expectantly, "What are we doing?"

"Well!" suggested Ivan, "I thought we might go to the Waterhole."

"Sounds great! Let's go! Ivan with me and Sam with Georgie."

Sam smiled sweetly at Georgie, "How about I ride your bike?"

She was trying to provoke a reaction and she got it. The immediate look of disappointment on Georgie's face prompted her to add, "Only joking."

We all knew how much Georgie loved riding his bike.

The Waterhole was about twenty minutes from the town, at the foot of the mountains. It was a quiet area surrounded by trees and was only accessible by bikes or off-road vehicles. Few adults used it and so it was a popular swimming hole for the youth of the town. Ivan was the only one of us who didn't have a bike, so he always rode with me.

I moved around the table to get Billy's attention and said loudly, "We're going to the Waterhole. Coming?"

He gave me a cursory glance and answered, "Okay! But later ... see you there!"

We left him chatting and laughing with his friends and walked home to gather our gear and bikes. It was almost two in the afternoon when we had finally pushed our bikes to the outskirts of town.

We rode across the noisy wooden bridge traversing the Karinya River and sped up the bitumen road towards the mountains. Ten minutes later, we turned off the highway onto a winding dirt road. The road gradually disappeared and became a narrow track as it coiled its way through the forest. All I could hear above the gentle hum of the 125cc motorbikes was the crackling noises of leaves and twigs beneath our tyres, as we raced along the forest floor.

Georgie was a fearless rider but his fearlessness often ended with him lying in a ditch because he was speeding or doing something else that required more forethought than he was able to summon. Today he had to follow me so there would be no silly accidents. For once, he had to ride in the slipstream of dust rolling back from behind my bike. The further we progressed, the denser the forest became, the shade canopy of the trees shielding us from the oppressive heat of the sun.

CHAPTER 2

THE WATERHOLE

About fifteen minutes later we arrived at the Waterhole and parked our bikes under a tree. We had our swimming gear on under our clothing so in a matter of seconds Georgie, Ivan and I were ready to dive into the water. Sam had moved away to the other side of the tree to remove her top and shorts and joined us shortly after. She smiled in amusement at our gaping mouths and transfixed eyes. Georgie gave a loud wolf whistle and smiled.

"What?" Sam asked with a grin.

She was wearing a black one-piece swimsuit and it was plain to see she had developed into a lovely young woman. The black swimsuit highlighted her curves and all we three males could do was stare. Our preoccupation was rather rude but Sam had certainly filled out in the last few months.

She repeated, "What?"

She laughed at our embarrassment as we tried to mask the fact we'd been ogling her. I knew that I could never again look at her as one of the boys—not ever. I glanced at the others and I knew instantly that they felt the same way. In a short time Sam had changed into a Samantha.

I mumbled, "Um . . . you look different."

"How?"

Her cheeky grin showed that she knew what I was thinking. In accord with her basic character Sam was enjoying seeing us squirm.

"The last time I saw you in swimmers you were a skinny kid just like a . . ."

My voice trailed off and I looked at Ivan for support but he'd turned away and pretended to busy himself tidying up his clothes. Georgie . . . well Georgie just stared, his mouth agape. Neither of them were any help.

Sam finished the sentence for me. "A boy?"

Before I could answer Georgie had recovered his vocal ability and blurted out, "You've got tits!"

Trust Georgie to be honest. Sam, Ivan and I burst out laughing. Georgie was puzzled for a moment but joined in when he realised we were laughing at his remark. He reached into a bag on the side of his bike and pulled out a bottle of beer. He tied a cord around the top of the bottle and gently lowered it into the cool water.

"Where'd you get that?" I asked, knowing full well he had stolen it from his dad's secret stash. I grabbed two packets of cigarettes from my bike and placed them on a rock under the tree. We all laughed again, in the knowledge that Georgie was not the only bandit in our midst, since I had taken them from my father's store.

"One day you two will get caught and cop it," grinned Ivan.

I scrambled down the bank and into the water. It was cool and the slippery mud oozed between my toes as I waded out to where the water was waist deep. Before I could turn to the others, I was bombarded by Georgie who threw himself into the water like an exploding bomb, quickly followed by Ivan and Sam. They stood up, shaking the water from their faces and laughing like little children. They had expected me to retaliate but I had dived under the water and disappeared temporarily, breaking the surface some five yards away. We dived and swam, enjoying the respite from the summer heat.

The Waterhole was at the base of a small waterfall that trickled down the mountainside. Oak trees stood like sentinels on all sides, their large overhanging branches protecting us from the sun. Intermittent rays of sunlight broke through and glimmered on the surface of the water that was largely shrouded by the canopy of leaves. The dark, tranquil water reflected the surrounding landscape. A tattered, worn rope hung from the branch of a gnarled oak and we used it to swing out and drop from a great height into the water. Here was a perfect spot to spend a relaxing few hours on a Saturday afternoon.

After spending almost an hour in the water we scrambled out and sat under a tree to smoke cigarettes and drink some of Georgie's cold beer. I really didn't like smoking or drinking beer but for reasons I could not deny, it made me feel more grown-up. Ivan declined both the cigarette and beer offered him.

By contrast, Georgie loved to imitate the actions of adults by dangling a cigarette from his mouth or trying, usually unsuccessfully, to blow smoke rings. Without fail, he would always deliver a loud gut wrenching belch after gulping down the beer and then look at us with a silly grin on his face, waiting for our response.

Sam was willing to try anything but after a puff on my cigarette and a mouthful of beer she screwed up her face and declared, "That's awful! My mum says kissing a man who smokes and drinks is disgusting. Now, I am sure she is right."

Ivan grinned, "So who have you kissed lately?"

"Don't be silly! Nobody . . . yuck!" retorted Sam.

This was an opportunity I couldn't miss. Sam took pleasure in making fun at my expense and now was my chance, for once, to turn the tables.

BURIED SECRETS

I teased, "Come on . . . I've seen you eyeing off Robbie Kirkland. I bet you kissed him."

"Yuck! I don't like him so there . . . What about you? Who have you kissed?"

That shut me up. Trust Sam to find a weakness in my makeup. My pride was salvaged by Georgie who had returned from the water's edge.

"Where ya going on ya holidays, Ivan?" he asked, as he scratched his legs. He had splattered mud on them and let it bake dry. He took great delight in peeling off the dry mud.

"We're going to Pindimar Beach—on the coast."

He grinned as the rest of us, po-faced and envious, sat staring into the water.

Our conversation was interrupted by the arrival of Billy and his friends. The Waterhole quickly became a noisy, frenetic place with plenty of loud squealing and laughter as members of the group dived and swam. After the beer, none of us was in the mood to join them so we sat and watched in silence. Finally, Sam decided to join a group of girls sitting near the water's edge.

Several boys dived and swam under water towards girls and tried to pull off their bikini tops, much to the delight of the other boys. Georgie revelled in this spectacle and was keen to get back into the water. Billy stood on the bank and chatted to Lauren, a beautiful blonde in a brief bikini. She had a reputation in town—the local scuttlebutt insisted that she had lost her virginity at age twelve. My outlook, albeit based only on flimsy personal experience, was that she and Billy were made for each other.

Sam yelled out to us from the water. I held out my arms and cupped my hands behind my ears to indicate that I couldn't hear her. She motioned for us to join her. I shook my head slowly but

— 11 —

Georgie needed no further prompting. He dived in and proceeded to demonstrate his skills as a swimmer—no doubt hoping the girls would be suitably impressed. Ivan and I joined him for a while but after ten minutes or so, left the water to sit and resume watching. Soon after, Georgie, who had been shunned by most of the group, came and sat beside us. These were Billy's friends, not ours.

"The girls certainly like him," I remarked as I watched Billy flit from one girl to another.

"Good luck to him," muttered Ivan, "I don't really care. I don't like him much."

"Me neither," chimed in Georgie.

All this time, Georgie had not taken his eyes from Billy and the girls. He was a little envious of Billy's popularity.

"He's okay!" I said, "At least he talks to us—not like some of the others."

Ivan agreed, "Yeah! I suppose so."

"How did Hank Jones become a member of Billy's gang?" asked Ivan. "It isn't because he can play sport, because he can't."

Hank was not typical of Billy's friends. His rather florid, fleshy face with dim beady eyes stationed above a bulbous nose and a large oversized mouth completed a most unappealing package. Straggly ginger hair sprouted from his head like a wet mop and all this sat atop a too-plump body.

"Nah! It's because his father has lots of money. Hank gives them treats like cigarettes and beer. I don't think any of Billy's group really like him at all," I answered as Hank strolled towards us.

I was about to suggest we pack up and leave when Hank walked over to Georgie and stood in front of him, his posture exuding menace.

Hank had one major behavioural flaw. It was he often said things on the spur of the moment, without thinking of the possible consequences. This, and the fact he was cruel and vindictive, meant he was not well liked.

Because it rhymed with his first name, he was nicknamed "Tank," although some members of the group maintained that he did, in fact, resemble a slow moving army tank. Since Hank the Tank delighted in teasing and taunting those who would not fight back, Georgie was always one of his prime targets.

"Hey Georgie! Bet you can't dive from that branch!" he smirked, pointing to a tree branch, overhanging the water hole. He knew that Georgie would take up the challenge.

"Leave him alone Jonesie!" I said sharply, moving towards him.

Georgie looked upwards. Despite his signature fearlessness, even Georgie knew that it was too high, his acknowledgement showing upon his face.

"Keep out of it Harmon!" Hank said, "Georgie can make up his own mind. Can't you Georgie? Or are you chicken?"

Hank bent over, placed his hands in his armpits and strutted up and down, imitating the sound of a chicken, much to the amusement of the other teenagers. He tried hard to compensate for his physical shortcomings by being a clown, continually cracking jokes as he aimed to keep everyone entertained. Their laughter encouraged him to persist with his taunts.

"What's the matter, chicken boy? No brains? No guts?"

Ivan stood up and moved towards Hank threateningly, his face twisted in anger.

"Why don't you do it, Tank? Let's see how brave you are. On second thoughts you'd better not . . . You'd break the branch with your weight," he growled, menacingly.

I had never seen Ivan so angry. In fact, I'd never even seen him involved in a confrontation, either physical or verbal. However, he was very protective of Georgie.

Hank's face darkened.

"Go back to your hole, wog boy," he muttered through clenched teeth.

Infuriated, Ivan charged at Hank. At the last split-second Hank stepped aside and pushed him to the ground. Before Ivan could get up to resume his attack, Georgie stepped forward and said, "Leave him alone; I'll do it."

"Don't be silly Georgie! It's not safe," I yelled; however, my warning was too late because Georgie had already scrambled halfway up the tree.

I grabbed Hank by the arm and threatened, "If he gets hurt, you'll pay for it Jones. I'll get you—you big fat turd!"

I saw the unmistakable flicker of fear in his eyes before he wrenched his arm away.

As he moved back to the safe proximity of his friends he retorted, "It's his choice. I'm not forcing him."

I glanced towards Billy but he was too pre-occupied with Lauren to notice. I helped Ivan regain his feet and we implored Georgie to come down but he was determined to prove to Hank he could do it. By this time, Hank and a few others were provoking Georgie and urging him to climb higher.

Ivan and I moved to the water's edge and prepared ourselves for the worst. Sam joined us. Georgie reached the branch but lost his nerve when he looked down.

He grasped the branch tightly, a mixture of terror and desperation etched on his face. I raced to the tree and began to climb. Hank and his mates continued to taunt their quarry.

One of the girls in the water shouted, "Leave him alone Hank! Can't you see he wants to come down?"

Another called out, "It's not funny anymore, Jonesie. Shut up!"

Sam chimed in, "He's had enough. Come down Georgie!"

I began climbing, directing Georgie to remain where he was. Finally, I got close enough to reach out to him, but before I could, there was a loud crack as the branch he clung to began to sag. Georgie looked at me, his eyes terror-stricken as I tried again to grab him. There was another audible crack as the branch gave way. Georgie uttered a cry as he plummeted into the water. I peered down. There was absolute silence as all eyes became fixed on the spot where he entered the water.

Ivan, followed by two other boys, dived below the surface to search for Georgie. I scrambled down the tree trunk and ran to the water's edge. Ivan and his two helpers surfaced with Georgie's motionless body; as they made their way towards me I dived in and helped bring him up onto the bank. Unsure of what else to do, I knelt down and put my head near his to determine if he was still breathing. He was.

We discovered that one of the group had done a first aid course and he took over. He began to resuscitate Georgie. Some of the teenagers gathered around, uneasy and tense, mumbling, "Come on Georgie!" The rest stood back, silent and watchful, their former joviality instantly forgotten. After a short time, Georgie's body convulsed and a stream of water gushed from his mouth. There was an immediate cheer from the onlookers. Georgie gazed up at me, his face ashen and miserable. He had a large gash on his head and the blood, mixed with water, ran steadily down the side of his head, making the injury look worse than it really was. He smiled weakly as he sat up, assisted by Sam.

"I showed him, didn't I Guy?" he whispered hoarsely.

"You sure did Georgie; you sure did," I whispered and then turned abruptly, looking for Hank Jones.

Everyone turned with me. Hank was standing apart from the group looking miserable, knowing full well that I was going to get him. He tried to remain defiant in front of his friends.

"I didn't make him go up there, so you can't blame me!"

He saw my face and stumbled backwards. I felt a sudden and almost irresistible urge to smash my fists into his face. I tried to temper the rage boiling within me but when I looked back at Georgie sitting on the ground clutching his bloody head, I clenched my fists tightly and rushed at Tank knocking him to the ground. Venting my anger, I punched him repeatedly. He staggered to his feet, blood pouring from his nose, as tears streamed down his flushed face. As he fled from my attack I turned to the group who had watched my actions in silence.

"Those of you, who egged Georgie on, are nothing but a bunch of shit heads. You make me sick!" I muttered, angrily.

Billy had never seen me in such a state of agitation and was taken aback but quickly recovered his composure. He shrugged indifferently and moved away. I helped Georgie to his feet. Ivan and Sam grabbed our gear as Billy dived back into the water. A few of the onlookers moved across to commiserate Georgie but most took Billy's lead and followed him, disciple-like, into the Waterhole.

Sam and I helped Georgie to the bikes and we set off home. Sam rode Georgie's bike with Ivan on the back while I took Georgie on my bike.

On the way home, none of the four of us exchanged a solitary word. When we arrived in Roxborough, we went to my house to tend to Georgie's head wound. The gash was about two inches long but the bleeding had almost been stemmed.

In fact, there were extensive bloodstains on the back of my shirt where Georgie had rested his head for the duration of the journey from the Waterhole to town. Sam took control of cleaning the wound and bandaging his head while I changed my clothes and also got a clean shirt for Georgie.

"I think you'll be okay," I said, "What ya going to tell your parents?"

"I suppose I'll tell them I fell out of a tree," Georgie shrugged.

"If you do that they'll probably ban you from going out to the Waterhole. They'll say it's too dangerous. Mine would," said Ivan.

Georgie had an anxious look on his face. "Don't worry! Just say we were mucking about and you weren't looking where you were going and you ran into the branch of a tree. They'll believe you," I reassured him. Georgie nodded.

Ivan grinned at me. "You sure sent Hank packing. You should have seen his face."

"Yeah! Well he deserved it. And those others, well, they egged him on. They were just as bad. I don't want anything to do with Billy or that group of his. They can go to hell! All of them!"

Georgie joined in, "Yeah! They can all go to hell."

Sam gave Georgie a hug, and then hugged both Ivan and me before she left. This was a first. Sam had revealed a new aspect to her personality, a soft side that I most certainly had been unaware of previously. Georgie and Ivan also left soon after Sam's departure, leaving me to clean up. I finished just as my mother arrived home with my brother and sister.

CHAPTER 3

THE GIFTS

Saturday night was movie night in Roxborough. Ivan's sister Anna took us to the movies in her car. Similar in appearance to Ivan, she had the characteristic clear pale skin, brown eyes and long blonde hair of a young woman with a mid-European heritage. She was nineteen and at University in the city so I didn't get many opportunities to see her.

Georgie didn't come so I took my brother, Marty and sister, Jan, both younger than me. The local cinema was in the main street, and for the younger folk. going to the movies on Saturday nights was a tradition, no matter what movie was playing. As usual there was a crowd but I was relieved not to see either Billy or Hank.

I didn't remember much about the movie because most of the time I was sneaking furtive glances at Anna who sat beside me. I looked slyly at the movement of her breasts beneath her thin blouse and at her shapely, tanned legs only partially covered by her brief shorts. Thankfully, Ivan and the others were too engrossed in the movie to notice my interest in her.

When we arrived home I sprawled on my bed and read until almost eleven o'clock. My eyes began to droop and the lids felt suddenly heavy, so I decided to go to sleep. As I moved to the window to pull down the blind, I noticed a light in the window of Anna's room next door. It wasn't really next door because there was a vacant block between our house and the Mavrak home. After the movie experience tonight I had been unable to erase Anna from my thoughts and I was definitely eager to see more of her so I clambered out the window and scampered across the vacant block to the Mavrak house. My pulse began racing, partly in anticipation of seeing Anna so close and partly because of the danger involved. I had never before done this—or even anything remotely like it.

I crept to Anna's window and cautiously peeped in. She stood in front of a mirror near the window. I shrank back, hoping she hadn't seen me. By the time I moved forward again, she had taken off her blouse and was about to shed her bra. I almost groaned out loud when I saw her firm, milky white breasts. My pulse quickened as I stood outside her window, transfixed by her beauty. When she reached down I knew she was removing her shorts but my eyes were below the level of the window sill and I couldn't see in. I stretched up on my toes but to no avail.

Thankfully, she moved back into the middle of the room and I saw she was wearing red panties. I waited for what seemed to be an eternity, in the hope she would remove them but to my extreme disappointment, she walked over to the window. As I crouched, Anna pulled down the blind and shortly after, the light went out. I returned to my room in a state of ecstasy, because it was the first time I had seen a young woman's breasts. For me, a naïve sixteen-year-old, this was indeed a big deal.

I was woken in the morning by something tickling me. Eyes still closed, I brushed at my nose several times, trying to get rid of the source of irritation. A girlish giggle followed and I opened my eyes to find Sam perched on my bed, feather in hand.

"Time to get up, sleepyhead! Your mum's got breakfast ready."

I rubbed the sleep from my eyes, sat up and mumbled, "Tell mum I'll be there in a few minutes."

"She told me you'd take forever. Come on! Up you get!"

She grabbed the bedclothes and tried to pull them from the bed. I resisted her efforts vigorously in an attempt to cover my modesty,

"Sam, I'm not wearing PJs. I'm in my underpants . . . nothing else."

Since before either of us had started school, Sam had often come to my house and woken me. However, things were different now. We were both growing up and I was not comfortable having a teenage girl wearing tiny shorts and a singlet top sitting on the end of my bed.

"Shy are we? Come on. I have a brother, so I've seen it all."

She tugged at the bedclothes again and gave a mischievous grin. Exasperated, I yanked back harder and she flew forward into my arms. She lay on my chest, her face inches from mine and her warm, soft body pressing down. She made no effort to roll away.

"My, my . . . Guy's blushing," she grinned.

I had every right to blush. I was uncomfortable because deep within me a horde of strange feelings was stirring. I tried to remain calm. Sam was enjoying every part of our interaction—our closeness, my discomfort and my embarrassment.

My unease magnified when my mum yelled out, "Guy! Are you up yet?"

Sam giggled as she reached forward and gave me a sisterly peck on the cheek. She rolled off the bed and ambled out the door.

At the table, whenever my eyes met Sam's, I blushed and she giggled. I was happy Marty and Jan were not around to ask those awkward sibling questions.

"What's with you? What's the big joke?" Mum had noticed my discomfort.

Sam replied, "Nothing really, Mrs Harmon. Guy's embarrassed. He's not used to seeing me dressed like this and he's a little self-conscious."

"I see. We've become so used to seeing you in jeans and shirt, Sam. Now you look very pretty. You are growing up quickly, right in front of our very eyes. Don't you agree, Guy?"

I could feel the blood rushing to my face again as they both laughed. I had nowhere to turn to shield my awkwardness, breakfast tables not being noted safe havens for sixteen-year-old boys in a state of conflicted emotion.

"That answers my question. Wouldn't you agree Sam?"

Sam smiled while I lowered my head and tried to eat breakfast. Ivan's timely arrival saved me from any more questions. I noticed him stealing a few glances at Sam and I had to concede that she had indeed blossomed into a very pretty young woman—worthy of more than just a few glances.

"Ready to get your hands dirty!" asked Sam as I finished the last of my breakfast.

"What?" I asked, knowing full well what she meant.

She screwed up her nose. "You haven't forgotten that you promised to help fix my bike today."

"Oh! That!"

"Yes, that!" she said, punching me on the arm.

I turned to Ivan. "What about it, Iv? Wanna help me fix her crappy bike?"

Sam punched me again and I smiled. We strolled down the street towards her house. She took us to the garage where I worked on the bike. Ivan, who knew little about bikes, was happy to sit and watch or hand me whatever tools I needed. Unlike Ivan, Sam could not stand by and watch.

The 'tomboy' Sam won a skirmish with the new-look Samantha and she rushed inside to change. When she came back out she was wearing an old pair of jeans and a long-sleeved checked shirt. It was a relief to work without her distracting me as we repaired the bike together.

By lunch time we had the bike repaired, ready once more for active duty. When we finished I wiped my oily hands on a rag but Sam decided to wipe hers on my face. What followed was a wrestling match as I attempted to prevent her covering my face with oil and dirt. It ended with war paint smeared all over my face and body. When Sam was a little girl it was easy to wrestle her, but now she was a young woman, I felt uncomfortable . . . uncomfortable and different. It was a totally new experience for me but one I had to admit I enjoyed. Ivan copped it too, much to his mock disgust but it was good natured fun that neither of us minded.

Sam hopped on the bike and roared down the street and back. This was not the girl who had woken me so many times over so many years.

"Let's go to the quarry after lunch," she said, after parking her bike.

"Okay. Wanna come Ivan?" I asked.

Even though Ivan didn't ride bikes I was always keen for him to feel part of the group. Maybe I could get him to ride my bike, once we got to the quarry. If not, he could watch Sam and me.

"I'll have to ask my mother but it should be okay," he answered.

Sam butted in, "You can ride with me, Ivan. I'm a much better rider than Guy."

"Says who?" I shot back.

"Says me. What about it, Iv. Do you trust me?"

Sam grinned. Ivan shrugged and replied, "Sure. No worries."

Sam's mum had prepared sandwiches for lunch but Ivan declined politely, saying that he was expected home. After eating we reunited and travelled out of town along a gravel road that twisted its way through the many farms on the northern side of the Karinya River. Ivan clung to Sam as she sped along. He hung on, no doubt enjoying the novelty of wrapping his arms tightly around a pretty girl. Eventually, we reached a rock quarry that had been carved into the side of the mountain.

The quarry was no longer in use and it was a popular spot for bike riders because of the mounds of soil and scattered rocks within its precinct. Although the quarry itself was filled with water it wasn't regarded as a safe swimming location.

There was a danger sign clearly visible on the fence that bounded the whole quarry area. However, we soon found an opening in the mesh and made our way in. Ten years ago, the story went, a young man had died in the quarry water after diving in and hitting a metal post hidden in the murk. The area was open to the sun and a dirt track encircled the water. Ivan perched on a rock under the only tree within the quarry site and watched as Sam and I roared around the track on our bikes, hurtling over mounds of soil as we raced in between the rocks.

After fifteen minutes, our clothes and faces were caked in dust so Sam stopped at the water's edge, dropped her bike and waded carefully into the water. She had to be cautious because there was a ledge that went out about ten feet. Beyond this ledge the depth of the water was about fifty feet.

Sam proceeded to wash her face and arms. I joined her and before long we were involved in a water fight. Ivan didn't want to miss this spontaneous fun so he too entered into the caper. Shortly, we clambered out of the water and sat on a large rock in the sun to dry out. To pass the time we chatted.

"Do you wear PJs Ivan?" asked Sam with a wicked grin.

Uncertain, Ivan answered with a deadpan expression, "Yeah! Why?"

"No reason. Do you know Guy only wears his undies to bed?"

I scowled, "Well, what do you wear to bed, Samantha?"

I expected her to clam up but she cheerfully answered, "Nothing . . . not a stitch."

She burst out laughing. "You should see your faces."

"Nothing? You mean . . . naked?" exclaimed Ivan.

"I'm joshing. I wear PJs, like you."

"Ha! Ha!" I said sarcastically, as I jumped from the rock and sauntered to my bike. The other two followed.

We arrived back home close to dusk and went our separate ways. Late that night I waited and prayed I might once again see Anna in all her natural glory—but no such luck.

The next day I didn't see Ivan but Sam came over to my place for a while. We sat on my bed and listened to records. I had time to observe her as she sat, cross legged on the bed, reading a record jacket. It was as though I was noticing her for the first time—blonde hair framing her delicate features, the blue eyes, the elfin face and soft, tanned skin. I had always thought of her as a 'mate,' like another sister, but now I had to learn to cope with other, unfamiliar, feelings stirring within me. Sam sensed my gaze and glanced across at me.

"What? Why you looking at me?" she grinned.

"Sorry! You've changed so much. Up till now you've always worn baggy clothes and a cap but now . . . well . . . now you look different."

"How?"

"I dunno . . . like a girl."

The wicked grin and the glint in her eye told me she knew what I was thinking. She laughed and hit me with a pillow. This led to the inevitable pillow fight.

For the next few days I hung out with Sam, Ivan, Georgie and friends and each night I waited patiently for the light to go on in Anna's room in the house next door. My wish was granted late one night, when I heard a car pull into the driveway next door and then five minutes later—to me it felt like a lifetime—sure enough, the light went on. I climbed out my bedroom window and moved stealthily to the edge of the vacant block. I felt uncomfortable because it was highlighted in bright moonlight—nowhere for me to hide if anyone chanced to walk by, or, worse still, hear me as I crept over to the house. I hesitated, undecided whether to return to the safety of home or press onward. The invitation issued by the light in the window overwhelmed my senses. Ignoring all thoughts of danger or discovery, I sprinted towards the Mavrak house, squeezed through a narrow opening in the fence and crept up to the window. I peered inside. My realisation that I was about to continue spying on Anna made the venture all the more exciting.

As I watched her undressing, another light went on in the house. Fearing discovery, I retreated hastily to my home. The next day the Mavrak family left on their vacation.

CHAPTER 4

AMY

After bidding Ivan a brief goodbye the following morning, I decided to take my bike and explore the mountain area by myself. As I followed the dirt road leading to the Waterhole I discovered a very narrow track branching off and wending its way up into the forest. The track was fenced in with a gate at the entrance. A sign on the gate indicated that it was private property but today I felt adventurous enough to ignore the warning and enter. I opened the gate and made my way at a leisurely pace, up the track. It was another hot day although the trees lining both sides of the track provided a measure of protection from the sun.

It was evident that the track was not in regular use as it was overgrown with dry, withered clumps of grass and occasional fallen branches. Since I hoped that it would lead to one of the abandoned gold mines I pushed on. In the late 1800s, there were many gold mines in the mountains surrounding Roxborough but they had ceased operations long ago. After couple of miles I came to a wire fence.

"Bugger!" I said aloud.

I could see the track continuing on the other side of the fence so I leaned my bike against the fence and proceeded on foot up the mountain slope. The sound of dry, decaying leaves crackling underfoot interrupted the silence.

Atop the mountain slope the tree line thinned out, enabling the sun's rays to penetrate the canopy of leaves like laser beams. From here the land sloped down into a small valley of open grassland. A creek, lined either side by trees, wended its way along the edge of the valley. I made my way down the slope towards it. Without the shade protection of the trees, the heat from the sun hit my body like a blast of hot air. Walking across the open ground under the gaze of that hot angry beast drained my energy, but the prospect of a shady retreat near the creek spurred me onward. A cool dip in the creek water would be refreshing and a welcome break from the oppressive heat.

When I reached the creek I was surprised by its size. I found a shady spot and sank to my knees near the edge. I scooped up a handful of water and splashed my face, before drinking to quench my thirst. The water was crystal clear and surprisingly cool. I untied the shirt wrapped around my waist and flung it on the bank before slipping quietly into the water. The uncomfortable warmth I had been feeling was replaced by a cool, soothing sensation. I could not help but notice the eerie silence—no breeze, no rustling of leaves and no birds. I had a sudden urge to shout but it quickly disappeared. I relished the peace and quiet.

I had not shouted as I had the impulse to do, but it was my own voice that broke the silence. Without realising it, I'd expressed my thoughts verbally.

"I'll go on for another ten minutes or so and then I'll turn back," I told myself as I clambered out of the water.

After this short break I pushed on, following the creek along the edge of the valley. The vegetation changed markedly as I pressed forward and I found it difficult to make my way through the thicket of shrubs and wild grass that hugged the creek banks. A breeze had sprung up, rustling the tall grass as I progressed, but it did little to lessen the heat.

Just as I was primed to turn back, I heard the sound of splashing somewhere close—up ahead. I crouched down and crept through the grass silently. The creek had widened as it made a sweeping curve and changed its direction. There was a rocky shelf on the curve of the embankment, overlooking a sun-drenched waterhole. I made out the indistinct shape of something swimming in the water, so I fell to my stomach and crawled forward. When I was close enough to distinguish the shape clearly, I had to brace myself.

It was not an animal as I had first thought. It was a girl. She moved to the creek bank and slowly climbed out. As she perched on the rock shelf to soak up the sun, I noticed that she was a teenager, probably about my own age. Long, dark hair framed an angelic face, and her slim tanned body was partly covered by a white T-shirt that just reached the waistline of her bikini. For the second time in a few days I was enraptured. What was this angel doing out here in the wilderness? Who was she? Certainly, I had never seen her before.

She arched her back and thrust her head backwards. Her long hair cascaded onto the rock. She shook her head, and a spray of water droplets flew into the air. The twin peaks of her breasts pushed against the thin fabric of her top. Aroused, I lay in the grass watching, my mouth dry and my heart racing. Droplets of water glistened on the girl's face and body. My gaze lingered on her breasts. As I moved forward to gain a better view I snapped a small branch with my hand. Her head turned sharply in my direction, so I hurriedly ducked. Not wanting to be discovered, I froze—and waited. A female voice broke the silence.

"So that's where you've been!"

I lifted my head slowly and saw an older woman standing at the water's edge. She was tall with tousled, sandy, shoulder length hair. Her thin body was wrapped in a rather plain, long, white dress. Her pale face betrayed obvious signs of tiredness, a sharp contrast to the exuberance and youthful vigour of the girl. Neither the woman, nor the girl I presumed to be her daughter, could have any inkling of my presence.

"The water looks so cool," remarked the woman as she reached down and traced circles in it with her hand.

She casually brushed aside strands of hair covering her eyes, and took a few hesitant steps into the water. She stopped to glance at the girl sitting on the rock shelf, dangling her legs in the water. The girl stood up and tugged the clinging T-shirt past her waistline.

The girl called out, "Come on mum . . . hop in and cool off. The water's great."

"I'd better not Amy. Too much work to do," her mother answered.

"Come on, mum. It's too hot to work. Just for a few minutes," Amy pleaded.

Amy spoke in a voice that was melodic and soft. She clambered down from the rock shelf, her movements lithe, catlike and sensual. I was completely mesmerised. She was taller than Sam and many degrees sexier. Sam was the image of the girl next door whereas this girl was 'the movie star model'.

The woman lifted her long dress, and stepped gingerly into the water, watched by her daughter. Still fully clothed, she now dived in, rising to the surface as Amy joined her. Both laughed and screamed in delight as they splashed each other. I lay watching. Despite my excitement I had no wish to reveal my presence as a 'peeping Tom' so I decided to crawl back along the creek, and then walk along the bank towards them. I retreated on my hands and knees for at least ten yards before standing.

I walked along the bank of the creek whistling loudly so the revellers would hear me. I hoped I could hold a tune well enough not to alarm them. By the time I reached the waterhole they were both out of the water. The girl hid behind her mother, who stood on the bank, in her wet bedraggled dress. She twisted her long, dank hair as it hung down over her shoulders, trying to squeeze the water from it. She paused when she saw me, and placed her arms by her side, tugging her dress outwards as its heavy wetness clung to the contours of her body.

In an attempt to allay any fears I introduced myself.

"Hi . . . I'm Guy," I said.

Clearly puzzled by my sudden appearance, the older woman's eyes swept the horizon for evidence the presence of others.

"I'm on my own. Just me . . . Guy. I didn't expect to see anyone out here. It's a bit of a shock to see you," I added.

She paused to compose herself before speaking softly, "You gave us a shock too. We don't usually see people up here. How did you get here? Where are you from?"

Understandably, she was suspicious. This place was isolated.

"I'm from Roxborough. I was out riding my motor bike and I found this track. I followed it into the bush and here I am," I answered.

"Where's your bike?"

"I had to leave it at a fence and walk."

"I see," she said. "You're a long way from home. What's your name again?"

"Guy . . . Guy Harmon. I thought the track might lead to an abandoned gold mine. If I'm on your property I'm sorry."

"It's fine, Guy. My name is Ruth and this is my daughter, Amy."

She stepped aside as she introduced her daughter, who looked up and smiled fleetingly.

"Looks like you've been trying to keep cool. I don't blame you," I said.

The girl stood alongside her mother, wide eyed and inquisitive, with her arms folded protectively across her chest. She was no doubt aware her wet shirt was almost transparent, and my eyes were firmly fixed on it. I was curious about why two women were up in the mountains, such a long way from civilisation.

"Do you live near here?" I asked.

I realised I was being rude so I quickly added a rejoinder, "Sorry! It's none of my business."

"We live in the house over there," the girl explained, and motioned in the direction of a distant clump of trees.

I turned and in the distance managed to make out a roof top peeking above the horizon. An awkward silence followed and I didn't know whether to leave or wait. Fortunately, the mother spoke.

"We need to get out of these wet clothes," she explained, once again peeling the clinging wet dress from her body.

"Oh! Okay . . . Well I'd better be on my way too. It's a long way back," I said, instantly resigned to the fact I would probably never see the girl again.

The girl whispered in her mother's ear and the two had a brief conversation. I turned and began to walk slowly—ever so slowly—away.

"Before you leave, would you like a cold drink?" asked Ruth.

Her tone betrayed what was obvious. She really didn't want me to stay. Under most circumstances, I would have declined the offer, but the thought of spending even a little more time in the presence of her daughter gave me cause to stop and turn.

"Thanks! That would be great but I don't want to inconvenience you."

"No problem. You look like you could do with a drink."

As we strolled towards the house tucked away amongst the trees, I surveyed the surrounds. There were no other houses nearby—nothing but paddocks of sundrenched grass and trees. Not the kind of place for two women living on their own, I thought. Why were they living here? Was there a husband and father? I kept my thoughts to myself.

Up close the house was a small, timber building, enclosed on two sides by a veranda, with a roof covered in sheets of rusting, corrugated iron. By any standard it was no palace. On the veranda were several large pots containing a variety of flowering geraniums. The house was set amongst tall pine trees at the base of the mountain. I spotted two horses grazing near an old Jeep that was parked under a tree near the house. A narrow dirt track passed by the house as it wended its way up towards the mountain. The house was old, but its outside timber had been given a fresh coat of paint, and evidence of a series of repairs that had been made only recently was noticeable. There were a number of new floorboards on the veranda and the railing had been fixed.

Ruth turned to me as we stood on the veranda, and made a grand sweeping motion. "This is our home. Not much—as you can see—but we like it. It's quiet and peaceful," she said.

"Do you have any neighbours?" I asked as I gazed at the surrounding bush.

"No! We rarely see anyone out here."

That admission explained why they had been so surprised to see me. Her voice trailed off and she took her daughter's hand.

Ruth continued. "I must admit it's not the best place for Amy. She has no friends to spend time with. How old are you Guy?"

"I'm sixteen."

Ruth smiled and put her arm around Amy's shoulders.

"What a co-incidence. So is Amy."

I grinned. I tried to convey the impression of calm and serenity; however, with a dry throat and a throbbing temple I felt as if my whole insides were trembling—and worse, that it was evident to anyone who might look at me. This was a new experience for me, at once pleasant and terrifying. My recent episodes spying on Anna were simply fuelled by lust and voyeurism but this was different—and I liked it. I glanced at Amy but she had lowered her head shyly.

The floorboards on the veranda creaked under our weight as we entered the house. I paused at the doorway and examined the interior. I stood inside a room that contained a tattered old sofa, two armchairs and a large bookcase overflowing with books. There was no television but there was a radio cabinet in one corner. A large throw rug partly covered the wooden floor near the sofa. The windows were covered by white curtains and I noticed the paint on the walls was faded. A small coffee table rested between the sofa and an open fireplace at the far end of the room. Adjoining this room was a small kitchen with the basic essentials—a stove, refrigerator and storage cupboards. On the kitchen table sat a colourful bunch of fresh flowers, artistically arranged in a large vase. This was the only bright, vibrant addition to the rather austere interior. Still, some ethereal quality made the house inviting and cosy.

Ruth noticed my eyes sweeping the rooms and said, "It's all we need—and you might have noticed, we do have electricity."

Amy had taken a large jug from the refrigerator and placed it on the table. Ruth took some glasses from a cupboard and said, "Thanks sweetheart! Why don't you go and get changed. I'll pour the drinks."

Ruth filled the glasses as Amy walked up the hallway. Even moving away she looked wonderful, full of that nimble sensuousness that had so excited me earlier. After handing me a drink and indicating a seat, Ruth also excused herself and left the room to change.

Hot in more ways than one, I devoured the cold drink in two or three hearty gulps. With this short interlude alone I stood up, topped up my glass and went to the bookcase to glance at some of the titles. I heard the tinkle of glasses and turned to see Amy, now in a pair of slacks and a blouse, sitting on the sofa. She sipped her drink and leaned back. She was much prettier, I thought, than my first impression of her. Her long, dark hair framed a beautiful face. She had brown, doe-like eyes and an inviting, sensuous mouth.

"Sit down!" she said. I sat in a chair opposite her as we sipped our drinks in awkward silence. Most of my exchanges with girls consisted of "Hi!" and not much else but I summoned up the courage to engage Amy in conversation.

"I haven't seen you in Roxborough. Where do you go to school?"

Amy leaned forward and put her glass on the coffee table.

"I don't go to school. You see, we've moved around a lot and it was too much trouble to enrol in a school and then leave a few months later," she answered softly.

"No school. You're lucky. I wish I could do that."

"I'm not so lucky. I still have to do schoolwork. Sometimes I have a tutor or I do it by correspondence. I'm sure you wouldn't like it. I don't! You don't get to have friends or do stuff like—you know—talk about things or play sport or meet others. I wish I could go to High School. Maybe one day . . ."

She sighed and stared into the distance. I didn't press her about the reasons for moving so often.

"Do you go into Roxborough? You know . . . shopping, the movies?" I asked.

Amy pulled her feet up onto the sofa and curled up like a kitten ready for an afternoon nap. She paused briefly before answering.

"We go into town to get groceries and things every couple of weeks but I've never been to the movies or met anyone there."

"Does your mum have a job?"

Amy stretched out and ruffled her hair. I was surprised at the easy to-and-fro manner of our conversation.

"Mum is an artist but she works at the High School as a cleaner during the week. Three days a week I go with her and have tutoring by teachers."

"I haven't seen you at High School."

"Mum goes to work in the mornings from six to eight and in the afternoons from four to six," she explained.

I wanted to discover everything I could about this charming creature so I continued.

"No wonder I haven't seen you. What kind of artist is your mum?" I asked.

"Mum has a studio behind the house and she paints flower stills and landscapes."

"I like to paint and draw, too. Do you paint?"

I hoped she did so we'd have something in common but she shook her head.

I continued, "Do you have any older brothers or sisters?"

She bit her bottom lip and her expression turned sombre. I'd hit a nerve.

"I'm the only one," she answered.

"It must be a bit lonely—not having others to hang out with."

Before Amy could answer, Ruth re-entered the room, picked up a drink from the table and curled up on the sofa alongside her daughter.

Beauty ran in the family, that much was indisputable. There were no tangible signs that a man lived in the house. I didn't ask.

"I suppose Amy has told you all about us," said Ruth.

She glanced at Amy who answered for me.

"I told Guy you were an artist and cleaner and that I didn't go to school. That's all."

"Did you say why?" Ruth asked in measured tones.

"Because we move around."

Ruth glanced back to me and began an explanation of sorts.

"We've had to move around in the last couple of years for reasons I can't tell you at this moment. We've been living here for five or six months. It's ideal for me because it's so quiet and peaceful but it is not quite so suitable for Amy. I was told that this was a miner's hut originally. You see . . . in the mountain behind us is an old abandoned gold mine."

My eyes widened and I leaned forward. I had been right about a gold mine. This news awakened my curiosity about Roxborough's mining past once more. I wanted to explore that mine—perhaps the summer break would be lined with gold.

Amy noticed my enthusiasm and said, "I've had a look but mum doesn't want me going into the mine because it's too dangerous."

"The old mine isn't safe," said Ruth. "There has been a rock fall and the tunnel might collapse so I told Amy to keep away from it. Are you going away for your holidays?"

"Nope!" I said.

"What do you parents do? I hope you don't mind me asking you these questions. Tell me to shut up if you think I'm being a busybody."

"Nah! It's fine. My dad owns the General Store in town. That's why I'm not going away, and mum . . . well mum just looks after us."

"That's a full-time job," said Ruth, who continued to pepper me with questions.

"Yeah."

"Do you have any brothers or sisters?"

"Yeah! One brother, Marty and a sister, Jan. They're younger than me," I answered.

I had expected Amy to ask me a few questions but she sat quietly and listened; not uttering a word.

Ruth glanced at a clock on the table and then outside at the ever deepening shadows. She stood up.

"It's getting dark. If you like I'll take you back to your bike in my Jeep."

The three of us left the house, climbed aboard the Jeep, and rattled down the track, until we reached the road leading to the Waterhole. The vintage Jeep was noisy and most uncomfortable, as it bumped up and down and from side to side, but I didn't mind. I was feeling few of the bumps as I continually stole glances at the lovely Amy. Ruth's property also had a gate and a warning sign. The turnoff to the track I had taken was about two miles back towards Roxborough. By this time the sun was well and truly behind the mountain. Sylvan dusk would soon be replaced by total night.

A slight breeze rustled the leaves of the trees above, and I could still feel the warmth of the summer's day, as the Jeep trundled along the track. In the distance a smoky, blue haze that drifted over the tree tops was still visible in the fading light, with the easily discernible scent of burning timber wafting on the breeze. A kookaburra's heartening laugh signalled the end of the day.

When we reached my bike, Ruth turned to me and said, "Guy. It was nice meeting you. It might sound a little strange to you but I'd like you not to tell anyone about meeting Amy and me. We do have reasons but I want to keep them private for now. Can I trust you?"

"Sure. No problems."

"Thank you! You are most welcome to come out and visit as long as you come alone. You see . . . I don't want a lot of people out here but it would be nice for Amy to have a friend. You can go horse riding or go for a swim."

Why would I tell anyone about meeting the girl of my dreams? I wanted to keep her to myself. I looked in Amy's direction for any hint of approval. There was no frown so I took that as a sign she wouldn't mind if I returned sometime soon.

"Thanks. I'd like to come out."

"Great! Come out tomorrow. We look forward to seeing you."

As the Jeep moved off I waved to Amy who had twisted around in her seat to say goodbye. On the trip home I mulled over the extraordinary events of the day, especially Ruth's guarded words.

Why didn't they want anyone else to find out where they lived? And why did they move so often? They didn't look like people running from the law. Maybe in time Ruth would tell me. Right then, I didn't really care.

CHAPTER 5

THE EXPLANATION

T he next morning, my mother admonished me at the breakfast table, for gulping down my breakfast too hastily. Breakfast in our house was usually chaotic, with my mother desperately trying to get the family to sit together and eat a wholesome meal.

My father had left for the store by the time I arrived at breakfast. Running a store was not easy. He had to serve customers, order goods, stock the shelves, clean the shop and complete the eternal tasks of book keeping and accounts. These tasks made huge inroads into Dad's leisure time and I helped him whenever he needed me. Most mornings he left us in our mother's capable hands. She rarely had a break from housework but I pitched in and helped her as much as possible.

My mother was the rock in our family—so quiet and imperturbable. Her sturdy presence was a genuine source of comfort to me in these, my mid-teenage years. Our respective personalities could easily have been labelled as polar opposites; for Mum was the eternal optimist while I . . . well I was a natural born pessimist.

With a wild younger brother and a "know it all" sister I had ample reason to welcome my mother's calming influence. She used any spare time to get out into the garden, or sit in an old sofa on the porch, either to read or knit. She poured me a glass of juice.

"Why are you in such a hurry?" she said. "You need to sit and eat . . . not bolt your food down."

"I'm not! I just want to make the most of the holidays," I mumbled, my mouth crammed.

My lame excuse presented my eleven-year-old brother the opportunity to embarrass me.

"Guy's off to see his girlfriend. That's why he's all dressed up," said Marty.

He was right. I was wearing my best shirt and jeans and my hair was neatly combed. I did look like I was heading out on a date. Marty had a mouthful of cereal and milk, and as he spoke, most of it dribbled down his chin. It was not a pretty sight.

"Marty! Don't talk with your mouth full," Mum scolded.

This prompted the youngest, Jan, to giggle and poke her spoon in his direction.

"Ha! Ha! Marty got into trouble from mum."

"Did not!"

"Did too!"

"Shut up frog face!"

Jan twisted in her chair and yelled out to mum. "Mum. Marty called me 'frog face'."

Mum said sternly, "We don't say those things in this house, Marty. Now both of you keep quiet and eat your breakfast."

This kind of behaviour was normal in our household at meal times but Mum took it all in her stride. She ruled the household but my dad was the boss. His word was final.

We knew that we would get the strap from dad if we did something bad and that was enough for us to 'toe the line'. If dad came home from the store angry or irritable, Mum would get him a beer and they would sit outside and talk to each other until once again her calming influence weaved its magic.

"Where ya going with your girlfriend, Guy?" Marty asked, with a wide, cheeky grin.

He swept his straggly, unkempt hair back from his face. Typical Marty—always untidy and messy.

I thumped him on the arm and gave him a steely glare. This didn't deter him.

Rubbing his arm, he grimaced and pleaded, "Can I go with you Guy? I could give you some pointers about girls."

We all laughed. Jan, who was nine-years-old, going on thirty, said, "No girl in her right mind would ever talk to you, Marty. Besides, Guy is nearly grown up and he can do what he likes . . . so there."

Mum looked at Jan and said firmly, "Guy is only sixteen and he doesn't need to worry about girls until he's much older."

She looked seriously at me and added, "It isn't a girl, is it?"

I didn't want Mum to know about Amy so I laughed it off.

"Come on, Mum. You know me. When was I ever interested in girls?"

Mum frowned as she cleared the dishes from the table. Yet what I had said was true. Until now I hadn't shown any interest in girls. Her frown was replaced with a smile. This seemed the perfect opportunity to leave before she extracted the truth. I said a quick goodbye, but before I left the house, I hurried to my room to change into an old shirt and jeans. If Marty noticed I was dressed up, then so would Amy and come to the same conclusion—that I was trying a little too hard. I glanced in the mirror and, satisfied with my casual appearance, dashed out of the house.

I didn't see Billy. I hadn't seen him since the Waterhole incident but his absence from my life didn't bother me. Georgie was a different matter. He hadn't come around for a while and I could not help wondering if he was all right. I decided to visit him when I returned from Amy's place. Sam was away visiting relatives for a few days so I didn't have to contend with her.

"Guy!"

I was on my way to the garage to get my bike when I heard my name. I turned and saw two school friends, Bobby and Mike, standing on the path, clutching fishing gear.

"We're going down to the river to do some fishing. Wanna come?" asked Bobby.

I really wanted to go to Amy's, so I lied. "I have some work to do at Dad's shop. Maybe later."

They could see me weakening so Mike pleaded, "Ah! Come on! We're only going for an hour. Can't the work wait a little longer?"

Bobby continued, "We can sit under the bridge, throw in a line and relax. Come on!"

It sounded too good an opportunity to miss, especially to go fishing, but I really did want to visit Amy too. Usually I would jump at the chance to spend time with them. I glanced at my watch. I decided that an hour with my friends might settle my nerves because I was uneasy about meeting Amy again.

"Okay! I can fish for an hour but then I have to go. I'll just grab my fishing gear," I said.

A few minutes later we trundled across the wooden bridge and scrambled down the embankment and onto the river bank. The Karinya River flowed along the edge of the town and down the valley. We did swim in it on occasions, but it was not popular, because the water was usually muddy, and there were no shady spots, except under the bridge. The river bank wasn't the most pleasant place, with hot, sandy loam, tufts of wild grass and clumps of stinkweed and bracken, all living in haphazard competition with each other. It was not an ideal place to repose. Being summer, we also had to contend with sticky, annoying flies. We found a spot, threw in our lines, stretched out and chatted. A half-hour passed before we had a nibble. We didn't mind, as our conversation ebbed and flowed as easily as the river current just a few yards away from where we sat.

Our conversation was interrupted a few times by traffic clattering across the bridge. After an hour, the only thing we'd caught was a small turtle which we promptly threw back. Soon I'd had enough of fishing so I decided to leave but the others said they were going to have a swim. I had other things on my mind so I waved goodbye and sped home to grab my bike.

It was nearly midday when I entered Ruth's property and hurtled along the dirt track towards the house. The whining noise of the bike announced my arrival and Amy came out onto the veranda and leaned over the railing. Shortly after, Ruth came out, wiping her hands on a towel.

"I didn't think you'd come back," she smiled, "but I'm glad you did and Amy will be too, I'm sure."

Catching the hint of a smile from Amy made me feel much better.

"Have you had lunch?" Ruth asked.

"No."

"Good. You can join us. We were about to eat when you arrived. After lunch, Amy can take you horse riding."

"Okay. Sounds great."

Over lunch Ruth politely asked me about my interests, high school, and my friends. I understood why and was quite happy to answer all questions. Amy entered the conversation only sporadically but she listened intently the whole time.

Ruth pushed her chair back and said, "You two go and enjoy yourselves. I'll see you later."

We helped Ruth clean up before we left. I followed Amy as she strolled towards the back of the house to the shed, where the horses were stabled.

"Grab a saddle and bridle from the shed will you?" she asked, stroking one of the horses. I picked up the gear and walked across to the horses. Amy slipped a bridle over the head of one of the horses and placed the bit in its mouth as I watched on.

"You forgot the blanket," she said and handed me the reins. She returned from the shed with a saddle blanket and threw it on the horse's back. The saddle went on next. She tightened the girth. I held the reins while Amy saddled the other horse.

"Have you ridden before?" she asked. Obviously she'd noticed that I wasn't too comfortable around the horses.

"Yes, but only a few times," I lied.

In fact, I was a complete novice but I didn't want her to know that. How could any girl fall for a boy who kept falling off his horse?

"You can ride Beauty. She's very quiet," she reassured me.

I watched her mount her horse and copied her actions. We travelled up the rough, worn track to the gold mine. Realising that I was far more at home on the back of a bike rather than the back of a horse,

Amy stayed at my side the whole journey. I watched how she held the reins and how she sat in the saddle.

The ground in front of the mine was bare—just gravel and rocks with patches of brown summer grass. A small tumbledown shack, with no roof and missing one wall, stood at one side, a stark reminder of the industry of yesteryear. There was ample evidence of the area's mining history, with large stockpiles of dirt and rocks and rusting machinery scattered around. In the side of the mountain was the narrow mine opening.

"Can we have a look?" I asked.

"Okay! But we can't go in."

Beauty stood quietly as I struggled to dismount. Amy had a wry smile on her face as she watched my clumsy effort. We strode to the mine entrance and looked in but heeded Ruth's warning not to enter.

After finishing our exploration, we travelled down to the open terrain of the valley where we were able to allow the horses to canter. Amy was an excellent rider but I was very ordinary, bumping up and down in the saddle like a bag of potatoes, while trying to convey the impression I knew what I was doing. I did enjoy the experience though. Near the creek, we dismounted and stretched out in the long grass under a tree, while the horses grazed nearby. A smattering of clouds and a soft, gentle breeze helped negate the stifling summer heat. We lay on our backs and gazed up at the azure sky. Since I knew nothing about Amy I seized the opportunity to ask her some things about her life.

"You know plenty about me but I know nothing about you," I said, turning on my side to face her. She was a vision of beauty. She had one arm behind her head and a blade of grass in her mouth as she looked upward. She was so relaxed and I hoped she hadn't noticed my nervousness.

She spat out the grass and faced me, smiling. "I don't know that much about you. I know you like bikes, play basketball and football, like art, hate school. Your friends are Ivan and Georgie, you like . . ."

"Okay! I'll answer your questions if you answer mine. Fair enough?" I interrupted.

She laughed, "Fine. Fire away."

"Besides horse riding, what do you like doing?"

"Well. I like music and reading. I like all animals, especially horses."

"What music do you like?"

"I like Elvis, Paul Anka, and Buddy Holly but I also like some Country and Western music. What about you?"

"Much the same."

Her expression told me she didn't believe me, so I added a disclaimer, "I'm not really such a great fan of Elvis."

I found out that she hated sport and the country life, which seemed at odds with her easy manner around her horses. We talked for nearly an hour. The only time she looked sad was when I talked about my friends and school. I found it easy to talk to her and I became more confident as time passed. Amazingly, it seemed as if I had known her for years. When I thought we had finished, Amy became more personal.

"Do you have a girlfriend?" she asked.

"Nup."

I didn't mention Sam because even though she was my best friend I didn't consider her my girlfriend.

"Why not?" she asked.

"I don't know. I really haven't spent much time with girls. They scare me."

Her body shook with laughter as a wide grin lit up her face.

"What do you mean . . . they scare you?"

"I'm not frightened of them. I'm just scared that if I ask them out they'll say no and laugh at me."

"Oh! I see," she laughed.

She leaned in very close to me and I could feel the warmth and sweet perfume of her body. I wanted desperately to kiss her but I choked on my feelings and stared at the clouds in the sky. I didn't know whether she was enjoying my discomfort or was just curious.

"Have you ever kissed a girl?" she continued.

"No. What about you?"

"What? Kissed a girl?" she answered, screwing up her nose and grinning.

"Nooo. I meant a boy."

"Yep! He was seven and I was six. It was awful."

There was an awkward silence. I decided to change the subject.

"Have you any friends you keep in touch with?" I asked.

"Not really. We never stayed in places long enough. I have a friend who writes now and again. We first knew each other when we were eleven," she answered. She grabbed another blade of grass and proceeded to chew it.

"What about your dad? Is he away working?"

Amy lapsed into a strange silence and I noticed she had clenched her fists tightly as a frown creased her forehead.

"Sorry! I shouldn't have asked you."

She sat up, took a measured breath, and answered. "It's okay. My dad left us a few years ago. I don't really want to see him again . . . ever."

"I'm sorry. You should've told me to shut up."

"No harm done. Let's walk down to the creek," she said. Her emphatic tone told me our conversation was over, at least for now.

She rose to her feet and brushed down her clothes. I scrambled to my feet and joined her. We walked down to the creek, and sat on the bank, dangling our feet in the water. To cool down, we splashed water on our faces, before giving the horses a drink. Amy led the way as we made our way back to the house. Ruth showed me her art studio while Amy rubbed down and fed the horses.

I had promised to take Amy on my motorbike so she hopped on behind me and put her arms around my waist. This was the first time any teenage girl had wrapped her arms around me, and my pulse quickened as I felt the warmth of her body. I rode down the track at a leisurely pace, but on the way back, I gunned the bike, causing Amy to wrap her arms tighter. When she rested her head on my shoulder it sent a wave of tingling sensations up and down my spine. This thoroughly agreeable feeling invigorated me as I accelerated towards the house.

"I'd better get going before it gets dark," I said as Amy hopped off the bike.

"Will I see you tomorrow?" she asked, glancing at Ruth, who had stepped out onto the veranda.

"Sure! If it's okay with you," I replied.

Amy nodded as Ruth called out, "You're welcome any time, Guy. See you tomorrow!"

They waved as I rolled down the track and out of view. On the way home I stopped at Georgie's house. He was sitting on the porch, playing with his pup.

"Watcha been doing, Georgie? I haven't seen you around," I said as I swung open the gate, and strolled up the path towards him.

"I've been working for Mr Davis on his farm. I start at six in the morning and I usually get home about four. It's hard work but he pays me well," he answered, as I sat alongside him, and playfully rubbed his pup's tummy.

"You look buggered," I said.

"Yeah! It's bloody hard work. That's why I haven't been round."

"How long you doing this for?"

"I'll be finished in another . . . um . . . four days, so I'll see you then," he said.

I honestly didn't want him around while I was with Amy. It was selfish but I didn't want to share her with anyone, not even Georgie.

"Fine . . . no worries . . . I'll see ya!" I said.

I made seeing Amy each day my foremost priority. We went horse riding, swam in the creek, listened to records and talked. No-one seemed to notice that I was disappearing from town as soon as possible every day and returning late each afternoon. On one or two occasions I had to stay and do chores or help out at the store but I still managed to spend a couple of hours with Amy and Ruth. Even after this short time I felt they had already become my friends, as the three of us had become more and more relaxed in each other's company.

A week passed by before Amy and Ruth took me into their confidence, to tell me their secret. I was ushered into the house and asked to sit down. They sat opposite looking grim faced. At first I was worried but Amy gave me a quick smile to put me at ease. Ruth spoke quietly and explained their secret.

"Guy! What I tell you today must never leave this room. After I tell you, you'll understand. Is that okay with you?" she said, her tone measured.

"No problems," I answered, leaning forward as my heart quickened.

Ruth continued, "As you might have noticed, there is no man around. You see, I divorced my husband several years ago after he abused and assaulted me and put me in hospital. He was a policeman and he would drink too much and then vent his anger and frustration on me. One night he was drunk and he tried to . . . to . . . to . . . molest Amy. He went into her bedroom and touched her inappropriately. When Amy screamed out I rushed in to find him on her bed. I yelled at him and told him to leave. That's when he bashed me and hospitalised me. You can imagine how Amy felt about what happened. It was terrible."

She paused, desperately trying to regain control of her emotions, holding Amy's hand tightly as they both struggled to stay calm.

"Did you go to the police?"

"Yes. Over the years I'd gone to them many times because of his violence. Being a cop, my husband had many friends on the force and he always managed to twist the facts to make me appear to be the villain. Nothing was done . . . not till he put me in hospital. Then the police had no choice but to arrest him."

This was not the secret I expected to hear. I was surprised and stunned at the story being told.

"What happened then?"

"Well . . . thankfully, he was put in jail for six years for bashing me and trying to sexually assault Amy. At his trial, he turned to me and yelled out he would get me and settle me once and for all. I believe him. He's a bastard! Pardon my language but he almost destroyed our lives. If he finds us he will kill me."

"He can't if he's in prison." I said.

"That's the problem. He has been released from prison and we've been on the run ever since. You see, as an ex-cop, he still has many friends that are willing to help him."

"It must be terrible having to move from place to place, not knowing if he'll turn up."

Amy turned away and buried her face in a pillow. What a life for her. I wanted to take her in my arms and comfort her. Ruth must have read my mind, because she put her arms protectively around Amy, and whispered in her ear, while brushing wisps of hair away from her eyes.

Ruth leaned forward and clasped my hand in a sign of trust. She spoke softly.

"We have been moving around for almost three years but we can't keep living like this for the rest of our lives. It's not great . . . not knowing if he'll find us. It would help if we had a friend who lived in Roxborough. I'm telling you this because I have come to trust you as a friend. Amy's at the age where she should have friends and live a normal life. Will you help us? You know; listen for any news of him or tell us if strangers come into town. It would take a burden off our minds."

"Sure. I'll do what I can do to help," I said.

Ruth jumped to her feet and pulled Amy up with her. I joined them.

She smiled. "Anyway . . . no more talk about this. It's spoiling your visit. You two go out and enjoy yourselves. It's another hot day. Why not cool off with a swim?"

She laughed and opened the door. Now everything made sense to me. I could read it on their faces, that Ruth and Amy were relieved after telling me their secret. I now understood why they lived alone. It was going to be difficult to keep all this new information a secret from Sam and Georgie.

CHAPTER 6

GREEN WITH ENVY

On the second Saturday of the month I travelled in company with Amy and Ruth to Roxborough for the first time, to buy groceries and other essential items. Ruth was apprehensive about my coming along with them, because she thought being in my company in public might draw unwanted attention to them. After I assured her I would introduce Amy as a family friend she agreed reluctantly, knowing that Amy had been looking forward to the trip.

While Ruth did the shopping I took Amy sightseeing. Our first visit was to the café to get an ice cream. Before entering Amy stopped and turned to face me. Her expression told me that she was nervous at the prospect of meeting my friends.

"You look terrific!" I gushed, "You'll knock them out."

She smiled and relaxed. Amy was prettier than any girl in Roxborough. For obvious reasons, I didn't want her to meet Billy. I didn't see him in the café but unfortunately I did see Sam. She was standing by a table chatting to friends. No cap or jeans today. Sam was a picture of teenage loveliness in a pink top and white shorts but her smile changed quickly to a look of disappointment when she saw Amy. Her face said it all. Instantly, I rued the fact I hadn't told Sam about Amy.

"Hi Sam," I called out. "Haven't seen you around for a while. How ya been?"

She ignored my greeting and swept past, brushing away tears.

"What's wrong with her?" I blurted.

A friend, Jan, answered, "Don't you know that Sam loves you, you brainless twerp? How'd you expect her to react when you turn up with a girl?"

I was lost for words. Apart from a very occasional peck on the cheek and a hug Sam hadn't given any indication that she considered me more than just a friend. I was a complete novice in the romance stakes—and it showed.

Amy whispered in my ear, "Is she your girlfriend? You told me you had no girlfriend."

"I don't. Sam lives near me and we've been friends all our lives. Nothing else. Never more than friends."

"Well! She obviously thinks differently. If you want to go after her I'll understand."

"No! We are just friends. It's not my responsibility if she thinks otherwise," I said testily.

Amy acknowledged my explanation. The other teenagers at the café accepted my introduction of her as a family friend and soon she was surrounded by an inquisitive throng. The boys, one and all, tried to capture her attention and she accepted this new development happily. I decided to go outside and see if Sam was okay but she had disappeared. I re-entered the café and stood in the background. As I watched Amy, somewhat envious of her popularity, I secretly wished she had worn some tattered jeans or something less feminine—perhaps an old army coat or even one of the horse blankets from her stable in the forest!

After leaving the café, each with an ice-cream, we strolled along the footpath, through the town centre. However, I made a huge mistake, one which I regretted immediately. I realised, too late, that we were passing the police station. That's where we ran into Billy, the last person in Roxborough I wanted to see. I turned to cross the street to get away from him but he saw my movement and stepped in front of Amy. He nodded a non-committal acknowledgement of my presence and then swiftly shifted his focus to Amy. His eyes lit up as he appraised her from head to toe.

"Hi! I'm Billy. And you are?" he asked; now completely ignoring me.

I interrupted to reply on Amy's behalf. "This is Amy. She's a family friend. She's visiting for a while."

Amy smiled and said in her soft, melodic voice, "Hi!"

I knew that Billy's mind was working overtime and he was getting ready to employ all his well-oiled charms.

"Are you staying with Guy? I haven't seen you around."

He struck a casual pose with his feet astride and his hands in his jacket pockets. Ruth had been worried and now so was I, but for a totally different set of reasons. I didn't want Billy anywhere near Amy. Unlike me, he knew how to appeal to the girls.

Before Amy could answer I interrupted with my own explanation. "No! Amy and her mother are staying out of town on a property. They're in town today only to get groceries."

There was no doubt Billy Jenkins planned to set a trap. Amy was the intended victim, unaware she was being caught in his silky smooth web, the fashionable clothes, the oily good looks, and his satin smooth delivery. Where was the Pest Control man when you needed him? I had to get Amy away from Billy. As if he read my mind he sidled closer to her.

"How long you staying?" he asked, a broad smile lighting his face.

Amy answered before I could interrupt. "Mum and I are hoping to stay for a long time. It all depends."

Glancing at my watch I said, "We've got to go. It's getting late."

I turned and motioned to Amy to accompany me as I crossed the street. I presumed that she would follow but when I glanced back she hadn't moved. In a very short space of time I had become the outsider, as the two of them only had eyes for each other. They continued their banter, each oblivious to the fact I'd moved away. I stared angrily in the shop window of the hardware store, trying to harness my emotions. I had no chance with Amy whilst ever Billy was in the picture. After only a few minutes he already had her under his spell. I didn't know whether to vent my anger or cry out in frustration because my vacation had suddenly turned sour. Infuriated, I kicked the brick wall of the building, and turning sharply, walked back to my father's grocery shop. I now had a stabbing pain in my foot to match the aching in my heart.

As I hobbled along the pavement I heard my name being called out. I stopped and glanced back, to see Amy running across the road towards me. Billy had turned and walked into the police station—mission accomplished. Amy's glowing face told me more than I wanted to know, or acknowledge, so I continued along the street without waiting for her. Finally she reached me and tugged my arm to slow me down. I halted to face her, angry and hurt.

"What's the matter?" she asked.

"Nothin," I muttered.

"Are you jealous because I talked to Billy?"

She grinned and placed her hands on her hips. I grimaced and lowered my head. She saw my reaction.

"You are jealous! Guy Harmon . . . well, I never knew you felt this way."

"No I'm not!" I said unconvincingly. Amy smiled and squeezed my hand.

"How sweet," she murmured.

How sweet indeed! To her I was just a friend, nothing more. I was devastated that she obviously felt the same way about me as I did about Sam. We didn't say a word until we reached the store. Finally Amy broke the silence.

"Billy asked me if I wanted to go to a place called the Waterhole tomorrow for a swim. He said you know it well and for you and Georgie to come too."

I thought 'Yeah! Right!' The only reason he wanted me to come along was because he knew that my presence would guarantee Amy would also be there.

Before I could reply she asked, "Where's the Waterhole?"

This was a subtle ruse to change the subject and confuse me, an art form at which, I was beginning to recognise, she excelled. I sat on a bench outside the store and Amy sat beside me waiting patiently for an answer. I told her where the Waterhole was but I also mentioned what had happened to Georgie.

"Billy was one of those that taunted Georgie and he made no effort to help him. He's no longer a friend of mine, if he ever was," I said firmly.

"Oh! That's odd because he seemed to think of you as his friend."

"Look! Billy has a reputation with the girls and I don't want to be forced to watch as you get hurt. Just be careful!"

I was badmouthing Billy because I was jealous but I couldn't help it. Amy probably saw through me and thought the same.

She gave me a reassuring grin, "It's fine! I can look after myself. Anyway, you'll be there to keep an eye on things."

Despite realising I was in the middle of a losing battle I persevered. "Listen! Billy's dad is a policeman. Be careful of everything you say around him. And I mean exactly that—anything!"

I was serious now. If Billy's dad knew about Amy's dad, there might be trouble. Amy's face darkened and she bit her lip and frowned. I could tell she was having second thoughts about going. For some reason, instead of feeling satisfied because I'd almost convinced her not to go, I felt guilty.

I sighed, "If you want to go . . . it's fine. I'll take you."

Amy leaned over and gave me a hug. I was sure she had already dismissed my warning about Billy's dad but I didn't care; I felt it was one of those things that had to be said, irrespective of the outcome. We had known each other only a very short time but I had decided I would rather have Amy in my life as a friend than not at all. I hoped that she would soon discover that Billy was a fraud and reject his overtures. It was wishful thinking on my part but it was all I had to console my wounded spirit.

She saw my miserable face and asked, "Are you sure it's okay? If you say we shouldn't . . ."

"It's fine. We'll go."

We sat in silence until Ruth came out of the store and headed towards us.

"There you are. Guy, would you help bring out the groceries please?"

"Sure," I answered, happy to oblige, because it would create a diversion that might help me erase Billy from my thoughts.

On the way back to their home, Ruth peppered us with questions about the day. Amy was eager to answer, while I slumped in the back of the Jeep, surrounded by boxes and bags of groceries. Ruth was delighted that Amy had met my friends and enjoyed herself. When Amy glanced in my direction a few times, I managed a weak smile, although within myself I was thoroughly miserable. When we reached the house, Amy told her mother about being invited to the Waterhole the next day. Ruth turned to me.

"Do you think it's a good idea?"

I simply nodded and said it was fine. Better to go right now, I told myself; the ride back to town might help clear my head. I bid Amy and Ruth a swift goodbye and walked to my bike. As I prepared to leave, Amy ran down from the house.

"Thanks for everything, Guy. You're the best . . . see ya tomorrow."

To show her appreciation, Amy leaned forward and kissed me on the cheek before dashing back to the house. I knew all too well what it was like to be kissed on the cheek. Always! It was the same feeling I always had when a relative greeted me. It was like a handshake or a pat on the head. It was my fault that I had not communicated to Amy how much I cared for her. Now I knew how Sam felt when she saw me with Amy.

As I rode away, I muttered under my breath, "Well done, Guy! You've lost your best friend, Sam and now you're about to lose Amy, too. Stupid! Stupid!"

I stopped at Georgie's house to see if he wanted to go to the Waterhole. I told him about Amy and I mentioned that Billy and his friends would be there. I expected Georgie to decline, given what had happened on our last visit there, but to my surprise he accepted. Obviously he was curious to meet Amy.

After dinner, while the rest of the family watched television, I lay on my bed listening to records, all the while sinking into the depths of despair.

Upon waking early the next morning I was greeted by a cloudless sky and a temperature that was already climbing. I had hoped it would be a cool, overcast day—too cold to go swimming. Georgie arrived and as we walked our bikes to the end of the street we were joined by Billy. There was no sign of Sam.

Billy asked politely, "Is it okay if I go with you to Amy's place?"

I was not in a forgiving mood and I answered rather abruptly, "Sorry! Amy's mum said that she didn't want anyone coming out to her house except me."

His polite manner changed and he snapped, "I don't believe you. Well, what about Georgie? He's going with you."

"Georgie is waiting at the roadside."

"Well, I'll come and talk to Amy's mum. She'll understand."

He was a persistent bugger but I wasn't going to back down.

"No! Amy's different from your other girls. I don't want you anywhere near her."

I'd let my guard down and allowed him to get 'under my skin'. In my estimate Billy Jenkins was little more than an arrogant, self-centred germ. His condescending smile and smug expression aggravated me. Couldn't anyone else see him for the snake he was?

He sneered, "Why? You scared I'll take her from you? I saw how you looked at her."

"You can try. I bet she'll have nothing to do with you."

I was ready to drop my bike and knock him down. He saw my reaction and backed off.

"It's okay, Harmon. I'll just follow you and you can't do anything about it."

He was right so I revved my bike and sped off, followed by Georgie, the pair of us leaving Billy in our wake. I continually sneaked glances over my shoulder as we rode along the road. To my dismay and annoyance he followed at a distance.

I halted by the side of the road and waited for Billy to catch up but he stopped about a hundred yards behind. Georgie had been totally silent to this moment, no doubt puzzled by it all.

I turned to him and said, "Georgie! You go ahead to the Waterhole! I'm going to get rid of Billy."

"How?"

"I'm hoping I can give him the slip and he'll follow you. Don't slow down, okay."

"Okay."

Georgie sped off and I followed. At the next bend in the road I braked sharply and veered off into the bushes and hid. Very soon, Billy roared past on his bike. I waited about five minutes before riding to Amy's house.

Amy and Ruth greeted me on the veranda. While Amy went inside to change I explained to Ruth about Billy wanting to tag along. I told her about Billy being the local policeman's son.

"I'm sorry!" I said. "I didn't think this would happen."

"Does Amy know about Billy's dad?"

"Yes! She said she wouldn't say anything about you or your secret."

Ruth sighed and grimaced. I thought that perhaps she was beginning to regret her former keenness for Amy to acquire a new circle of friends.

"All right . . . what is done cannot be undone. Nothing we can do about it now. Let's hope everything will be okay. You'll need to keep an eye on her," she said.

"Got ya gear?" I asked when Amy joined us.

She responded by lifting up her top to reveal a red, one-piece swimsuit. She kissed her mother on the cheek and walked to my bike carrying a canvas bag.

Ruth called out, "Enjoy yourself. Have a great day."

As her mother, Ruth had wanted Amy to mix with other teenagers and I understood her trepidation. I imagined it was just like sending a child to school for the very first time. Ruth still had that concerned look on her face so I moved towards her and tried to reassure her.

"It'll be okay. I'll look after her," I said.

She gave a faint smile and called anxiously to Amy, "Amy! Stay with Guy! Okay!"

Amy waved and yelled back, "Okay! See ya Mum."

We arrived at the Waterhole to find a large group of teenagers splashing about in the water and mingling on the bank. Georgie joined us. When he saw Amy, his jaw dropped and, open mouthed, he stared at her. First there was Sam and now Amy.

"Close your mouth Georgie before you swallow a bug or something. This is Amy; Amy—Georgie," I said.

"Hi! Georgie," she said with a smile.

Georgie replied with an almost inaudible 'Hi'. Billy had been with his friends but when he saw Amy, he ran over to us.

He muttered, "Round one to you, Harmon. We'll see who wins round two."

He smirked as, without any encouragement from her, he took Amy by the arm and escorted her over to his friends. Georgie and I watched from a distance as he introduced Amy to them.

The clear cloudless sky had fulfilled its promise to turn on a hot one. We stripped down to our shorts and grabbed the rope on the tree. We swung out over the water and dropped down into the murky depths. We swam by ourselves because we didn't want to mix with Billy or his group. I noticed that 'Hank the Tank' was not with them. True to my promise to Ruth, I kept an eye on Amy throughout the afternoon. Billy was using all his bogus persuasion and mock charm on Amy and, from my perspective, it seemed to be working. She giggled and smiled happily as she mingled with his friends. When she took off her clothes to go swimming, she drew whistles of appreciation from all the boys present, who admired her figure in her one-piece suit. She responded with a pose, before wading out into the water, where Billy quickly joined her.

Georgie and I lounged under a tree, all the while watching the group. Georgie asked me countless questions about Amy, and not surprisingly, his eyes never strayed from her. Like Billy, he too was captivated by her charms. Disappointing to both of us, Amy chose to spend the afternoon with Billy and his friends, and it wasn't till she climbed out of the water, that she came over to the tree. She flopped down beside me and shook her head vigorously, grinning as I copped a spray of water.

She grabbed my arm and declared, "This place is great! Thanks for bringing me."

"I'm glad you're having a good time," I muttered.

"You are okay with me and Billy, aren't you? If not, we can go," she said, taking my hand.

"Nah! It's fine. Have a good time."

Once again we were interrupted by Billy, who grabbed Amy's hand as he asked her to join him for one last swim. While they swam, Georgie and I tinkered with our bikes until Amy indicated she was ready to leave. She approached us while Billy waited near his bike.

"Billy asked me to go with him. Is it okay?" she asked.

"What will your mother say?" I asked, "She might not want Billy going to your house."

"Why?"

"You're showing Billy where you live. Don't forget he's the son of the local cop."

"So?"

I was angry because she didn't want to listen to reason. Had she forgotten why she had been forced to move from town to town over the last three years?

"What about your secret . . . you know! Your mum will not be happy about this."

"I won't tell him anything. He's just taking me home. What's the harm in that?" she said defiantly.

There was nothing I could gain by arguing further. Amy was determined to forge a relationship with Billy. He was charming and handsome and anything I might be able to tell her could be interpreted only one way—that I was jealous and mean spirited. What could I say? No! Keep away from that creep!

"Fine! Go with him."

Amy hopped on Billy's bike and they set off along the track. Georgie and I followed at a safe distance. When we arrived at the house we saw Amy in earnest conversation with Billy. They stopped talking and separated when they saw us approaching.

Billy turned and rode past us, giving a casual wave, before he roared off down the track. Amy waved goodbye and moved towards the house. I didn't want to try and explain to Ruth, so I turned and followed Billy. As we sped off, I glanced back, and saw Ruth and Amy in conversation on the veranda.

My summer was rapidly becoming a summer of lost love. By the time we reached home, I had decided that I would not visit Amy the next day, so I asked Georgie if he would like to go shooting with me.

CHAPTER 7

BEST FRIENDS

The following morning, Georgie and I rode into the mountains carrying our rifles and a few brightly coloured targets. We travelled along the road to the quarry, but branched off near it, to take a narrow, winding track up the mountain. The track led to a clearing in the forest that was used regularly by the youth of the town for target practice because it was isolated and its backdrop was a cliff face. I set up an assortment of targets on a large log in the middle of the clearing, including tin cans and bottles as well as the cardboard targets.

After completing this task I grinned at Georgie and asked, "What's your aim like Georgie? I bet you can't hit them all."

He grinned and replied cockily, "Easy! I once shot the bull's-eye of a target from four hundred yards."

"Rubbish! You're telling another one of your tales."

"No I'm not! I did. You can ask my dad."

I laughed. Telling tales was part of his nature and Georgie was prone to exaggeration. He once bragged he could hold his breath under water for four minutes but when Ivan and I timed him, he lasted forty seconds. Of course he had an excuse. He always had excuses but we took everything he said with a grain of salt. Other teenagers delighted in 'leading him on' and made fun of him but it didn't seem to bother Georgie.

Georgie wrapped the rifle strap around his arm, just as he had seen soldiers do in the movies, and closed one eye as he aimed carefully at the target. He squeezed the trigger and fired, but managed to hit only three targets. Typical Georgie—he complained that the sun was in his eyes, which of course was untrue.

Georgie could be said to be a kindred spirit to a giant Labrador dog—gangly, awkward but lovable. I took aim and shot but deliberately missed all but two of the targets.

"Bad luck," Georgie grinned, "maybe next time."

"You're too good today, Georgie. I'll get you next time."

Georgie was clumsy and uncoordinated. He'd trip over his own feet but if you gave him a tiny creature to hold, he became a totally different person. He handled animals easily, because I think they sensed he wouldn't harm them, and they trusted him. He was always bringing home sick birds and animals to nurse back to health, so when we went shooting, he refused to shoot live targets.

"How's Troy goin?" I asked as I grabbed some targets.

"Great! I'm trying to teach him some tricks. He can roll over now when I tell him," he replied.

His 'best friend', Trixie, a Kelpie dog had died of old age six months ago and Georgie was devastated. To ease his pain, his father gave him a puppy.

Georgie called the pup 'Troy'. As a companion, Troy often rode with Georgie on his bike, his tiny, furry head poking out the top of Georgie's shirt. It was easy to see why he loved his animal friends so much—they loved him unconditionally and they never teased or put him down.

I set up five targets.

"Here we go, Georgie," I said, "just imagine all these are Billy Jenkins."

Remarkably, when we fired, we hit all of them. Our mounting resentment of Billy had certainly improved our aim.

When I returned home, my mother told me that I had to help my father do a stock take at the store in the morning. I wasn't eager to visit Amy again so I really didn't mind the prospect of helping out.

Next morning Sam met me at the front door. After the incident at the cafe I thought our friendship was well and truly over, or at best had been placed in a holding pattern and under the most extreme stress. Sam's miserable expression indicated that she was hurting. I felt guilty. We exchanged greetings and walked out onto the lawn in silence. I tried to explain Amy to her.

"Sam . . . Amy . . . I'm sorry I didn't tell you about her. I'm sorry if I hurt you. I'm a complete and utter dickhead."

"Hurt me? Hell . . . I'm not hurt . . . much . . . It's your life, and yes, you are a dickhead."

I knew Sam didn't mean it. Her friendship was important to me—and she was aware of it. Sam sat on the swing hanging from the tree in our front yard and stared at the ground. As she slowly swung back and forth, she shuffled her feet on the bare patch of earth under the swing. I stepped in front of her to get her attention and she stopped. She looked up at me with tear stained eyes. I hated seeing her like this.

"Amy lives with her mother on a property out of town. She has no friends and her mother asked me to show her around," I explained.

"Is she your girlfriend?"

"Not really. She likes Billy."

"Billy? Lover boy Billy? Why do girls go for him? I think he's a slime bag. You're much better."

"I wish Amy thought so. Sam . . . you're my best friend but . . ."

"I know . . . but not your girlfriend. It's fine. If you ever get tired of this Amy . . . well you know."

She stood up and moved away so I couldn't see her face. I didn't blame her.

"Sure! Still friends?" I begged.

"Yeah! No matter what, I'll always be your friend."

"I have to help Dad in the store for a couple of days, starting this morning. Wanna help too?"

Sam hesitated before answering. I tried to sweeten the deal.

"You'll get free drinks and ice creams. And . . . you'll get to spend time with your best friend."

"In that case, count me in. But I can't help today; see ya in the morning."

She smiled briefly before departing; leaving me to ponder what might have been between us. If Amy had not entered my life Sam and I might have been more than just friends.

Sam helped out at the store for the next two days. I enjoyed her company and her wicked sense of humour. She delighted in playing practical jokes on me. Sam and I never talked about Amy again. I now accepted that she had feelings for me even though I was emotionally committed to Amy, at least for the time being.

CHAPTER 8

THE FIRST INCIDENT

I hadn't seen Amy for three days, and although her involvement with Billy had been an impediment in my relationship with her, I was still keen to meet up with her again. My enthusiasm for her was curbed somewhat, when I arrived at Ruth's house, only to discover Billy's bike parked outside. Ruth came out onto the veranda to greet me. When she saw me looking at Billy's bike, she moved quickly to explain his presence, even though she had taken great pains to tell me that she didn't want people coming out to her house.

"Billy has come out to see us every day. I know it goes against what I said to you before, but he has been the perfect gentleman. He and Amy seem to be having a great time," she said.

This news, so casually revealed, infuriated me. Of course Billy would be the perfect gentleman for a while to gain their confidence. Then he would pounce. I thought that as a mother Ruth should have known better, the more so in the wake of her recent negative experiences.

"I don't trust Billy. Don't forget he's the son of a cop," I said.

"That's why I need you here to look after Amy. I know you have feelings for her but you have to realise she hasn't spent much time with boys and girls of her own age. Give her time. She will learn. Right now Amy and Billy are swimming in the creek. Why not go join them?"

I shook my head and walked away. I didn't want to join Amy and Billy, but as I picked up my bike to go home, I decided that I would venture down to the creek and let Amy know how I felt. As I came closer to the water hole, I heard laughing and splashing. The revellers didn't hear me approaching because I reached the waterhole in time to watch them as they locked in an embrace, kissing. Amy was learning . . . quickly.

They disengaged when they saw me on the bank. Amy was embarrassed, but not Billy. He grinned and put his arm around her shoulder, a gesture of ownership that declared 'she's mine now'.

Amy moved towards the bank to greet me but stopped when I said coldly, "Don't let me interrupt you. Just came to say hello. I'll leave you alone."

Amy frowned and pleaded, "Come and join us, Guy. Please?"

"Nah! I'll just go and have a talk to Ruth. Round two to you Billy. See ya."

I tramped back to the house, seething with fury. Billy had wormed his way into Amy's life and now I was on the outer. I sat and watched Ruth in her studio as she painted. She painted delicate flowers in watercolour, handling the brushes and paint with the skill of a surgeon. Her talent inspired me to try some drawing of my own so I picked up a sketch pad and began drawing. Ruth obviously had some insight into how I was feeling because she didn't ask any questions. Time seemed to fly and eventually I forgot about Amy and Billy.

Ruth and I had a short break for lunch and Amy and Billy arrived just as we commenced washing the dishes and plates. I heard them giggling happily as they walked onto the veranda. I took that as my cue to leave.

"Ruth! Do you mind if I go up to the mine to do some sketching?" I asked.

"That's fine. See you later; but just remember what I told you about the mine."

I passed Amy and Billy as they entered the house, ignoring them completely and rode up to the abandoned mine. I spent an hour sketching and was packing up in preparation of returning to the house to say goodbye when I saw a horse and a solo rider approaching. It was Amy.

Her face was flushed and she had the look of a wild beast ready to rip me apart and devour me. If looks could kill, I was already dead. She leapt from her horse and strode towards me. As she stomped across the bare earth, tiny clouds of red dust trailed behind her. I stood motionless, almost hypnotised by her icy glare. She halted about three yards in front of me and placed her hands on her hips in an aggressive stance. I waited for the explosion that came soon.

She blurted out, "What's wrong with you? You don't come near me . . . You come up here and hide. You don't visit for three days."

Angry tears spilled down her cheeks. However, I was just as angry.

"If you don't know, I'm not going to tell you," I muttered.

"Is it because of Billy? What about us?"

"What about us?" I repeated, shuffling my feet.

"I thought we were friends," she said, wiping away tears. "Don't you like me?"

"Friends!" I scoffed, "You and Billy aren't just friends are you?"

I stared at the ground and kicked angrily at the loose gravel before slouching against a large rock nearby.

"All we did is kiss. Nothing else."

"You never kissed me like that. You can't say it was nothing."

I glanced up at her. She moved in and gently kissed me on the lips. Her soft lips sent my spirit soaring. I had to be close to heaven. She pulled back and grinned at the stunned expression on my face. I lunged forward to kiss her but she stepped back and giggled. I was confused and baffled by her actions. I'd seen her in a passionate embrace with another boy, she berated me for not understanding—and then kissed me! To add to my confusion, she moved away when I tried to kiss her. Did that mean she still looked upon me as a friend only or was she doing it on purpose to frustrate me? Even now, at sixteen and with very little experience, I was beginning to grasp that I would never understand women. It was exasperating.

"Have you only kissed him or has it gone further?" I asked.

I wanted to find out her true feelings for Billy. Was it love or lust?

"What do you mean . . . further?" she asked, seemingly innocent.

"You know . . . more than kissing. Do I have to spell it out?"

Amy's mouth opened in shock and she gasped out loud. She slapped me on the arm as if to say 'how dare you?'

"NO! No way. We've only kissed."

I put my hands up in mock horror but changed my attitude the instant I saw the hurt in her eyes. I quickly apologised for my remarks which she had so obviously found offensive.

"Sorry! I should have known you wouldn't do anything else."

I paused briefly before adding, "But Billy would!"

Amy glared, "Billy has been a gentleman; stop picking on him!"

"You know I don't trust him. I can't help how I feel."

"Maybe you're just jealous and don't want him around. Think about that!" she said angrily.

"Maybe I am but Billy Jenkins is dangerous. You'll see!" I barked. I wasn't going to back down.

Amy turned on her heel and without another word, strode to her horse and swung up into the saddle in one fluid movement. She turned the horse's head and galloped off, leaving me to grab my gear and follow on the bike. When I arrived back at the house she was unsaddling the horse in the yard. She ignored me as she brushed the horse down. I strode up to the yard and held out my hand.

"Friends?"

She disregarded my peace offering and continued to tend the horse. I slouched against a post and watched in silence. After a short time, I'd had enough of the stony silence so I turned and walked away. I'd only taken a few steps when I felt her hand on my shoulder twisting me around. She grinned and offered her hand.

"Friends."

Before I could respond, she wrapped her arms around me in an embrace. This was followed by 'Race ya!' and she dashed to the house with me in hot pursuit. We both entered and collapsed on the sofa, giggling like little children. Ruth entered from the back of the house.

"Well, you two certainly seem happy. What happened?"

Amy grinned, "Nothing. We're just happy to be friends."

Ruth smiled and sat opposite us. She looked at Amy.

"Before Billy left, he asked me if he could take you to a movie tomorrow night. I told him it was okay and that I would drop you off at the theatre and pick you up after," she said.

I was puzzled. Ruth had appeared deadly serious when she told me her secret and pressed me not to tell others. Yet, here she was, happy that Amy was going out with the son of a local policeman. I was beginning to have doubts about the honesty and integrity of Ruth Parkinson. All was not what it seemed.

"Why don't you go too, Guy? I really would like you to go for Amy's sake," Ruth added.

I grimaced. I didn't want to watch a movie and watch Billy and Amy cuddling and kissing as well. I glanced at Amy who stood up and moved behind the sofa.

"I can look after myself, Mum," she said.

However, my remarks about Billy must have sown the seeds of doubt in her mind because she added, "But it would make me feel better if I knew Guy was there too."

I tried to convince myself that it was okay to accompany Amy to the movies even though she would be with Billy but I could not dupe myself. I was too emotionally involved with Amy, whether I liked to admit it or not.

"I can't go. I have to work at home. Mum asked me to help her. Sorry!"

Amy knew I was lying. She slumped down on the sofa, her lovely features downcast.

She said, "Well, if Guy can't make it, then I won't go either. I'll go some other time."

The expressions on their faces and the tone of Amy's voice indicated they were both bitterly disappointed. Whatever transpired, I couldn't win. I had won because Amy wasn't going but I had lost because she was so unhappy. A stronger, more disagreeable person would have enjoyed the victory—but not me.

I sighed and muttered, "I'll go with Georgie but . . . we won't sit anywhere near Amy."

Amy's face lit up, Ruth smiled warmly and I . . . well . . . I felt trapped.

It is accepted that at the movies, the couples who want to make out sit up the back away from prying eyes and so it was no surprise to see Billy Jenkins take Amy to the back of the theatre when we went the next night. Georgie and I sat together in the middle rows, in the stalls at the side and away from them.

Several times during the movie I peered through the darkness and saw them snuggling up close together. I felt such searing hurt inside that it became an ordeal to remain seated. I wanted so much to separate them and knock Billy down.

Halfway through the movie I was surprisingly joined by a distraught Amy. Her clothes were in disarray, her blouse hanging out from her skirt and her face wet with tears. Several buttons on her blouse were undone. I sprang to my feet and turned in the direction of Billy but he had gone. I took Amy's arm and sat her down beside me. She rested her head on my shoulder and whispered in my ear. Apparently, Billy had wanted more than a kiss—and Billy was used to getting his own way.

Georgie went outside to look around but Billy had disappeared. I put my arm around Amy to comfort her for the rest of the movie while Georgie kept an eye on the door in case Billy returned.

After the movie we waited outside in the cool, night air for Ruth's arrival. Amy had composed herself and re-arranged her clothes. I didn't ask about the incident, mindful that I could I upset her again but after a time she decided to take me in to her confidence.

"I'm glad you were here. Billy put his hands under my blouse and touched my breasts. I told him not to but he wouldn't stop. He had his hands all over me. In the end I told him you were here and I was going to sit with you. That made him stop but he was so angry. He left when I came down to you. You were right! I should have known better," she whispered softly with a tremor in her voice.

I smiled the lofty smile of someone whose opinion has just been vindicated but inside, my heart was dancing a wild tango. I had been proven right and after tonight Billy would never again be part of Amy's life. It would have been quite a shock for Billy to have a girl rebuff his advances, especially the prettiest girl in the Roxborough district.

Georgie, who had developed a secret crush on Amy, finally spoke up.

"If Billy Jenkins comes near you again . . . I'll . . . I'll smash him into little pieces!" he told Amy.

To emphasise his point, he slammed his right fist into his other hand. Amy smiled in gratitude as she touched his hand. A matching smile spread over Georgie's face and he poked out his chest as if to say, 'I am your bodyguard and I will protect you from all evil'.

Because I knew Georgie so well, I hoped he wouldn't do anything silly that would generate trouble. Amy asked us not to say anything about the incident to Ruth. She didn't want to alarm her mother and I guessed she didn't want her mother to place restrictions on her going into Roxborough. Georgie and I said our goodbyes shortly after Ruth arrived. It would be up to Amy to maintain a brave face and keep the incident to herself.

CHAPTER 9

THE SECOND INCIDENT

With Billy out of the picture I had Amy to myself for a few days. I took her on my bike to show her Roxborough and its surrounds. On one or two occasions, Georgie tagged along with Troy tucked into his shirt. I remained uneasy about Billy because I reasoned it was out of character for him to give up so easily with a girl, especially one so lovely as Amy.

On Sundays, I usually attended church with my family. It had been a week since the movies and I was reluctant to go to church because I wanted to go out to Amy's but my parents were insistent that church was a family event. It was about two in the afternoon when Georgie and I arrived at Amy's house, to be greeted by Ruth.

"Boys! Amy's not here. Billy came about half an hour ago to see her. I told him she went horse riding up past the old mine. That's where he headed," she said.

Obviously she knew nothing about the incident at the movies so she showed no trace of concern; however, her words sent instant alarm bells ringing in my head.

Trying to remain calm, I said, "Thanks Ruth. Georgie and I'll ride after them. Let's go Georgie!"

On reaching the mine site I spotted Amy's horse but there was no sign of either Amy or Billy. The horse wasn't tethered and its bridle dragged on the ground. I jumped off my bike, sprinted to the mine

BURIED SECRETS

entrance and peered into the eerie gloom. I shouted Amy's name but all I heard was an echo of my own voice. Georgie joined me.

"If Billy so much as touches Amy, I'll kill him," I growled.

The untethered horse was a worry in itself. I surveyed the surrounding landscape. There was no sign of either Amy or Billy.

I turned to Georgie and said, "I'll go on up the mountain past the mine and you go down towards the creek. Give us a yell if you see them. Okay?"

"Yeah!" he answered. He swivelled on his heels and proceeded towards the creek line.

As I trudged up the mountain slope I constantly yelled out Amy's name, hoping to hear a reply. After ten minutes I swung down towards the open ground near the creek. The sweat was dripping down my forehead, stinging my eyes as I ploughed through the long grass. The thought of Amy being molested by Billy gave me plenty of motivation to find her. I now realised that Ruth should have been told about the movie incident. If she had known, I was sure she would have told Billy to leave. I quickened my pace, continuing to call Amy's name and praying silently that she was safe.

A piercing scream interrupted my thoughts. I swivelled my head, looking in every direction but my line of sight was blocked by trees bordering the creek. Another scream came from the direction of the creek. I hurtled through the undergrowth like a startled rabbit, zigzagging through the trees, blindly hoping I would find Amy, for I was certain these were her screams. I halted, scanning the terrain for signs of her. I thought I heard faint but audible sobs coming from my left. I sprinted through the grass and bushes to be confronted by the sight of Amy slumped on the grassy bank of the creek. Her body heaved as she sobbed loudly. Just as I reached her, Georgie also arrived. I took Amy in my arms and tried to comfort her.

— 79 —

Her blouse was ripped open to the waist and her shorts were undone. As I gently raised her head I saw her bruised and bloody mouth. The blood, mixed with the tears that ran down her face.

Carefully, I wiped her face and comforted her as best I could with reassuring words. Georgie paced up and down nearby, angrily muttering to himself. There was no sign of Billy.

"Did Billy do this?" I whispered softly.

Through muffled sobs she managed to answer, "Yes."

She held her blouse together with one hand while attempting to pull up her shorts with the other.

"Where'd he go?" I asked, looking around.

After a few moments, she managed to control her sobbing and sat up, rearranging her clothes.

Pausing for breath, she answered, "When he heard you calling out he ran off."

Georgie growled, "I'll get him!"

In spite of my objections, Georgie dashed off towards the mine. I hoped he wouldn't catch Billy because in his present state he might kill him. I turned back to Amy.

"Are you okay?" I asked. It was a mindless question but I asked it anyway.

She nodded but her whole body was trembling so I took off my shirt and wrapped it around her.

"Why did you come to the creek with him?"

"I didn't. I was here when he arrived. Mum probably told him I was here."

"I found your horse up near the mine."

Tears welled in her eyes again but she blinked them away.

"Billy said he was very sorry. He promised it would never happen again," she said.

"Billy is an arsehole!" I muttered, "He is a low life—a maggot!"

"I told him to get lost but he pushed me backwards to the ground. He ripped open my blouse and he groped my breasts. I fought him but he pinned my arms to my side. I screamed and he hit me in the mouth. That's when we heard you calling out," she cried.

She crumpled on my chest and her body shook as she cried. These were not tears that flowed down her cheeks but great wracking sobs that came from deep down inside, shaking her shoulders and making her gasp for breath. Eventually, her sobs quietened as she lay resting against me, exhausted, drained.

"I'd better get you home," I said, helping her to her feet.

"I'm going to be sick," she gasped and sank to her knees and vomited.

She stared blankly at the ground as she tried to recover. Her face was a ghastly, ashen colour. As I watched this scene with an unpleasant mix of helplessness and anger, I was unable to prevent tears spilling down my cheeks. This latest ordeal had rendered Amy exceedingly weak so I lifted her into my arms and carried her back to the mine and to my bike. With her clinging to me I slowly rode back to the house.

Ruth was sitting on the veranda reading but when she looked up and saw Amy, she gasped in horror and dashed down the steps. Without a word, she helped me carry Amy into the house and onto the sofa. While I sat beside Amy and held her hand, Ruth began tending to her daughter's bruises and cuts. Ruth's face drained of colour when Amy opened my shirt that had concealed the torn blouse.

She looked at me and whispered, "What happened? Did Billy do this?"

I nodded and told her the story. She listened intently with tears flowing down her cheeks. Her face was pale and her lips trembled as she held Amy in her arms as she would a baby. She was visibly relieved to learn Billy had not raped Amy.

She gave me a hug and said, "Thank you Guy. Amy's lucky to have you as a friend. I never saw Billy come back. He must have sneaked past and grabbed his bike. Where's Georgie?"

I jumped to my feet.

"I forgot about Georgie. I'd better catch up to him before he finds Billy. Who knows what he might do to him?" I said.

Amy grabbed my arm and cried out, "NO! You can't go! Billy might come back. Don't leave."

She began to weep again so I sat down and took her hand. It would be difficult to leave her but I also had a responsibility to find Georgie.

"Your mother's here to protect you. You'll be all right. He wouldn't dare come back now."

This did not console her and she turned to Ruth and cried, "Mummy! I don't want Guy to leave. Please make him stay. Please!"

Amy was like a frightened and traumatised child. This had been an unspeakable torment for her, especially as it came after the prior incident at the movies and Billy's subsequent assurance that he would never again act that way towards her. I glanced at Ruth. I could see by the look on her face that she wanted me to stay for Amy's sake.

Ruth pleaded, "Could you just stay the night, Guy? It would help Amy so much if she knew you were here."

I explained, "If I don't go home, my parents will be worried sick."

Amy had buried her face in a pillow, sobbing quietly. I dearly wanted to stay but I knew I had to go home as I also had Georgie to think about.

Ruth's face lit up and she exclaimed, "I can drive into Roxborough and tell your parents I've invited you to stay over because you're camping near the old gold mine with Amy and a few friends. I know it is a blatant lie but I don't know what else to do."

I shrugged and said, "It might work but I'm still worried about Georgie."

Ruth quickly added. "I'll try and find him as well. Okay?"

There wasn't much I could say so I nodded my head in assent.

"Good! That's settled," Ruth said, "Now! If you go and bring the horse back, I'll give Amy a bath and prepare some food before I leave for town."

I brought the horse back from the mine, removed the saddle and bridle and fed both horses. I had helped Amy do this a few times so I knew what to do. I hurried back to the house to find Amy, dressed in a bathrobe, curled up on the sofa. I gave her a warm smile and joined her. She reached out, took my hand and gave a faint smile in return. Ruth was busy in the kitchen making sandwiches. We ate the meal in virtual silence, each engrossed in our own thoughts. I was thinking about Billy Jenkins and Georgie—a different set of thoughts for each of two very different people.

Before Ruth left to drive to town, she took me aside and whispered, "Thanks for staying Guy. Lock the doors when I leave but leave the veranda light on."

I nodded and asked, "Are you going to the police? You do know Billy's dad is a cop?"

"I know. It's a bit awkward. I've got to be careful. There's the matter of Billy but also our secret. But Billy did assault Amy and he has to be punished."

Any other mother, no matter what dark secrets they harboured, would have gone directly to the police but not Ruth. I tried to understand her concerns but there was no way I was going to remain impassive whilst Billy got away with hurting Amy. I promised myself I would not allow this to happen, even if it meant taking the law into my own hands. Ruth frowned as she moved to Amy's side.

"Sweetheart! You've got to trust me. I need to be told. If you had told me about what happened at the movies I wouldn't have allowed Billy near you. You know I'm not going to yell at you or punish you if you do the wrong thing. Do you understand?"

Amy burst into tears. Ruth held her in her arms and whispered soothing words.

Amy gathered herself, wiped away the tears and replied, "I'm sorry Mum. I know I should have told you. It won't happen again. I promise."

Ruth kissed her and sat her down on the sofa. She picked up the keys to the Jeep and left the house. I locked the door behind her and sat beside Amy.

She sat up and said in a weary voice, "I think I'll go to my room. I'm feeling a little tired."

I helped her to her room and prepared to leave but she motioned me to stay so I sat at the foot of the bed while she curled up under the bedclothes.

"Would you like some music?" I asked.

She nodded so I placed a stack of records on the record player and sat back down.

Amy pointed to the pillow beside her and said, "Come here beside me. I won't bite you."

I felt rather self-conscious and awkward as I lay on top of the bedclothes alongside her but in time I began to relax. We lay in silence, listening to the soothing sounds of the sixties. Eventually, Amy moved over and nestled in my arms, her head resting on my chest.

It wasn't long before she fell asleep. I dared not move for fear of waking her. It was exhilarating and enjoyable to have a warm, lovely girl asleep in my arms. I thought about the events of the summer so far—it was a summer I would never forget.

When Ruth returned and entered the bedroom, I gently disentangled myself from Amy and slid off the bed. Ruth showed me to a small room at the back of the house where she had made up a bed.

I asked, "Did you see my parents and Georgie?"

"Your parents were fine. I didn't find Georgie or Billy Jenkins but I saw one of Billy's friends at the café. He told me Billy had been there earlier but had gone home."

"Maybe I should go and check on Georgie. I don't want him getting into trouble," I said.

"Look! It's late and I'm sure he's gone home by now. You might as well stay here and see him in the morning. Amy would feel much better if you were here to greet her in the morning."

"I suppose so," I said reluctantly. I was worried about Georgie but agreed to her request.

"Thanks Guy. I really do appreciate your help. I'll see you in the morning. Goodnight."

She left the room and I stretched out on the bed and stared up at the ceiling. I remembered how self-conscious I had been when Amy first kissed and hugged me. I felt we connected because of a shared innocence and naivety about life and love. I wondered what action Ruth might contemplate regarding Billy. Would she go to the police and perhaps risk disclosing her secret? Would she ban Amy from going into Roxborough? I fell asleep with these thoughts whirring around in my brain.

Early the next morning I awoke to find Amy bending over me.

"Guy! Are you awake?"

I sat up and rubbed the sleep from my eyes. She smiled sweetly and gently kissed me on the cheek.

"Are you okay?" I asked.

"I'm fine. Thanks for staying. Mum's got breakfast ready."

She turned to leave but at once changed her mind and sat down on the bed.

She spoke softly, "Look! I know very little about boys or love. Billy was a new experience for me and so were you. What I'm trying to say is . . . even though I had these feelings I should have been more careful. I'm sorry."

"Why should you be sorry? You've done nothing wrong. Billy has had lots of girls wrapped around his grubby little fingers. Don't blame yourself for what happened."

"Even so, I feel I've let you and Mum down."

"Rubbish! You did the right thing in saying no to Billy. Not all boys are like him, you know."

"True! The perfect boy was here all the time."

"Who?"

"You, silly."

She smiled and left the room. I basked in the warm glow of her affection for me. Things were definitely looking up in our relationship. As a teenager, smitten by first love, I was only too eager to forgive her for her dalliance with another boy.

CHAPTER 10

A LOST CAUSE

It was almost mid-day when I got home, aiming to find Georgie and clear up the matter of Billy Jenkins. I had a quick shower and put on a change of clothes before heading across to Georgie's house. I was greeted at the door by Mr and Mrs Henderson, who were clearly upset. There was no sign of Georgie and their faces told me that something had happened. I feared the worst as they invited me inside and sat me down.

Pat Henderson was a quiet, unassuming mum and her husband, Tom was a mechanic at the local garage. He was a tall, thin man, who like his wife, was rather quiet. The Hendersons had four children—Georgie, the eldest, Max and Johnny who were twelve and ten respectively and Mary, the youngest. Considering the Henderson parents' usual reserved demeanor, I was surprised to see them so angry and upset, but when I heard the full story, I understood. Georgie, because of his intellectual disability, had always been a concern for his parents and they had tried their utmost to protect him throughout his childhood and teenage years.

What had happened was something they had secretly dreaded for years. Georgie was in hospital recovering from a beating at the hands of Billy Jenkins and his friends. One of our friends, who witnessed the incident, told the Hendersons what happened. Apparently Georgie had followed Billy to town and finally caught up with him at the café. Georgie accused Billy of attacking Amy and threatened to bash him if he ever went near her again. Billy just laughed at him, called him a 'retard' and told him to 'piss off'.

Billy then went on to add that Amy was a 'slut' who wanted to have sex with him and that she had been all over him. When Billy refused, she was the one who attacked him. He and his friends started calling Georgie more derogatory names. That's when Georgie lost his cool and grabbed Billy in a bear hug. Georgie was a tall, strong youth and he lifted Billy up off the ground and shook him violently.

Billy wasn't able to break free so his pathetic friends pulled Georgie away and dragged him outside. They took him around the side of the building and pinned his arms by his side while Billy laid into him. When they threw Georgie to the ground, Billy kicked and punched him until he was unconscious. Our friend sounded the alarm to the owner of the café who intervened before Billy could inflict more damage on his hapless victim.

As a result of this cowardly attack, Georgie was left with several broken ribs and a broken nose as well as numerous cuts and bruises. I felt sick to the stomach upon hearing the extent of his injuries. I had been worried that Georgie might harm Billy, not the other way round. I had a foul, unpleasant taste in my mouth and tears burned my eyes as I listened to the story.

"Have you gone to the police?" I asked.

Pat Henderson began to sob on her husband's shoulder as he raised his voice in anger, incensed by the mention of the police.

"Police? Police? This town doesn't have police. You know what I was told by the police. They said the café owner had contacted them about the incident. They interviewed the teenagers at the café and were told Georgie had started the fight. He had accused Billy and then attacked him. Billy and his friends were defending themselves. Can you believe it? They were *defending* themselves. The police said Georgie had brought it upon himself and no charges would be laid. What a joke!"

Tom Henderson banged his clenched fist on the chair and put his head in his hands, shaking it from side to side in sheer helpless frustration.

"What about the café owner and those who were not Billy's mates?" I asked. "Surely they told the police what really happened."

Tom Henderson lifted his head. His lips were pressed tight together as his face screwed in anger. His voice was harsh.

"Yeah! They told the police what happened but the police didn't believe them. Billy told his father lies about the café owner not liking Billy and his friends because they had been skylarking in the café and had broken some furniture. As for the others, Billy convinced his dad that they were Georgie's friends, all of them hell-bent on getting Billy into trouble. They did not say why, of course. They believed Billy. And why not, when your old man's a policeman? You can't win. If I see Billy Jenkins in the street I'll kill him. I swear I'll kill him."

Mrs Henderson took his hand and said softly, "No Tom. If you do anything you'll end up in jail and this family doesn't need that right now—or any other time. There's an old saying 'What goes around, comes around'."

She saw my puzzled expression and was quick with an explanation. "Guy. It means that sooner or later Billy Jenkins will get what he deserves."

I didn't want it to end there. It was unfair that one of my closest friends was in hospital as a result of a cowardly assault. The victim was an intellectually disabled teenager who had no chance of properly defending himself—and yet nothing was being done about it.

"What if we get Amy to tell the police about Billy attacking her? They would have to charge Billy then, wouldn't they?" I argued.

Tom Henderson sighed and held his wife's hand. He clenched his fist and once again his face twisted in anger as he answered.

"Georgie told us what happened so I went to the police and told them about the attack on Amy. You'll never believe their answer."

"What? That Amy made up the story?" I said.

"Yep! They said it was Amy's word against Billy's. Billy told them it didn't happen. When I told them about her being hit and her clothes being torn, they said she might have hurt herself falling down or even done it herself. Billy told them that Amy was a vindictive, jealous girl. He told them that Amy wanted to have sex with him and she became furious when he refused. So what can you do? Nothing! It's so galling."

"That's rubbish! I heard that Billy got a girl into trouble in the city and her father made sure that Billy and his dad were moved to the country. His dad knows what Billy's like. That's just an excuse," I growled angrily.

Tom Henderson stood up abruptly and walked away, clearly upset. It was a lost cause. Billy Jenkins would get away with it. I decided that I would take action and give Billy Jenkins the thrashing of his life and put him in hospital. I clenched my fists and muttered an obscenity under my breath. Pat Henderson noticed my reaction and seemed to read my mind because she put her hand on my shoulder before quietly warning me.

"Leave it be, Guy! Don't do something you'll regret. For the moment, just leave it be and we'll see how things level out. I'll tell you now—Billy Jenkins will not get away with this."

For the moment I was prepared to wait before seeking revenge. I didn't know how this news would affect Ruth and Amy. No doubt, they would be upset and furious at the non-action of the police.

I went with the Hendersons to visit Georgie in hospital. His face was almost unrecognisable. One eye was swollen, his mouth bruised and twice its normal size. His broken nose was bandaged. The only feature easily recognisable as belonging to Georgie was his thick, curly hair. I squeezed his hand and said "'Hi." He whispered a reply. Tears threatened so I turned away to take a few deep breaths.

After the visit I went home and decided to tell my parents about the incident. I didn't want someone relaying Billy's fabricated version of recent events to them. Mum was standing at the sink, humming to herself, as she washed some dishes.

"Mum! Georgie's in hospital. He was bashed by Billy Jenkins and his mates," I said, my voice cracking with pent-up emotion.

Mum stopped cleaning and turned to face me. Soapy water dripped from her hands onto the floor. She wiped them on her apron and stared at me with a look of sheer disbelief.

"What? How did it happen?"

I tried to control myself but the words gushed out in staccato fashion,

"Billy assaulted Amy Parkinson and Georgie went after Billy. Billy's friends held Georgie while Billy bashed him."

"Who is Amy Parkinson?"

I told her about Ruth and Amy living on the property out of town and how I had made friends with them.

Mum frowned as she asked, "Why didn't you tell me about this Amy? And what's this to do with Billy?"

"I didn't tell you about Amy because . . . well . . . because I didn't think it important and Billy . . . well . . . Billy was going out with Amy and he wanted more than a kiss . . . if you know what I mean. When Amy rejected him he attacked her."

"I see. And now Georgie is in hospital. Is he okay?" she asked. She bit her lip, worriedly.

"He's got some bad cuts, a swollen eye and a few broken ribs, but yes, he will be okay in time. The police won't do anything because they believe Billy's story rather than Georgie's. They claimed it was Georgie who started the fight. It's not fair! Jim Jenkins is a policeman and Billy gets away with it. It's just not fair!"

Mum wiped her hands again and sat down at the table. I joined her. Billy was like a son to her so she was clearly upset by the news and hesitated before continuing.

"I agree, but what can be done? If the police won't do anything about it, there's not much you can do. You can't go off 'half-cocked' and take the law into your own hands or it will be you who is in trouble with the police. It's best to wait and see."

"Billy will not get away with this. That's a promise!" I muttered through clenched lips.

My mother shook her head and reached out to take my hand.

"Calm down. He won't get away with it but you have to promise me not to go after him. Promise?"

I nodded and whispered, "Promise."

She then decided to give me the third degree about Amy and Ruth.

She said, "I don't think any woman should live up in the mountains by herself, especially with a teenage daughter. There's no reason they couldn't both live in Roxborough."

I couldn't tell her about Ruth's husband so I replied, "She is an artist and writer and she needed a quiet, peaceful place—somewhere she could concentrate on her work without interruptions."

I was surprised by my mother's cross-examination. She accepted people with all their faults and yet she was ready to criticise Ruth, a woman whose existence she had known nothing about until a few minutes ago. My brow furrowed and I tried to control my frustration as I continued to listen.

"It's not Mrs Parkinson's fault, or Amy's. It's Billy's!" I said gruffly.

Sensing my angry mood, my mother apologised.

"I'm sorry Guy. If you like her, that's good enough for me. I trust your judgement. Be careful though! Billy is a policeman's son. I don't want you involved in any kind of trouble."

"Thanks mum. Ruth and Amy are good people."

I rode out to Amy's house to break the bad news to her and her mother. Both mother and daughter registered disbelief and shock as I told them what had happened. Tears flowed, but after a time, outrage set in.

"I'm furious that the police are not going to do anything about it but I understand why. The boy is a policeman's son. He's popular in town. Georgie has a disability and he's bigger than most sixteen-year-olds. Amy is not local. The police would favour Billy and his friends. Not right—but understandable," said Ruth calmly and rationally.

She paused and continued, "If it wasn't for our particular situation, I would press the police further. I don't want to see Amy hurt any more. So it's best to heed Mrs Henderson's words and leave it be, at least for the time being."

She took Amy in her arms and kissed her on the forehead. I felt helpless.

My voice shook as I blurted, "I'm sorry! This would not have occurred if I hadn't met you. It's my fault. Maybe it would be better if I left you alone. I'm only bringing you trouble."

As soon as I uttered this Amy was in my arms, her face pressed against my neck. Ruth stepped forward and put her arms around both of us.

She whispered, "Nonsense! Don't even think about it being your fault. You are the best thing that has happened to Amy. You're more important to us than any trouble. You are not going to stay away from us. Do you hear me? You're one of the family. We can handle any problems. We've had to do it before, so don't worry."

Amy raised her head and cried, "If you leave I'll . . . I'll never forgive you Guy Harmon. You won't, will you? Leave, I mean?"

I looked at them both and grinned, "Well . . . If you can stand having me around I'll stay."

They both smiled warmly and hugged me. I stayed with them for the remainder of the day as we tried to forget the ordeal. However, uppermost in my thoughts was Billy Jenkins—and revenge!

CHAPTER 11

THE AFTERMATH

When Billy arrived in Roxborough from the city I felt sorry for him as a newcomer trying to adjust to life in a new town, but there was neither defence nor explanation for him attempting to rape Amy and then bashing Georgie. The fact he showed no remorse for his actions justified my opinion of him—he was a scumbag.

I visited Georgie in hospital regularly and although he still nursed bruises, broken ribs and a busted nose, he was able to get out of bed and move around. He was quieter and more distant than usual but this was natural considering his recent ordeal. As a joke I wanted to say the beating had improved his looks but thought better of it. Georgie told me that he'd been thinking about Billy and his mates and, like me, he wanted retribution. Whereas I could control myself I wasn't sure about Georgie.

"If I see him I'm going to kill him!" Georgie muttered through gritted teeth.

"I thought about doing that too but your mum advised me not to go near Billy. He's a cop's son and we could get into real strife if we bash him."

"But . . . he bashed me and Amy. He deserves whatever comes his way."

"I know. But we have to be careful. Don't do anything without telling me! Okay?"

"Okay."

"It doesn't mean we can't think of ways to get back at him," I said.

We pondered the many ways of exacting revenge. Georgie's ideas always resulted in Billy's death and I had to tell him repeatedly—if we killed Billy we would both end up in jail. Foolishly, I did mention we could make his death look like an accident. Georgie grasped my statement with relish and came up with drowning Billy and making it look like an accident, or crashing his motorbike into a tree, or having a shooting accident. He even thought of running Billy over with a car or truck, as well as many other impractical ideas. Impractical though the ideas were, they did give us a chance to forget about the ordeal, for a short time at least.

As I arrived home after visiting Georgie, Sam appeared on the doorstep. She was upset about Georgie and wanted to know the full story.

"How's Georgie? Did Billy really bash him?" she asked.

"Billy and his friends put Georgie in hospital."

"Why? I was told Georgie attacked Billy but I knew it couldn't be true because Georgie wouldn't attack anyone—unless he was provoked."

I realised I had to tell Sam the whole story so we sat on the steps and I explained what had happened. Sam listened in disbelief as I went back over the events that had led to Georgie's beating. After my re-telling, Sam sat in silence, shaking her head.

"How's Amy?" she asked, "No girl should have to put up with that."

"She's okay. A little shaken but she's fine."

"What about you? It's a wonder you aren't out looking for Billy. I would be."

"He's a cop's son so I can't beat him up. Sooner or later I'll get my revenge. Don't worry," I answered. It was infuriating and frustrating to know that Billy Jenkins wasn't being punished.

"I hope I'm there when you do."

Sam placed her hand on my shoulder and stood up to leave.

"I suppose this means you'll be seeing more of Amy now," she said.

"Not really. You and I can still do things together."

"I'll think about it. See ya!" she said and stood up to leave.

"Bye!"

Sam left me sitting on the step. I wanted to keep a close eye on Georgie in case he planned to exact revenge on Billy. A workable plan was to take him along with me to Amy's place in the afternoons. For the next week I spent time with Georgie and Sam in the mornings and saw Amy after lunch.

Georgie's recovery was slow, so he couldn't engage in any physical activity. To pass time a little constructively we fiddled with our bikes or played with his pup. On a couple of occasions, Sam took Georgie on her bike to visit an aunt who lived on a farm outside Roxborough. I tagged along as well.

One Sunday afternoon towards the end of summer vacation, Amy and I explored the uppermost corner of the valley. We discovered that it ended abruptly at a rocky cliff face. Nearby, we heard the dull, continuous roar of falling water, so we struggled through a thicket of trees and bushes till we reached the creek. Before us a waterfall tumbled down the steep cliff face and into the creek, launching large clouds of spray into the air. The noise was deafening. Trees sheltered the creek from the summer sun and the air under their green canopy was dank and misty. We didn't need an invitation to cool off so we sat at the water's edge, took off our shoes, before jumping in, fully clothed.

The horses had followed us down and drank thirstily while we took shelter from the heat.

After a time, we dragged ourselves onto the bank to dry off. Amy's wet clothes clung to every curve of her body. I wondered whether she knew the effect she was having on me. Not wanting Amy to see how aroused I was, I rose and clambered up towards the waterfall.

I was amazed to find a huge cave chiselled out of the cliff face, completely hidden from view, behind the waterfall. Amy joined me and we both made our way carefully over the slippery, wet rocks near the entrance.

"Wow! What do you know?" I declared, peering into the gloom.

"It's huge!" yelled Amy, above the roar of the falling water.

"Let's go in," I shouted back, moving inside the entrance.

Amy shook her head vigorously and grabbed my arm.

"No Guy. It's too dark in there. We need a torch. Let's leave it for now."

"Well, we can come back tomorrow. I want to see inside," I said earnestly, as we made our way back to the water's edge.

As I scanned the horizon, I noticed rain clouds threatening the sky to the east. The wind began to pick up.

"Looks like rain. We'd better get back!" I said.

We swung up onto our horses and set off for the mine. As the wind swept towards us, the grass rippled like waves in the sea. A loud crack of thunder galvanised us into action and we galloped across the open ground. The sky darkened as rain droplets began to drift down intermittently. Lightning flashed, signalling the onset of the heaviest of the rain. It pelted down, raindrops nipping at our skin like sharp needles, as we urged our horses to go faster.

We were saturated by the time we reached the shed near the house. We slipped off the saddles and stabled the horses. Amy wiped her face with a cloth and swept her hair back before tending to the horses. I stood at the doorway, watching the rain hissing as it struck the soil in a pulsating rhythm, producing tiny dust clouds. The raindrops formed rivulets that spread rapidly, creating puddles. The sweet smell created by rain on the hot, dry earth rose up to meet me. I loved summer storms with the staccato beat of raindrops resonating on the tin roof. By the time Amy joined me, the rain had subsided to a slow drizzle. Our clothes clung to our bodies as we made our way back to the house, dodging the muddy puddles scattered across the ground. As it was late I said goodbye and departed.

The following afternoon, Georgie joined Amy and me as we set out on horseback to explore the cave. I had fanciful visions of uncovering treasure or gold hidden by miners while Georgie was excited about the possibility of finding a human skeleton. Amy, ever the romantic, hoped the cave would lead us to another realm or a hidden valley on the other side of the mountain. All our wishes were dashed when we entered the cave, torches in hand, to find it was a large hole in the cliff face and nothing more. Our discovery was a huge let-down.

When we arrived back at the mine I decided to take a peek inside, to compensate for the disappointment of finding nothing in the cave. I ignored the large warning sign outside the mine entrance.

I turned in the saddle and said to Georgie, "Let's look inside."

As I dismounted, Amy warned, "Don't be silly, Guy! It's too dangerous. Remember what Mum said."

I grabbed my torch and replied, "I just want a quick look. I won't go in very far. Don't worry."

"If you kill yourself I won't speak to you ever again."

"How true," I grinned.

Amy was not in a jocular mood so she said forcefully. "You know what I mean. Talk to him, Georgie,"

She was surprised to see Georgie waiting at the mine entrance, torch in hand.

"Fine. Go in but I'm staying out here," she said, folding her arms and giving us the 'look'.

I didn't want to argue with her so with Georgie following, I entered the mine. Amy plonked herself down on a large rock and stared off into the distance. With a degree of caution, Georgie and I made our way in, sweeping the sides and ceiling with our torchlights to spot possible dangers.

"Watch your head!" I signalled to Georgie.

The low ceiling forced us to stoop as we progressed, stumbling at times over rocks and clods of earth. Timber beams had been used to strengthen the walls and ceiling of the tunnel. As we travelled further along the tunnel, the air became mustier and cooler. The tunnel narrowed and I began to feel claustrophobic. I didn't want to venture too far because of the lurking element of danger. My misgivings were confirmed when our progress was halted by a large pile of fallen rocks and timber. I shone my torch beyond the mound of debris and could see the mine tunnel continuing further but decided not to proceed.

"Let's go back," I whispered.

I don't know why I whispered. Probably because I thought that if I spoke too loudly the ceiling might collapse. We turned and retraced our steps. Near the entrance I heard Amy's muffled voice calling our names.

I whispered, "Let's play a trick on Amy. You run out and tell her I'm trapped under rocks."

Georgie frowned. Amy was still recovering from the ordeal with Billy and I don't know why I thought a practical joke should appeal as being funny. I realised later that it was a rather childish trick to play. The only explanation I could offer was that I wanted to see Amy's reaction—nonetheless, it was a thoughtless, selfish thing to even contemplate.

"I don't think we should. She'll be upset and mad," Georgie argued.

"Well then. Say that I've had a fall and twisted my ankle. That's not so bad."

"I still think it's wrong."

"Come on Georgie. Don't worry! I'll take the blame," I pleaded, "Okay?"

"Okay! But I know she'll be mad at us."

He raced out of the cave yelling, "Guy's hurt himself. He fell and hurt his leg."

On hearing this, Amy cried out in anguish and ran into the cave into my open arms.

I laughed and said, "Got ya!"

She stormed out of the cave and waited for me at the entrance. When I appeared, she thumped my chest with her fists.

"That was mean. I hate you Guy Harmon."

She continued to hit me as I made a hasty retreat. Georgie's assessment had been correct—Amy was upset. I tried to placate her by repeating over and over again that I was sorry but it took a minute or two before she settled down. I now realised what a heartless fool I was.

"Don't you ever play tricks on me again!" she yelled, shaking her fist at me in anger.

When she saw my dismal, contrite face she relaxed and moved towards me. Not understanding the meaning of this sudden movement, I quickly stepped back and sprawled unceremoniously on the ground. While I lay there, a puzzled expression on my face, Amy and Georgie stood over me laughing hysterically.

"Here!" she said, offering her hand, "Get up you silly goose!"

I took her hand and rose slowly to my feet, dusting myself off, while she watched in amusement. It seemed she had forgiven me.

It was late in the afternoon when Georgie and I reached Roxborough. Mum reminded me that I had to help my father in his store the following morning.

My father had lived in Roxborough for over twenty years and was a popular citizen involved in many community activities. People came into his store not only to buy goods but to spend time chatting to him about everything from politics to the weather. My dad loved to talk, a trait I hadn't inherited. His store was a meeting place for customers to gossip and get together. A strong, wiry man with rugged features beneath a receding hairline, he looked more like a logger from the timber mill than a shop owner.

The store was an old brick building built at the turn of the century. The high timber framed ceiling and stained, worn floorboards that creaked when you walked on them, immediately transported store customers back in time. With only a few small windows, the store was poorly lit, a characteristic that added to its charm. Apart from the noisy ceiling fans and new shelving, the old building hadn't changed in appearance since the 1890s.

I, for one, was happy my father hadn't attempted to modernise the store and as a child I had spent countless hours searching every nook and cranny of this grand old store. I remembered with fondness the many times as a child I had curled up on a window seat soaking up the warmth of the sun while reading a book or watching my father behind the counter serving customers. I often closed my eyes and absorbed the pleasurable aromas that permeated the store.

There were other, more modern shops in town but older folk still preferred to come to my father's store. He told me that sooner or later the store would close because the younger generation was shopping elsewhere but whilst ever he had the support of his faithful customers our store would stay open for trading. I helped him do a stock take, then swept the floors and cleaned the bench tops before heading home to get a bite to eat.

CHAPTER 12

THE UNWELCOME VISITOR

It was after midday when, after running an errand for my dad, I ran into Tom Henderson who was leaving the police station.

"How ya going, Guy?" he asked. He was wearing overalls covered in grease and oil—a legacy of his job. He took a cloth from his pocket and wiped his hands, as he glanced angrily back at the police station. It was obvious he'd just had another run—in with the police.

"Fine, Mr Henderson. How are you?"

"Not so good. I've been to the police again and told Bob Ridgeway a few home truths. I said that if anything else happened to my Georgie I would take matters in my own hands. Of course, Bob just stood there and warned me. Some nerve! It was a waste of time. I don't trust the cops in this place. By the way, I overheard Bob on the phone to some fellow who was making enquiries about a woman and her daughter. I heard the name Ruth mentioned. Bob said he'd leave a note for Jim Jenkins. Your friend . . . what's her name?"

"Amy?" I answered.

"Yeah. Amy. Well she lives alone with her mother doesn't she? I'm sure it's not her but you never know."

I was stunned. Was this Ruth's husband? I hoped Tom didn't notice my alarm.

I answered quickly, "Yes. She does but I don't think it would have anything to do with them."

"I'm sure you're right. Anyway! Must be off. See Ya!"

He pushed the cloth into his overall pocket and strode briskly down the street.

"Yeah. See you Mr Henderson," I called after him.

I stood outside the station deep in thought. Who was this person? What would Billy's dad do? He knew about Amy but did he know Ruth's name? Billy did and that was cause for worry.

I dashed home to get my bike to ride out and relay the news to Ruth. Before I left, I went to Georgie's home and asked him to go into town and keep an eye out for any movements from either the police or Billy.

I reached the house in the forest in record time and was greeted warmly by both mother and daughter. They sensed something was wrong by the glum look on my face. We went inside and sat down. Ruth and Amy had their eyes fixed unwaveringly on my miserable face, waiting for me to speak. They both turned ashen as I told them about the telephone call as told to me by Mr Henderson. I tried to remain positive and reassure them there was no proof it was Ben Parkinson; however, I could tell from their faces they thought it was.

"How long ago was this?" Ruth asked. Her face was grim as was Amy's.

"Not long ago. I came as soon as I heard. You know . . . Billy might not hear about it," I answered, trying to be optimistic.

"He'll find out and he'll tell," Amy muttered, "I don't trust him . . ."

"If it's him I'll stay with you. He won't try anything while I'm here—surely," I said.

"Thanks Guy. But I don't want you involved in this. My husband is not a man to be trifled with. Amy and I will have to leave," Ruth said and took Amy's hand.

"What about the other cop? You know . . . Bob Ridgeway. Maybe we can go to him," Amy whispered.

Ruth answered, "He might be okay but I can't see him helping us. Billy's dad will influence him and he's not likely to confront a fellow cop. Besides, we don't know if it is my ex-husband. The police won't act unless they're certain and even then they can't act unless he does something wrong. No! We will pack and leave tonight. Let's hope he's not close by."

This was the sensible thing to do but I didn't want them to leave. Amy began to weep quietly and Ruth tried to comfort her. My bottom lip shook and I knew that if I tried to say anything the tears welling in my eyes would break free and run down my cheeks so I rose from the chair and went to the window. As I stood there, I cursed under my breath. Ruth and Amy didn't deserve such wretched luck. Ruth finally broke the silence.

"Well, we can't waste time," she declared, "We'd better start packing. Thanks for your help, Guy."

"I'd better go into town to see if there's any news but I'll come back tonight to help out. Don't leave without saying goodbye, okay?"

"Of course not. Thanks again Guy. We'll see you tonight," Ruth answered and turned towards Amy.

Amy had curled up on the sofa, her head buried in her lap, so I quietly left the house and walked down to my bike. As I reached it, I heard the door slam and turned to see her running down the path towards me. She flung her arms around my neck and collapsed, on my chest.

"I don't want to go without you," she cried, "It's not right! I'll die without you."

Tenderly, I lifted her head and looked at her sad face.

"I love you," I said, kissing her gently on the lips.

She kissed me in return and answered softly, "I love you, too."

"Don't worry! Everything will be all right," I said as I disengaged myself from her warm embrace and mounted the bike.

Her slim body shook uncontrollably as she wept. As I rode down the track, I turned and waved but she didn't respond. I knew she was inconsolable but I needed to return to town to check with Georgie. I found him waiting near my home. He had no news. I figured this meant Ruth's ex-husband was not close by. Hopefully, it would take him many hours or even days to reach Roxborough, so it would give Ruth time to pack and leave.

"I'm going out to Amy's place tonight to help them pack and leave," I told Georgie.

"Do they have to leave?" he answered, "It mightn't be Amy's dad."

"It's better to be safe than sorry. Remember he said he'd kill Ruth if he found her. They have to leave."

"Then I want to go with you," Georgie pleaded.

"Okay! I'll meet you here at seven. Don't tell anyone Georgie! Keep it to yourself."

"My lips are zipped . . . tight!"

I went indoors to try to prepare for whatever may lay ahead. Thoughts raced around inside my head—asking questions, weighing possible scenarios, so much so that my head was spinning. If necessary, I was prepared to leave with Ruth and Amy. I even took a rifle from my father's gun cupboard. If Ruth's husband did show up, I could threaten him with the gun. I didn't think about the consequences of such an action. I was definite about one thing. If Billy Jenkins told his father about Ruth and Amy he was dead.

I told my mum that I was going to Amy's place with Georgie because we'd been invited to spend the evening with them. I didn't mention anything about their leaving, or Ruth's husband. I knew that if I told her, she would contact the police—and I didn't trust the police. I thought that I was grown-up enough to handle it myself. Mum was quite surprised when I gave her a hug and kiss before I left.

Georgie and I made our way along the well-worn route to Amy's home. Tonight might be the last occasion we would tread this now familiar track. We rode along the narrow track up to the house. It was a moonlit night and the stars were brilliant, shedding a soft light over the countryside.

The outskirts of Roxborough provided a surprisingly tranquil backdrop as we cruised slowly along the track with our motorbikes humming softly and the cool night air caressing our cheeks. My thoughts were focused on the pending urgent departure of Amy and her mum. The trees and surrounding landscape were bathed in the ghostly glow from the moon, creating a surreal effect. It was very still, with no wind to ruffle the treetops, no sound of crackling leaves, not even a song from any of the many wild birds as they sought resting places for the night. The atmosphere was soothing and peaceful but I perceived an underlying menace I could not help but feel was a portent of things to come.

As we neared the house I spotted an unknown car parked near the Jeep, so I killed the lights and cut the motor, motioning to Georgie to do the same. Beneath the luxuriant moonlight we coasted silently up to the house and glided to a halt near Ruth's Jeep. I looked anxiously towards the house lights. I placed my finger on my lips to warn Georgie not to make a sound and grabbed the rifle. I crept up to the car and peered inside. It was empty. I moved towards the house, with Georgie following closely, our eyes searching the gloom for any sign of either Amy or Ruth.

As we approached the veranda I came to a sudden stop on hearing Ruth's unmistakable voice. She was arguing loudly—with a man. Georgie dug his fingers into my arm as we stood listening to the argument. The sound of the man's guttural voice filled my heart with dread. My stomach churned and my heart began to tick like a time bomb. I began to shiver uncontrollably as fear invaded my being. Obviously the desire to help Amy and Ruth had given me the courage I needed to stay, rather than turn and run.

I whispered, "You stay here! If I need help I'll call out."

Immediate relief showed on Georgie's face and he nodded his head vigorously. I didn't hear Amy's voice and all I could do was hope she was safe. My prayers were answered when she appeared from the shadows and motioned to us. We crept over to her hiding place near the veranda.

"Thank God you've arrived. It's him. He's found us," she whispered, her voice tremulous.

"When did he arrive? Is there anyone with him?" I asked.

"He came about ten minutes ago by himself. Mum is trying to reason with him but he's getting very angry and he's been drinking."

"Has he got a gun?"

"I didn't see one. What are we going to do?"

Her eyes were fixed on the rifle I held in the crook of my arm as she spoke.

"The rifle isn't loaded. It's only to intimidate him," I said.

The rifle was loaded and I was willing to use it if necessary although I honestly didn't know what I would have done if confronted by a malevolent, brutal man who thought nothing of hurting others. Full of trepidation, I made my way along the side of the house. The argument in the house was escalating and I knew I had to intervene before something dire happened to Ruth.

"I'm going in the back of the house," I whispered and proceeded to make my way to the back door.

I'd expected Amy to stay with Georgie but was surprised to hear her behind me. I stopped and faced her.

"Where do you think you're going?" I whispered, grabbing her by the arm.

"I'm coming with you. Don't try and stop me, Guy. That's my Mum in there."

I let her arm go and put my fingers on my lips.

"Okay! But stay behind me!"

We entered the house, tentatively making our way past Amy's room into the kitchen. The argument between Ruth and her ex-husband continued unabated and I was amazed that Ruth could be so aggressive and demanding. I reasoned that any mother would fight to the death to protect her family from harm. Amy and I crouched in the semi-darkness observing the verbal fisticuffs of the two adults before us. The man was almost unintelligible but I did make out words such as 'prison, my money, framed, you'll pay' but not enough to understand what he was actually saying.

Ruth was sitting on the sofa, her face red and angry, facing a tall, broad shouldered man. He wore dark trousers and a jacket. Ben Parkinson had a weather-beaten appearance. His face was unshaven and lined and his bloodshot, piercing, dark eyes exuded an evil, threatening presence. His face twisted in anger as he stood in front of Ruth. He clasped a bottle of whisky in one hand as he tried to remain steady. My hands were wet with perspiration and my mouth was dry as I waited in the kitchen. The rifle in my hand gave me some small measure of courage but I wasn't sure I could shoot this man, even if he threatened me.

Unfortunately at that moment, Ruth stood up to move away from Ben Parkinson and he reached out and grasped her arm tightly. She tried to wrench free but his iron grip forced a scream from her. She swung her free arm and hit him in the face.

He rubbed his red cheek slowly and growled, "Bloody hell, woman. You stupid bitch"

Before she could escape his clutches, he hit Ruth hard with his open hand, sending her sprawling on the floor. She screamed in pain and raised her arms to protect herself as he bent down threateningly. He hit her again as she tried to crawl away. He was an imposing figure, strongly built and seemingly devoid of any compassion. I knew that he could easily pick Ruth up and throw her across the room like a sack of potatoes so I stepped out from my hiding place in an effort to protect her.

Before I could call out, Amy ran from behind me and screamed, "Leave her alone, you bastard."

Her father struggled to remain steady on his feet as he turned to face Amy.

"Keep out of this Amy! This is between your mother and me," he slurred, wiping his mouth with the back of his hand.

He saw me standing near Amy with my rifle pointed at him and froze; however, he quickly recovered his composure. Then his lips curled in an expression of utter contempt.

"Put the rifle down sonny, or you just might get hurt!"

He sneered and stumbled towards me. His body reeked of alcohol. Amy stepped in front of him.

"Please leave us alone. Please go!" she pleaded.

His answer was an open-handed slap to her face, its force knocking her to the floor. He stood belligerently before me, his hands on his hips.

"Well sonny. What are you going to do? Look . . . you're shaking. My! My! The boy is scared of little old me. Be careful or you might wet your pants, girlie. Now! Put the gun down before I knock you down, you little piece of shit!" he yelled.

He could see the fear in my eyes and arrogantly took a step towards me. I tried to summon up the courage to fire but I couldn't move. The stale smell of whisky on his breath made me want to gag.

I glanced down at Amy and in that instant Ben Parkinson reached out and grabbed the barrel of the rifle. He wrenched it from my grasp, sending me sprawling across the room. He lurched clumsily after me, crashing into a chair but managed to hang onto the rifle. At the same time the whisky bottle smashed onto the floor, scattering glass. Ben Parkinson ignored the glass shards. His sole purpose right then was to punish me. He had temporarily forgotten about Amy and Ruth.

"Say goodbye, sonny!" he sneered arrogantly, "Little boys shouldn't play with grown-up toys."

I looked up to see him aiming the rifle while trying to remain steady on his feet. Colour drained from my face as I crouched on the floor, frozen in terror. Amy moved to protect me but before her father could squeeze the trigger, a loud noise, like a car backfiring, broke the silence.

Ben Parkinson looked down in utter surprise at the blood seeping from a wound to his chest. He swayed unsteadily and crashed backwards to the floor. He raised his head and struggled to stand, the rifle still clutched in his hands but as he did, a second shot struck him in the chest. He fell backwards and the rifle tumbled from his hands. A guttural, choking sound issued from his mouth. It changed to a wheezy, rattle of death. Blood oozed from the bullet holes in his chest and a dark red stain spread slowly across the front of his shirt.

Amy and I, stunned by the sudden turn of events, stared in absolute horror at the body before turning around. Ruth stood at the entrance to the kitchen, a rifle in her hands. She let out a harsh sobbing noise like a beast in agony and dropped the gun. A low moan of despair issued from her lips as she slowly sank to her knees. She collapsed on the floor, her head in her hands, and sobbed. While Ben Parkinson had been threatening Amy and me, Ruth had crawled silently from the room and grabbed her rifle.

We sat on the floor speechless and unable to move. Ruth curled up and rocked to and fro, sobbing silently. Amy slid across the floor to hold her mother in her arms while I hauled myself up to stand beside the body.

I looked blankly at the crumpled body of Ben Parkinson, mesmerised by the pool of blood emanating from the two bullet wounds. I knew I would never forget his lifeless, cold eyes staring up at me. I began to tremble and took a couple of deep breaths in an attempt to compose myself; however, it was too late.

My stomach churned and I promptly placed my hands over my mouth as I stumbled outside. I leaned over the veranda railing and vomited. I held onto the railing for a minute or two but my legs betrayed me and I eased myself down to the floor. There I crouched on my haunches with my head between my knees, inhaling large mouthfuls of air as I struggled to clear my head. Georgie raced up the steps, his face a deathly white.

"What happened? I heard shots," he asked.

"He's dead, Georgie," I croaked in a husky voice, "Ben Parkinson's been shot."

"Is Amy okay?"

Georgie stared at the doorway and moved towards it. I grabbed his arm.

"Amy and Ruth are both okay. Don't go in, Georgie!" I ordered. "Wait for me!"

I stood up and peered into the surrounding landscape for any sign of intruders. Luckily, Ruth's house was well hidden from the main road. I joined Georgie and we entered the house. Amy was comforting her mother, who was sitting up, her head resting on Amy's chest. They were both crying.

"Are you sure he's dead?" asked a wide-eyed Georgie.

I whispered hoarsely, "He hasn't moved Georgie. He's dead."

"What are we going to do?" I cried, tears filling my eyes. Hysteria was threatening to envelop me as I stood rooted to the spot, trembling all over.

Ruth took control. She climbed to her feet and stared coldly at the body of Ben Parkinson.

"Guy! Grab a blanket from the linen press in the hallway!" she said softly.

Amy tried to stand up but Ruth said in a firm voice, "No! Stay there sweetheart till I've covered the body!"

As Ruth threw the blanket over the lifeless body of Ben Parkinson, I helped Amy to her feet and we sat down on the sofa averting our eyes. Ruth searched for a bottle of whisky. She told us whisky would help steady our nerves. After rummaging through several cupboards, she found a bottle and poured a small amount into each of three glasses. She told us to sip the whisky not gulp it down. We sat and sipped the drink in silence. I was still trembling but the liquor did help to settle my jangled nerves almost immediately.

Eventually, Ruth placed her glass on the coffee table, kissed Amy on the cheek and left the room. She returned moments later, wearing a coat and carrying a purse.

"What are you doing?" I asked.

"I'm going to report this to the police. I'll tell them exactly what happened. He was going to shoot you. It was self-defence," she answered as she took the keys to the jeep from her purse.

I didn't want anything to do with the police after the way they had treated Georgie and Amy. I didn't trust them at all. Billy Jenkins had probably told Ben Parkinson where Ruth lived.

"Hold on!" I argued, "Let's think about this. He's an ex-cop. You shot him. What did the police do about Georgie and Amy? Nothing! I don't trust Billy or his father. They could charge you with murder and you might end up in jail."

I had regained my nerve and actually began to think calmly. I didn't know why—maybe it was the whisky or the mention of the police, or even a simple instance of self-preservation.

"Guy's right, Mum," agreed Amy, "they could twist everything around so you could end up being judged guilty of murder. We need to think about this."

"That's well and good," Ruth sighed, "but nothing can change the fact I killed my ex-husband and there's a body on the floor. If we don't go to the police, what else can we do?"

"We could get rid of the body."

Those profound words were uttered by Georgie.

"Georgie's right. We have only two choices—go to the police or get rid of the body," I said. "If no-one else knows he came out here tonight we could rid of the body but if Billy knew we could be in trouble."

Ruth sat back down on the sofa. I had sown seeds of doubt in her mind.

"Someone had to show him how to get here," Amy said, further complicating our predicament.

"There's nobody else here is there?" I said, "I'd say Billy showed your dad the turnoff to this property but didn't come any further. He wasn't by the roadside when we came out so he wouldn't know if your dad left after seeing your mum."

"I suppose so," sighed Ruth. I was slowly convincing her to not go to the police.

I continued, "If the police ask we can tell them Ben Parkinson did come here to talk to you but left soon after. They have to believe you, especially if there's no body."

There was silence as we pondered the pros and cons of getting rid of the body. I'd run out of ideas and my worst fears were realised when Ruth spoke to the three of us.

"I still think the best thing to do is go to the police," she said firmly. "If we try to dispose of the body we will only risk getting into more trouble."

I knew she was right but there was also a very real possibility she could end up in prison. I didn't want Ruth going to the police so in desperation I pitched one more argument to try and change her mind.

"If we hide the body somewhere for a few days and nothing happens . . . you know . . . no-one comes asking for him, we'll know he came alone. If Billy or his dad asks we can tell them he was here but left soon afterward. I think it's worth taking this chance. It could mean the difference between jail and freedom, certainly for you, and perhaps for Amy, Georgie and me as well. We could bury the body down a mine shaft or in the cave behind the waterfall. He would never be found," I said.

It was a plausible argument and both Amy and Georgie agreed with me. Ruth remained skeptical.

Amy pleaded. "Mum! You saw what happened with Georgie and Billy. I don't trust Billy or his dad. I agree with Guy. Let's wait a few days before deciding what to do. Please?"

"That's fine but what do we do with a body for two or three days? We can't shove it in a cupboard. This summer heat will decompose it and it'll begin to smell," Ruth argued.

"Keep it cool!" Georgie stated.

"Georgie's right," I declared, "but how?"

Ruth came up with a feasible answer.

"We don't have a freezer but there is a large drum in my studio. A body could fit in it. I don't know how we can stop it decomposing though. Perhaps we can pack salt in with it. You know, salt is used for preserving things; but a body? I don't know. Oh! What am I saying! Too many things can go wrong. Anyway, I don't like the idea of a dead body near this house, if only for a couple of days," she said, shaking her head.

Before she had time to think it over any further I said, "We can put the body in the drum in the studio. I can get bags of salt from my dad's store. You lock the studio and then, if all is okay after three days we can bury the body in the mine."

"It's the correct thing to do Mum," pleaded Amy. "He was a horrible, evil man. He would have killed us. He deserved to die and you don't deserve to go to jail. Let's wait the three days. Please?"

Ruth closed her eyes and sat silently with her head in her hands.

Amy implored, "Please Mummy! It can't hurt to try it."

Ruth took Amy's hand, sighing as she did so.

She said softly, "I know that your father had a falling out with his family and hasn't spoken to any of them for at least ten years so I suppose he would have no-one asking about him. So . . . Okay! We will store the body in the drum for three days and see what happens. I will clean out the drum and I'll get a plastic sheet to wrap the body in."

We breathed a collective sigh of relief. I only hoped we were doing the right thing. Time would tell. We followed Ruth to the studio and while Amy helped Ruth clean the drum, Georgie and I found a large sheet of thick plastic and took it back to the house. I placed the sheet alongside the blanket and carefully rolled the body over onto it. Congealed blood covering parts of the blanket caused me to dry retch but I continued.

I felt the warmth of the body through the thin blanket and this awareness sent shivers down my spine. Once again, I became overwhelmed and I gagged before dashing from the room and 'heaving' over the veranda railing. Georgie joined me soon after. The cool night air steadied us both and we returned to complete the task. The sight of the blood and the body proved too much to handle and we sat down on the sofa, trying to steady our nerves.

Ruth came back from the studio, took one look at our pale, miserable faces and took over. She bent down and completed the task of wrapping the plastic around the body of Ben Parkinson. I summoned the grit to help her, being careful to avoid the pool of blood and the slivers of glass on the floor. Amy's dad was a big man so it was going to be a formidable task to carry him.

"Get the wheelbarrow from the studio!" Ruth directed Georgie. "We'll put him in that. Guy, get some towels from the cupboard in the hallway to mop up this blood!"

Luckily, the floor was wooden, so it could be washed and cleaned after we disposed of the body. Georgie returned with the wheelbarrow and with his help, we lifted the body into it. I helped Georgie push the wheelbarrow outside to the studio and Ruth tipped the drum onto its side. She and I tentatively pushed the bundle into the drum. Because of his height, Ben Parkinson's legs had to be bent, to fit into the drum. This job I left to Ruth. Amy didn't watch and Georgie and I both turned a definitive shade of green. Handling a dead body was not on my top-ten list of things to do, and I breathed a sigh of relief when the lid was finally in place on the drum.

"I don't think I could stand having this drum here, even if it's for three days. It's too close to the house," Ruth said.

Amy agreed, "I don't want it here either. It will give me nightmares."

"Where?" I asked.

"There is a small shed at the back of the horse stable. We could make room in there," Amy said.

Ruth nodded her head in agreement.

"Can we roll the drum up to the shed?" I asked.

"Yes! The ground is reasonably flat. If you and Georgie roll the drum, Amy and I will go ahead and make room for it."

The shed was only a short distance from the studio and it wasn't too onerous a task to roll the drum up to its door. As we moved it across the open ground, I looked nervously around, because the moon illuminated everything in its glow. Georgie halted midway and listened.

"I thought I heard a noise in those bushes over there. Listen!" he whispered. Our eyes scanned the bushes as we listened for a sound.

"Your mind's playing tricks on you. There's nothing there," I said.

At that moment a rustling noise in the bushes interrupted the stillness of the night. I peered into the gloom but saw nothing. Was it

Billy, spying on us? I took my hands from the drum and crept towards the bushes. I stopped suddenly as a small animal scurried across the ground in front of me and into the darkness of the surrounding trees. I smiled and turned back to Georgie.

"It was only a rabbit," Georgie said, mightily relieved.

We continued rolling the drum towards the shed. The doorway was narrow so we had to stand the drum upright and manoeuvre it inside. Ruth covered it with a piece of canvas.

"I feel much better now it's away from the house," declared Ruth, closing the shed door.

"I'll bring the salt out tomorrow," I said as we returned to the house.

We entered the room to be confronted by the chaos of a blood-stained floor littered with broken glass.

"Don't step in the blood!" Ruth ordered.

Ruth used a broom to sweep up the glass before she mopped up the blood. Amy went outside and returned with a mop, bucket, scrubbing brushes and detergent.

"Boil some water, dear," Ruth told Amy as she placed the blood-soaked towels in plastic bags.

She asked Georgie and me to burn the towels in an empty drum outside, at the back of the house. Georgie stayed to keep an eye on the fire burning in the drum while I returned inside to help Ruth.

Walking back to the house, I noticed Ben Parkinson's car parked alongside the Jeep. Ruth was on her hands and knees, busily scrubbing the floor when I entered. Perspiration glistened on her face, as she laboured to eradicate all signs of blood from the floorboards and the cracks between them. It was an arduous task and she barely looked up when I entered.

"Ruth! What about the car outside?" I asked.

She stopped scrubbing, arched her back and scratched her head.

"I forgot about that. Maybe I can drive it out of town somewhere."

Amy sat up and cried out, "What if someone sees you? You might get caught."

"Fine! Instead, we'll hide it in the bush. No, that's not the answer. It would be very difficult to hide a car in the bush. I really don't know."

I had a brainwave. "I know. We can hide it in the cave behind the waterfall at the top of the valley or . . . or . . . dump it in the creek."

Ruth agreed and said, "Wait till I've finished and I'll drive it. You can show me the way."

When Ruth finished cleaning we made our way down to the car. Luckily, the keys were in the ignition so Ruth and Amy clambered in and Georgie and I hopped on our bikes. I led the way as we travelled past the mine, across the open grassland and towards the waterfall and cave. Our progress was slow because of the terrain and the darkness, even though the moon was a source of light. I had to stop on two or three occasions to check where we were heading but eventually we arrived at the waterfall. There were several large rocks near the cliff face but with much loud scraping and bumping, Ruth managed to squeeze the car into the cave, leaving the headlights on to give us even more light.

As she climbed out of the car she said, "If anyone finds this cave they'll know who owned the car from the rego and number plates."

"I'll get the number plates off. There must be a tool kit in the boot," I shouted above the roar of the waterfall. When I opened the boot I found a screwdriver but was surprised to find a suitcase of clothes.

"We can't hide these. We need to burn them," said Ruth.

Then I had another brainwave.

"Why not burn the whole car? There's petrol in the tank. If we burn the car nobody will be able to recognise it."

"Are you sure? Petrol is dangerous and the car might blow up," Ruth asked uneasily; her face showing concern.

"It'll be okay. I'll make a wick to put in the tank. That will give us time to get away," I answered displaying more bravado than good sense.

Ruth reluctantly agreed to my proposal so while I took the number plates off the car, Georgie grabbed a shirt from the suitcase. I gave the plates to Ruth and twisted the shirt to make a wick. Amy searched the car for matches and found some in the glove box.

I shoved the wick into the opening of the petrol tank.

"Are you sure you know what you're doing?" asked Amy.

"No, I'm not but hopefully I can light this shirt to ignite the petrol in the tank and give me time to escape."

"I don't like this. You could be blown up with the car. Isn't there a better way?"

"I'll be all right so don't worry. Now! You all need to get the hell out of here . . . well out of the way."

I waited until they had disappeared from view before I tried to light the wick. The matches would not ignite the dry cotton material so I pulled the wick out and turned it around so I could light the end soaked in petrol. Very carefully I struck a match, reached out and touched it to the material. I turned and fled from the cave at breakneck speed, stumbling across the rocky surface and into the night. The others waited several yards away, huddling together under a tree.

After a short time there was a whooshing sound followed by an explosion as the car burst into flames. I could feel the intense heat from the fire and see the flames from behind the curtain of water.

"What about these number plates?" asked Ruth. "Maybe we can bury them or throw them in the creek? That's no good is it? They would be discovered."

"I'll take them home with me and hide them for now. I'll get rid of them later," I answered.

I took Ruth on my bike and Amy went with Georgie as we wended our way back up the valley towards the mine. I glanced back and noticed a dull, dim glow but by the time we reached the mine, there was no sign of the fire at all. I was satisfied that all evidence of Ben Parkinson—and his demise—was concealed. All we had to do now was wait and hope that everything would be all right. It was midnight when we arrived at the house.

"It's late! Georgie and I should go," I said, declining Ruth's offer of hot chocolate.

"You can stay if you like," offered Ruth.

"No thanks. We'd better go. My parents will be expecting me home. We'll come out tomorrow. You'll be okay here, won't you?"

"We'll be fine. I'll sleep with Amy tonight. That's if we can get any sleep at all after what's happened."

I knew what she meant. I was still trembling and nauseous. The next three days would be difficult in the extreme, certainly nothing a teenager from Roxborough was equipped to handle.

"What about your rifle?" Amy asked.

"I'd better take it home. Otherwise Dad will notice it missing."

Ruth went inside and brought out the rifle. She cleaned it with a cloth before handing it to me.

"I'll put my rifle in the shed near the drum," Ruth said. "We'll get rid of it later."

Georgie and I said goodbye and made our way back to the road. On the trip back to town, I constantly scanned the surrounding landscape for any sign of either Billy or his dad. When I arrived home I whispered to Georgie not to tell anyone about the death of Ben Parkinson or events of the night. He nodded and left. As it was after midnight my family had long gone to bed.

I hid the number plates at the back of our garage and put the rifle back in the gun cabinet and went to bed. It had been the worst night of my young life—a night I would never forget. A night that altered the entire course of my life.

CHAPTER 13

THE AFTERMATH

Sleep did not come easy to me as I was visited by nightmares. I tossed and turned in bed, reliving the harrowing events which had culminated in the death of Ben Parkinson. Several times during the night I sat bolt upright, gasping for air and sweating profusely.

My appetite at breakfast the next morning was non-existent. I had not been able to rid myself of the demons. I felt wretched, expecting the police to knock at the door at any moment. I nibbled a slice of toast and sat staring at the table, stony faced. My mother showed genuine concern at my appearance because usually I ate extremely swiftly before making a hasty exit.

"Are you okay, Guy? You look very pale," she asked.

"I didn't get much sleep last night. I might be coming down with a cold or something," I croaked with as much conviction as I could muster.

"Do you want anything for it? Maybe you need to see the doctor."

"No, I'll be fine . . . It'll probably go away. If I don't feel any better by this afternoon I'll go see the doctor."

I managed a weak grin and tried to put on a cheerful face. I knew what I suffered from could not be cured by medicine or a doctor. I left the house to pick up Georgie.

Like me, Georgie had not been able to sleep. Before heading out to Ruth's house, we walked into town, searching for Billy or his father; our efforts drew a blank. However, we did bump into the other Roxborough policeman, Bob Ridgeway. The colour quickly drained from our faces as we faced him but there was no reaction from him so I concluded that the police were as yet unaware of Ben Parkinson's death and disappearance.

This knowledge raised my spirits and I proceeded to my father's store and grabbed two large bags of salt from the storeroom. Georgie and I placed the bags on my bike and we set off to Ruth's house.

When we arrived, our jaws dropped. A police car was parked outside! I had a sinking, sick feeling in the pit of my stomach as I glanced at Georgie. I hoped he wouldn't panic and reveal anything about the events of last night.

I dragged the bags of salt and placed them behind a tree, before heading towards the house. Georgie followed rather uneasily. I was stopped in my tracks by the appearance of Jim Jenkins on the veranda. Ruth was with him.

"Hello boys," he said pleasantly enough, as he walked down the steps.

When he was level with me he stopped. He took his cap off and brushed his hair back. His keen eyes fastened on mine and he asked, "Maybe you can help me boys. Have either of you seen a blue dodge sedan in town?"

Both Georgie and I shook our heads vigorously and I glanced nervously in Ruth's direction. She stood on the veranda impassively, her arms crossed. Billy's father wiped his brow with a handkerchief and placed his cap back on his head. He turned back to Ruth.

"Thanks for your time Mrs Parkinson," he said and walked to his car.

Georgie and I continued up the path to join Ruth on the veranda and we watched the police car slowly make its way down the track and out of sight.

Remaining silent, Ruth wiped her brow with her hand and entered the house, followed by Georgie and me. She slumped down on the sofa alongside Amy, who had entered from the back of the house. Georgie and I sat opposite her, both of us expecting the worst.

"What happened? What did he want?" I asked anxiously.

Ruth sat up, rubbed her eyes and frowned.

She answered, "He wanted to know if I had seen Ben. He said that Billy had told him that he'd met Ben in town. Ben had been driving a blue Dodge and when he told Billy that he was visiting me, Billy offered to show him the way. Billy said that he left Ben at the gate to this property and rode his bike back to town. Billy told his dad all this. That's why Jim Jenkins came out today to check on Ben's whereabouts. I told him that Ben arrived here in the evening, drunk. We had an argument which lasted a long time before he stormed out and drove off. I said I hadn't seen him since and I didn't want to see him again—ever."

"Do you think he believed you?"

"I'm pretty sure. If you think about it for a few seconds, except for the last part, it was all true."

We breathed a collective sigh of relief but I knew this saga was far from over. There were two more days before we disposed of Ben Parkinson's body; however, one obstacle had been overcome.

"I've brought the salt," I said.

"I'll get it!" said Georgie and he raced from the room, returning a few minutes later with the bags.

Ruth led the way to the outside shed and prised open the lid on the drum with a screwdriver. With eyes averted, she emptied the bags of salt into the drum and then sealed it. I had no idea if the salt would help slow down the decaying process. It was pure conjecture. I knew that dead animals, exposed to the air, began to smell after a few days, and we had three days, so I was reasonably confident it would be okay.

"I'll go up to the mine and find a place to bury the body," I declared.

"Don't be too impatient!" warned Ruth, "We have two days . . . remember!"

"Yeah! But I'd like to check it out now to see if it's suitable or not, rather than wait. What do you think, Amy?"

Amy screwed up her face and muttered, "The mine's not safe! I want nothing to do with your plan."

"Then, what do we do with the body? Leave it where it is?" I argued.

"No, silly. We could bury it in the forest."

Ruth interrupted, "Guy's right, sweetie. If we bury it in the forest, it stands a far greater chance of being uncovered, but no-one will dare venture into the mine because it's unsafe."

Amy grasped onto the last word with relish.

She declared, "It is unsafe. What if there's a rock fall? Guy could be killed."

"I didn't think of that. Perhaps it should be me who goes into the mine, then."

"No Ruth! Georgie and I will go. We'll be extra careful," I said firmly.

"I'm not sure, now. Perhaps it would be easier to go to the police after all," Ruth said, a resigned look on her face.

"No! You can't turn around now and change your story. You will definitely end up in jail. Georgie and I are leaving for the mine now. Let's go Georgie!"

As we hopped on our bikes, Amy ran down the path and clambered on behind me. She wrapped her arms around my waist and shouted in my ear over the engine noise.

"Don't think you can get rid of me so easily? Someone has to keep an eye on you."

She pinched me firmly, causing me to cry out in pain as I roared up the track. She stayed at the entrance to the mine while Georgie and I, torches switched on, made our way inside. We crept along the tunnel to the rock fall.

"You stay here! I'll crawl through to the other side," I said.

The tunnel ahead was narrow and dark so Georgie was only too willing to comply. I crawled through a narrow opening at the top of the rock fall and proceeded onward until I reached a smaller opening branching off. I followed this for a short distance before it ended abruptly. At the end of the tunnel I discovered that the miners had dug down about six feet before stopping. Obviously they had come to the realisation that there was no gold bearing deposit here. The hole was an ideal place to bury a body, I concluded. I turned and made my way back to Georgie and together we retraced our steps back to the entrance.

"I found a hole we can use to hide the body where nobody would ever find it. We can fill it in and block up the tunnel at the rock fall," I told Amy.

When we returned to the house we managed to eat the light meal Ruth had prepared. Georgie had to leave and go back to Roxborough, so Amy and I saddled the horses and rode up the valley. It was another hot, cloudless day but the heat was tempered by a soft, cool breeze. We cantered down to the creek where we dismounted and sat on the bank under the shade of trees. Amy snuggled up close to me and rested her head on my shoulder as we sat quietly gazing into the water. In time, Amy broke the silence.

"Do you honestly think the police will find out?"

I answered, "I don't think so. If your father had friends or relatives who really cared about him there might be an inquiry but if he was alone, we might be lucky. I hope so."

"I can't imagine anyone missing him. He was a cruel, violent drunk!"

"Was he always like that?" I asked.

"Well . . . I was very young when he left so I can't really say."

She was defensive when it came to talking about her father, as if she was concealing something. Maybe she was harbouring another buried secret. If so I really didn't want to know.

Noticing my expression she continued, "Mum told me that he had a temper and when he started drinking he used to become violent. Things just got worse. Do you think we shall go to jail if the police find out what happened last night?"

"Probably. But I think they would go easy on us because of your father's threats and what he tried to do."

"I think we're doing the right thing, don't you?" she asked, turning to face me.

"Yeah, for sure!" I answered, trying to sound confident.

On the way back to the house we didn't speak. I was thinking about having to wait two more days before we could dispose of Ben

Parkinson for good. Since I couldn't imagine a man such as he had been having friends who would be too concerned about his whereabouts I was quietly confident no-one would be aware of his disappearance, let alone investigate it.

When we arrived at the house, I went with Ruth to check the drum in the shed. We were both relieved to find there was only the merest hint of odour. It would have been different if the body hadn't been sealed in the drum because the shed's tin roof intensified the summertime heat.

I said, "It might be difficult getting the body out of the drum to bury . . . I think we should leave it in the drum and bury the drum. That way it won't smell as much. To be truthful I don't fancy handling the body at all."

"I agree," she replied, "If we can get it to the Jeep and up to the mine. The drum might roll along the tunnel."

"Georgie could help me roll it. We won't know until we try."

"You're right but we're getting ahead of ourselves. We still have two days. Let's wait till then."

Soon after our chat, I returned to town. Over the past couple of weeks I had spent most of my time at Ruth's place. Some friends spoke to me in the street and I joined them at the café. Back home, I grabbed my brother Marty and shot a few hoops with him. Sam, whom I hadn't seen for a while, arrived and joined us. Marty was surprised when I offered to take him on my bike for a ride. Sam tagged along. It was a pleasant change to do something without thinking about Ruth, Amy or Amy's dad. After the ride, Marty went inside to watch television while I sat on the steps with Sam.

"You're very quiet. Anything wrong?" she asked.

"Nah! I'm okay. It's been a long day."

"Well you look like crap. How's Amy?"

"Thanks. I feel like crap, too. Amy is fine I guess. What about you?" I asked, changing the subject.

"Haven't been doing much—Helping Mum; listening to records; hanging out with friends; thinking of you. You know. The usual stuff."

I smiled, "You'll never give up will you?"

"Nope! Never! The first day I clapped eyes on you I said to myself, 'Sam . . . one day you'll marry Guy Harmon'."

When I first met Sam she was a skinny kid with pig tails, exuberant and friendly. Over the last decade, her physical appearance had changed but not her personality. I looked at her slender body and enticing smile. She was beautiful.

I mumbled self-consciously, "Sam . . . You know if it wasn't for Amy I'd . . . You and I . . . You know . . ."

Sam interrupted, "Yeah! I know what you mean. Gotta go! See Ya!"

Her statement was terse. It was obvious that she was annoyed with my continuing relationship with Amy. Sam and I had lived so much in each other's company and I didn't want us to drift apart because of the presence of Amy in my life. This delicate situation with Sam and the ongoing drama surrounding the death of Ben Parkinson combined to ensure I had another sleepless night.

CHAPTER 14

THE BURIAL

I managed to eat a small breakfast to please my mother but I was edgy and tense. Waiting for two days to bury Ben Parkinson was a ticking bomb, one that was ready to explode at any given moment.

"You look a little better today," Mum said, as she collected the dishes from the table. "Before you go anywhere I need you to do some jobs for me."

"Fine, Mum."

I completed the chores by mid-morning, with some help from Georgie. We saw Billy in his front yard, also working at a few household chores. He glanced our way but continued working. Having avoided us for the last two weeks after his hateful interference in our lives, his decision to keep his distance was a wise choice. Georgie, more than anyone, wanted to punish Billy for his contemptible deeds.

"If he sees us leaving, he might follow," I muttered under my breath. "Let's go into town for a while. We have plenty of time."

We walked to my father's store where we offered our services for an hour. Dad gave us money to buy a hamburger at the café. After lunch, we strolled back home to get our bikes. Billy was nowhere to be seen. As we rode out of town I glanced back several times to make sure he wasn't following. We spent the remainder of the day with Amy, trying to relax. Late in the afternoon we returned home knowing that in twenty-four hours Ben Parkinson's mortal remains would be sealed in the abandoned and dangerous gold mine—forever.

It was midday when Georgie and I arrived at Ruth's house the next morning, ready to relocate the body, neither of us looking forward to the task. Ruth and Amy were sitting on the veranda waiting for us. We joined them for a cool drink and discussed the situation.

"How are you boys coping?" asked Ruth.

"Not great!" I replied. "I'm not getting any sleep. It's nerve-racking, just waiting and waiting."

"Amy and I are the same. Waiting for something to happen is a living hell."

The events of the past week had taken their toll on all of us. We all looked jaded.

"We need to bury the body in the mine," I said. "We can't leave it in the shed in this hot weather and if Billy or his policeman dad come prying, they might discover it."

Ruth declared, "Well! It looks like you were right. No-one's been around asking questions so I'll move the Jeep up to the shed. You and Georgie can move the drum out."

Amy said, "I'll keep a look out down the track."

This was her way of saying, "I don't want to be around when you do this."

With difficulty, Georgie and I managed to move the drum out of the shed and place it on its side. Ruth backed the Jeep up to the shed and we placed two large wooden planks and ran them from the back of the Jeep to the ground. The added salt and the body made the drum quite heavy and it took the combined muscle power of the three of us to roll the drum up into the back of the Jeep. I was thankful that

Georgie had the strength of an adult. I put shovels, torches, the planks, Ruth's rifle and rope into the Jeep before we climbed aboard. We set off for the mine, picking up Amy on the way.

At the mine we unloaded the drum and with Ruth leading the way, rolled it along the tunnel until we arrived at the rock fall. Georgie and I began the onerous task of shifting rocks and soil until we had fashioned an opening large enough to accommodate the drum. After completing this task, which took some time, our clothes were saturated. Although the mine was relatively cool compared to the heat outside, we were working in a confined space with minimal air.

We returned to the entrance to join Ruth and Amy, who had parked the Jeep in the shade of a tree. They had cool drinks and we sat in silence drinking and reflecting on the work still to be done. Ruth's face mirrored Amy's—both looked weary and sad. I tried to remain positive about the situation.

"Once we bury the drum your worries will be finally over," I said.

Ruth screwed up her face and sighed, "It will never be the same. Even if the body is not found, our worries will not be over. The only reason I agreed to this was because if I went to jail, Amy would be alone. Even if I elude jail, I don't think we can stay here. There are too many bad memories."

This was not the news I wanted to hear. My mouth dropped open. I couldn't speak. Amy reacted in a similar way but managed to utter her concerns tearfully.

"Do we have to leave here, Mum? What about Guy and Georgie? I don't want to leave them. Can't we stay for a while at least and see how things are?"

"I know how it will affect you and Guy—Georgie too. We will need to sit down over the coming weeks and discuss this. I'm not planning to leave right away so don't get upset—any of you," Ruth insisted.

She was trying to alleviate our concerns but it was too late. I already had a bagful of misgivings and felt that my future with Amy would soon be ruined. I was hurt and disappointed to think my summer would end in such a way. I stood silently and motioned Georgie to follow. We entered the mine leaving Amy and Ruth in earnest, animated conversation.

We managed to push and coax the drum past the rock fall and along the side tunnel to the vertical shaft. We couldn't push the drum into the hole because the drop was too deep and the fall would most likely break open the drum. My idea was to tie the ropes around the drum and lower it by hand but I decided against that because it was too heavy.

"I don't think we can hold this. It's too heavy!" I said, "Let's go back and grab the planks, shovels and Ruth's rifle."

We brought the planks back and slid them at an angle into the hole. We used the ropes to carefully lower the drum down the planks. Unfortunately, the weight of the drum was too much for me to handle and halfway down the ropes slipped through my fingers, Georgie desperately held on but the drum broke loose and crashed with a loud thump at the bottom of the hole. I shone my torch down and saw that the lid had dislodged and part of the body was revealed.

"I'd better go down and fix the lid back on," I said, dreading the prospect of being near the body.

I drew in several large breaths. Georgie nodded and I cautiously eased my way down the planks. My heart was pounding as I drew in a deep breath but the stench of decay was strong and I fell back, hand over my nose. The need to yell was overcome by the need to retch. I collapsed on my haunches and vomited. I stood up, wiped my mouth and looked up at Georgie.

I gasped, "Bloody hell! I can't stand this, help me out!"

Georgie lay on his stomach and leaned over the edge with an outstretched hand. I tried to climb the plank to grab his hand but failed and fell back to land near the body. I scrambled like a startled rabbit up the plank to grasp Georgie's hand. He hauled me out and I lay on the edge, gasping for breath.

"Shit! That was awful!" I muttered.

When I had recovered, I helped Georgie pull up the planks and throw them to one side. I threw the rifle into the hole and grabbed a shovel.

"Okay! Let's fill it in!"

Because of the depth of the hole, it took nearly an hour of shovelling rocks and soil to completely cover the drum. We rolled loose rocks, gathered from the tunnel floor into the hole to cover it completely and prevent wild animals digging up the body. By this time, we were exhausted. My muscles began to protest and my back ached from bending over. My arms felt as if they were on fire. Wearily, we retraced our steps to the rock fall, satisfied that the only way the body would be discovered was if someone was to mine again, a most unlikely happening.

Amy and Ruth were waiting for us. Ruth said, "Boys! Go out and have a drink. You look like you need a rest. Amy and I will seal up the hole in this rock fall."

It was late afternoon when we returned to the house. We were covered in dust and soil so while Ruth and Amy went inside to wash, Georgie and I used buckets of water from the tank near the house to wash the grime from our bodies. Ruth provided towels and a drink as we sat on the steps of the veranda, silently gazing at the sun setting behind the trees, a deep orange glow, deepening to a dull red. The sun painted the grass and trees with its own special range of pastel colours.

The countryside was silent, almost reverent, as though every living creature was paying homage to this glorious sight. It took my mind off the aches, pains and events of the day temporarily at least. Ruth and Amy joined us on the veranda and Amy sat beside me, her head resting on my shoulder.

"What a beautiful scene!" murmured Ruth, breaking the silence.

"We had better go before it gets too dark," I said, helping Amy to her feet. "I'll come out tomorrow."

"I can't come out," declared Georgie, "I'm going to the timber mill to see if I can get a job."

Georgie had left school and was joining the workforce. He hoped to join Ivan's father at the mill or if that was not possible, he planned to work for his dad as an apprentice mechanic.

"Oh!" said Ruth surprised by his words, "Well! Good luck Georgie. I'm sure you will get a job. What about you Guy? What does the future have in store for you?"

"My mum and dad want me to finish school and go to college or university but I wouldn't mind becoming an artist. I haven't made my mind up yet. What about you Amy?"

Amy shrugged and answered, "To be honest I haven't thought about it. Maybe I'll get a job as a waitress or marry and have seven or eight kids. Who knows?"

"You're so pretty you could be a model or a movie star," Georgie declared loudly.

He lowered his head in embarrassment, while Amy blushed.

"Georgie's right!" I murmured, "Amy could become a model. Isn't that so, Ruth?"

Ruth nodded her head and put her arms around Amy's shoulders. Amy didn't say a word.

"You boys better go!" smiled Ruth, "you've embarrassed her."

I grinned and, with Georgie following, strolled down the path. As I reached my bike, I heard the rush of footsteps and turned to see Amy plant a kiss on Georgie's cheek.

She twirled around and flung her arms around my neck, kissing me first on one cheek, then the other before kissing the tip of my nose. Her sweet perfume invaded my senses as she pressed her lips tenderly against mine. She murmured 'thank you' in my ear then left to join her mother on the veranda. Georgie touched his cheek and from his glazed expression I knew he wouldn't wash his cheek for days, or even weeks.

As we travelled back to Roxborough I had time to recall the events of the past week. Today we had laid the body of Ben Parkinson to rest. He was now out of sight, hopefully permanently. I considered I had grown up a great deal in the past few weeks—battle hardened you might say. Deep down though, I knew that the slaying of Amy's dad would haunt me for a long time to come.

I glanced at Georgie, riding alongside me. Poor Georgie! He was the butt of cruel jokes and put downs and most girls had never made the effort to get to know him. Sam and Amy were exceptions. Having Amy as a friend meant the world to him.

As we pushed our bikes along the footpath towards my home, I noticed that Ivan and his family had arrived back from their holiday. His return presented a new problem. How would I explain Amy? Even though he was my friend, I couldn't tell him about the incidents of the past weeks. I would have to keep my relationship with Ruth and Amy from him.

"Georgie. We can't tell Ivan about Ruth and Amy," I said. "Do you understand? He can't go with us out to Ruth's place. It's for Amy's safety. We have to keep it a secret even if he asks. Okay?"

"I won't say anything. Mum's the word."

I reiterated firmly, "No-one must ever know about her dad—never!"

Georgie nodded and left. I went inside and stretched out on my bed. Ivan's return brought with it the realisation that the summer vacation had almost ended. Battling fatigue, I drifted off to sleep.

CHAPTER 15

THE DEPARTURE

The arrival of Ivan, who looked suntanned and very relaxed, interrupted my breakfast the next day. He sat opposite me and rambled on about his holiday. I nodded my head a few times and pretended to listen but my thoughts were elsewhere. After breakfast, we strolled into town and met up with some friends at the café.

Naturally, Ivan didn't have a clue about Billy Jenkins and his involvement with Amy and the bashing of Georgie. In fact, Ivan knew absolutely nothing of Amy's existence so when Billy entered the café; Ivan was puzzled by my reaction.

I ignored Billy completely by turning away. As for Billy, he walked past me, chatting to one of his cronies. I stood and left the café and Ivan followed me outside.

"Are you still upset with Billy over what happened to Georgie at the waterhole?" he asked.

"Not just that. Billy and his mates bashed Georgie for no reason; they put him in hospital."

"You're joking aren't you? Why?"

I fabricated a story that Georgie had been taunted by Billy and his friends at the café and when Georgie grabbed Billy for calling him a retard, Billy's friends held Georgie while he belted him. Ivan listened in silence.

"I never liked Billy Jenkins," he muttered.

"Worse still," I said, "Billy is not sorry. He's scum of the earth."

Ivan believed my story. It was going to be difficult trying to avoid Billy but sometime in the future all these matters would come to a head. Billy Jenkins and I were on a collision course and we would have an altercation. For now, I was prepared to heed the advice of Georgie's mother. I told Ivan I had to help my father in his store after lunch and suggested that he and Georgie go for a swim.

I didn't intend to help Dad at all. It was a sly ruse to spend time with Amy. I felt guilty about telling lies but I considered Amy worth it. Georgie now had a job at the timber mill and was due to begin work in a few days, so he would be able to hang out with us only on weekends. I was happy for Georgie because he wouldn't have to put up with the jibes from Billy and his friends at school.

Without the spectre of Ben Parkinson's presence, Amy and Ruth appeared more relaxed when I visited them. Ruth didn't mention leaving Roxborough and I hoped that she would reconsider her plans. With this in mind I determined that I would spend every day with Amy.

Unfortunately, I ignored Ivan and one afternoon after returning home from Amy's home, he confronted me. His face clouded with anger and I knew what was coming.

"What's going on?" he asked. "You've been avoiding me since I got home. Is something the matter?"

As upset as he was, I couldn't tell him about the incidents of the past two weeks and I knew that sooner or later he would find out that I was seeing Amy. I tried to explain what had happened.

"I'm sorry!" I answered, "After you went on holidays I met this girl and I've been seeing her."

I could see the hurt in his eyes. He and I had shown little interest in girls and to be told that I now had a girlfriend must have been disheartening.

"I see! Well, you could have told me. Who is she? Do I know her?" he asked.

"You don't know her. Her name is Amy and she lives out of town. She's new to this area."

"So that's where you go every day?"

"Yes! I've been spending a lot of time with her because she might be leaving soon."

"Oh! I see," Ivan said, resigned to the fact that I was now in a relationship.

His face said it all. I know he felt betrayed. With Georgie now working, Ivan was destined to be alone for the bulk of each day. He bowed his head sadly and shuffled dejectedly along the path to his home.

I called out, "Look! We'll get together . . . soon! Okay?"

Without stopping, he mumbled, "Fine!"

I spoke to Amy about Ivan and she suggested I spend the mornings with him and visit her after lunch. Ivan was surprised when I took him swimming and fishing. We hung out with our group of friends in town and being able to spend this time with him for a few days took my mind off my troubles.

Besides, I enjoyed our time together. The sleepless nights and nightmares continued, although they had become less frequent. My friends and my family had noticed my mood swings. My mum asked me why I was so often 'in the dumps' and my dad, bless his soul, passed it off as a hormonal thing, common in teenagers.

Ivan noted my change in disposition as well. "You've changed Guy. Are you annoyed with me because I'm taking you away from Amy? I mean . . . If you want to spend all day with her, go ahead. I don't care!" he said, after spending another morning enduring my gloomy, pessimistic behaviour.

"Nah! Sorry I've been a shit. Amy's has a few problems; that's all," I explained.

It seemed to me that the only good thing in my life right now, besides Amy, was the fact that no enquiries had been made about Amy's father. Sam's visits to our home were now sparse. I didn't blame her if she loathed me. I am sure I would have felt the same way in similar circumstances.

A week passed and the summer vacation was over. I travelled the now well-worn path to Ruth's home on the last day of the holidays. Amy had informed me that she and her mum had discussed leaving Roxborough but nothing had been decided.

As soon as I entered the house and saw Amy's flushed face I knew that a decision had been made and they were leaving. Ruth asked me to sit down and I awaited the bombshell.

"Guy! You've been a wonderful, dear friend to Amy and to me. We will always treasure your help and companionship," Ruth said, in a polite attempt to soften the blow we both knew was coming.

It felt as if a noose had tightened around my neck, as I sat uncomfortably, waiting for the inevitable. I glanced at a disconsolate Amy curled up on the sofa.

"I thought very seriously about remaining here but there were many factors to consider," said Ruth. "I had to think about Amy and her future. If we stayed here she would come into contact with Billy Jenkins at some time and I don't want that. There was also my ex-husband buried in the mine and the possibility that in the future questions might be asked about his whereabouts . . . doubtful, but a possibility all the same. Leaving and re-locating to another town would give us a chance to begin a new life."

Before I could reply she continued. "I also had to consider Amy's feelings and her friendship with you. In the near future you will probably go to college or uni or get a job and you will have some decisions to make as well. So, after much soul searching I have decided to leave and start afresh in another town. We can keep in contact with you; you know, by phone or letter and there's no reason why you can't visit us. It's for the best. It's the most sensible thing to do. I do hope you understand."

She reached across, took my hand and gave me a weak smile. Of course she was right but when the love of my life, my first love, was leaving me, I was hurt and disillusioned. I fought back tears as I struggled desperately to compose myself.

"I know what you are doing is for the best. It just would have been great if you could have stayed for a while," I murmured, my voice breaking.

My stomach was twisted into a sharp, gut wrenching knot and it felt as though invisible metal bands were being tightened around my chest, compressing it and squeezing the essence of life from me. Even though I had sensed this would happen, it was still quite a shock when it actually happened.

Amy suddenly burst into tears and fled the room, prompting Ruth to speak for her.

"It's been difficult for Amy. She loves you dearly but she doesn't understand the full implications of us staying. Naturally, it is heartbreaking for her to leave you but in time she'll accept my decision and I hope you will too. Right now, I think you need to spend a little time together before we leave."

"When are you leaving?" I asked, fervently praying it was not too soon.

"Next week!" Ruth answered, "We'll need to pack up and get everything settled. I was only renting this house so there's no need to sell it."

"What about the horses?"

"They were here when we arrived. One of the conditions of the lease was to look after the horses. Amy is heartbroken at leaving them. Maybe our new house will have plenty of space for a horse. Who knows?"

Amy and I spent the afternoon trying to come to terms with her impending departure. One week and she would vanish from my life, perhaps forever. With heavy heart I departed late in the afternoon. On the way home I cried without restraint, tears flowing down my cheeks freely. My journey with Amy and Ruth was ending. Sadly, it wasn't going to be a happy ending.

Georgie and Sam were sitting on the steps of my home when I returned. I took my time putting the bike in the garage because I didn't want them to see how upset I was. It also gave me the opportunity to wipe my face and regain my composure. Even so, I couldn't hide my grief and when Sam saw my miserable countenance she moved forward with a concerned expression.

"Are you okay, Guy? What's wrong?" she asked.

I bit my bottom lip to stop it trembling and tried to put on a stoic face.

"Amy and Ruth are leaving."

"Why? What's happened?"

"Is it because of . . . ?" Georgie asked. He realised what he was about to ask and stopped abruptly.

I glared at him and replied, "It's family business. Nothing else."

"I'm so sorry. I liked Amy," Sam said.

I didn't know if she was telling the truth or just trying to be supportive. Right then, I didn't care.

"When are they leaving?" Georgie asked in a gruff voice as he, too, fought back tears.

"The end of next week."

Georgie was as crestfallen as I had been. He lowered his head and silently stared at the ground. Sam put her arm around his shoulders and we sat on the steps in silence, contemplating life without Amy.

I broke the silence finally and whispered, "I'll see you tomorrow. Bye!"

I dashed inside, leaving Sam and Georgie on the steps. I flung myself onto my bed and the tears flowed. I woke next morning with my pillow damp from crying.

Every available moment during the next week was spent with Amy and as each day went by, it felt as if another dagger was being thrust into my heart. The school term had started so I visited Amy after school. On the last two days of the week I didn't attend school so I could be with Amy and Ruth. Ruth continued to promise that they would keep in touch but this did little to ease my heartache. The realisation—that they were leaving—hit me as I stood outside their house, watching the Jeep trundle down the track out of sight, with Amy waving a sad goodbye. A feeling of isolation enveloped me as they disappeared from view and there was a lump in my throat that threatened to choke me. The end of summer. Too soon!

CHAPTER 16

LIFE AFTER AMY

After the departure of Amy and Ruth I attempted to get on with my life in Roxborough. Once settled in a new home, Amy wrote to me regularly. These letters I treasured. At high school I succeeded in avoiding Billy Jenkins but things changed when Deanne, a friend at school, informed me that Billy had been spreading malicious rumours about Amy. That was the final straw. I confronted him after school and we had a fight. Watched by a crowd of his cronies, I thrashed him. As he lay on the ground, I stood over him and shouted so everyone could hear me.

"You're a prick! You attacked Amy because she didn't want anything to do with you. You tried to rape her. If I had my way I'd shoot you, you lousy shit! As for Georgie, your gutless mates held him while you bashed him. If I hear you've ever uttered another bad word about Amy I'll kill you."

My outburst silenced the crowd. A few of my friends clapped and cheered but the majority stood in stunned silence as I walked away. Revenge was sweet.

Billy yelled out to me, "I know what happened at Ruth's house that night."

I froze. The news I had dreaded so long drained the colour from my face as I turned slowly to face him. He wiped the blood from his mouth and smirked.

"I know! Watch your back, Harmon. You won't get away with what you've done. I'll see to that."

Did this mean he knew about the Ben Parkinson's death? Or was he trying to frighten me by guessing what might have happened? His remarks brought up old wounds, which now soured my victory. He knew his remarks had upset me and the smirk on his face broadened. I turned and left.

News of the fight spread quickly and later that afternoon Georgie arrived on my doorstep. A huge grin lit up his face.

"Sam told me you had a fight with Billy Jenkins. Is it true?" he asked expectantly.

"Yes! He said Amy was a slut so I thumped him."

"Wow! That's great! Was he bleeding? Did he cry?"

Georgie wanted all the details. He'd been waiting for this moment since Billy had put him in hospital.

"I gave him a black eye and a bloody nose . . . He didn't cry but he did look a mess."

"He got what he deserved, then. I'm glad you did it."

I must admit I gained a great deal of satisfaction in fighting Billy, but I needed to know if he was at Ruth's house on the night of Ben Parkinson's death. I wrote to Amy and told her about the fight and I also mentioned Billy's remarks. I asked if he had contacted them at all.

When I received her reply, Ruth had written a brief comment in the margin, informing me of her belief that if Billy had been there that night, he would have gone immediately to the police. The fact that the police had not become involved indicated that he had no idea about what happened and he probably said those things to unnerve me. He had not contacted them, so she told me to ignore the possibility of his presence on that fateful night. Amy's reaction was to call me her hero. Her loving comments kept me on cloud nine for weeks after. Georgie asked me if she mentioned him in her letters so I wrote and asked her to include him in them. From then on, whenever I received a letter, Georgie would come over to my house and his face would glow like a lovesick puppy when I read Amy's personal message to him. It always finished with, 'love and kisses to my sweet Georgie'.

Her letters were the glue that kept me from falling apart. I relied on them to boost my ego whenever I felt depressed or lonely. She wrote to me every week and this kept our love alive but not being able to see her or hold her weighed heavily on me, as did the death of Ben Parkinson.

I found school arduous and my zest for learning had greatly diminished. I sat in class and daydreamed of Amy and what might have been. Consequently, I found studying for the final exams all but impossible. At night I read her letters over and over and listened to our favourite music rather than doing school work. Mum and Dad received a letter from the school about my work. They confronted me one evening and their glum faces indicated it wasn't a social call.

Dad growled, "We've got a letter from the High School about your schoolwork. According to them your grades have dropped a considerable margin this year. Unless you put your head down and work harder they say you don't have a chance of getting into university. Can you explain this?"

"Well . . . since Amy left I can't concentrate on school. It's hard," I mumbled unconvincingly.

"Rubbish! That's just an excuse. You've become lazy. Don't you want to go to uni?" he said, shaking his head.

"I dunno!"

My nonchalant remark infuriated him but luckily, Mum intervened, before he could vent his anger.

"Ivan and Sam are working hard to get into uni. I thought you wanted to be with them. I know you miss Amy but it shouldn't prevent you from doing your school work," she declared.

Dad was trying to control his anger. It had always been his hope for me that I go to a college or university, so my newfound attitude had him baffled and fuming.

"It's not good enough! You need to grow up and get your act together or you'll find yourself out of school and with no prospects at all," he snapped.

Mum, ever the diplomat, tried to solve the problem quietly.

"If you can't study here, why not study with Ivan?" she asked.

"I don't think his parents would allow it and besides we don't spend much time together anymore."

"What about Sam?"

"I suppose so but she's a girl and her parents might think I'd be a distraction. You know," I answered. My answers certainly gave the impression that I was trying to wriggle out of any form of study.

A deepening frown on my father's face warned of his increasing impatience with me.

"You're coming up with excuse after excuse. I'll go and talk to Sam's parents and see if you can study with Sam in her house. If they agree will you do it?" he said.

His expression told me not to resist or I would cop a tongue lashing, so I nodded and agreed. It was arranged that three times a week I went to Sam's house in the evening to study. At first we studied in the kitchen and I had to admit Sam helped me with my studies and my grades began to improve steadily. She was a kindred spirit who knew me completely, and this helped keep my mind on the work. For the time being, my parents and the school were satisfied that I was making an effort.

As the year progressed, most of my spare time was spent with Georgie and Sam, but my relationship with Ivan had changed. He became increasingly occupied with study because he wanted to go to university and become a lawyer. Consequently, I rarely saw him.

Sam helped make my life more bearable without Amy. We became almost inseparable and our friends presumed that she was my girlfriend. We laughed at this, but in the upper reaches of my mind, I often speculated upon what might have happened between us if I had not met Amy.

Many of the young men in Roxborough had asked her out, but she chose my company. I didn't know why. Maybe it was because we knew each other so well. We had similar interests and had developed a comradeship from childhood. Sam knew that Amy and I wrote to each other but this didn't seem to bother her. I made sure that I didn't mention Amy in Sam's presence unless she asked about her.

Over time, our study habits changed. Sam convinced her parents she and I could study better if we were in her room. She had to keep the door open at all times, but her parents rarely checked on us and gradually we found ourselves spending the study time either talking or listening to music. Our friendship moved from platonic to a more romantic one that September.

Sam and I were in her bedroom trying to study but inevitably we began chatting and listening to records. She was wearing a short sleeved blouse unbuttoned at the top and a pair of skin tight shorts. I didn't know if it was a deliberate act on her part to arouse me, but it certainly worked. As she bent down to pick up a record I caught a glimpse of her breasts. She noticed I was staring and smiled. It was a mischievous, all-knowing smile. It was enough to make me want to hold and kiss her. She read my mind and closed the bedroom door. Before I had a chance to recover, she had wrapped her arms around my neck and kissed me. Her lips were soft, moist and warm and I felt a tingling sensation enveloping my whole body.

I was completely lost in her cosy, passionate embrace for what seemed an eternity. After a few minutes we separated to catch our breath.

"That was nice," Sam whispered, "just how I imagined it."

For a moment I stared at her—speechless. I was bewitched by her beauty and captivated by her sensuality.

"Didn't you enjoy it?" she asked when I didn't respond. I found my voice again and answered.

"Sorry! You caught me by surprise. It was great . . . just great," I croaked hoarsely.

"On a scale of one to ten, how would you rate it?"

"It was a definite ten. You're a terrific kisser Sam."

"I've wanted to do that for a long time. I know your girl is Amy but I have feelings for you, too," she said softly with a grin.

"You sure do. Wow!"

If Amy had not been in the picture I would have jumped into bed with Sam then and there. I gathered myself and sat on the edge of the bed.

"No harm done. It was just a kiss, no more," I said huskily, trying to disguise the fact that I was aroused by her.

Sam grinned and with a wicked glint in her eyes, brushed her lips against my cheek and stood up. She casually rearranged her clothes and opened the bedroom door.

"Just a kiss hey! I'm gonna keep at you til I've won you over. I'm sorry to do this Amy but Guy Harmon is mine," she chuckled.

"You can try but I won't give up Amy without a fight," I grinned and hit her with a pillow.

Naturally it ended up with a pillow fight with our first kiss being forgotten for the moment. From then on, studying took second place to 'snogging'. With her parents in the house it was only a matter of time before they became suspicious and investigated. One night we were caught kissing and embracing by Sam's mum, who asked me politely but promptly to leave. That was the end of our study arrangements.

My relationship with Sam became stronger after this episode and I delighted in warding off her advances. It became a game where she tried everything to show her love for me and get me to reciprocate. It happened whenever we were alone—at the Waterhole or at the movies. Sam was a free spirit. She didn't mind that I fondled her breasts and on one occasion she placed her hand inside my jeans and touched me but that was as far as it went. In a direct contrast, Sam was like a wild sexual beast whereas Amy was a sweet, innocent angel. They were opposites in so many ways and I found myself attracted to both for a variety of conflicting reasons.

Amy continued to write to me. She and Ruth had settled down in Sheffield Plains, a large country town in the centre of the wheat belt. Ruth rented a house on the outskirts of the town and worked as a waitress in a local restaurant four nights a week to supplement her income as an artist.

Amy was attending the local high school and was enjoying her time there. I didn't tell her about Sam. I did feel guilty about my rekindled relationship with Sam but the guilt surfaced only when I read a letter from Amy or I wrote to her. I knew I wasn't being fair to either of them but I couldn't help myself. I was a seventeen-year-old boy with two beautiful female friends. To me it was a situation sanctioned in bliss, but deep within my being, I realised I would have to make a decision sooner or later, about the girls.

At the end of the year I wasn't surprised to miss qualifying to go to university and neither were my parents. Sam and Ivan both met the criteria to enter uni and that meant that I would only see Sam when she had a holiday break.

After Sam broke the news to me, I rode my bike up the road towards the Waterhole to have some quiet time alone. On the spur of the moment, I decided to travel out to Ruth's old place. I sat on the steps of the house and re-lived the great times I'd had with Amy. In my mind's eye I could picture Amy and Ruth there with me. Then I thought about Sam leaving and tears pricked the corner of my eyes. My emotions overwhelmed me and I broke down and wept.

Finally, I stood up and yelled, "Wake up you prick! Crying's not going to change anything. Grow up!"

The outburst helped calm me and I took a deep breath as I wiped away the tears. I needed to make firm decisions about my life and my relationships with Amy and Sam.

In need of even more solitude, I rode up to the mine to check it out and then made my way across the grassy valley to the waterfall. The skeleton of Ben Parkinson's car, burnt and black, sat in the cave, a stark reminder of that fateful night. The buried secret was safe—for the time being.

It was late afternoon when I made the journey home. A sleepless night followed—not because of my nightmares but because of what I feared the future held for me and the decisions I would be forced to make, sooner rather than later.

CHAPTER 17

THE SAWMILL

With both Sam and Ivan at university, my only friend still in Roxborough was Georgie. For a while I worked with my dad in his store but standing behind a counter all day didn't appeal to me. Georgie convinced me to seek work at the sawmill. I asked if I could work with Georgie and luckily the plant manager agreed. Georgie worked outside cleaning up the yard and doing odd jobs. This type of work suited me and Georgie was 'over the moon' when I joined him at the mill.

It didn't take long for me to see that Georgie was treated like dirt. The other men teased and taunted him mercilessly. I couldn't comprehend why grown men, so called adults, would act this way. Maybe it was because Georgie was different or he bragged about all the things he could do or maybe it was just that Georgie provided an unmissable target for them. Whatever the reason, I was disgusted with their behaviour. At lunch on my first day there as I sat with Georgie against the wall of a shed, away from the other workers, I asked him about it.

"Georgie? Do these men always treat you like this . . . you know . . . calling you names and pushing you around?"

"Most of the time; but it doesn't worry me. I'm used to it," he answered with a shrug of his shoulders.

He had become conditioned to this treatment because from an early age he'd been a focus for abuse and his transition into the workforce had changed nothing. It wasn't fair.

"It's not right! You've got to stand up for yourself. They've no right to push you around."

"I don't want to cause trouble. I might lose my job."

He was probably right but I knew I couldn't stand by and let him continue to be treated in this fashion. I glanced up and saw one of the millworkers swaggering towards us. He was short, stocky man in his thirties, with long straggly hair swept back from a dirty, unshaven face. He stood in front of us with a leer on his face and yelled loudly so his mates could hear him.

"Hey! Shit for brains, who's your friend?"

Quietly, Georgie replied, "This is Guy."

"Well Guy. Why you hanging out with this retard?" he sneered; a silly grin on his face.

This oaf reminded me very much of Hank Jones. Despite the menace of his strong, powerful build I was not going to allow him to put Georgie down. I slowly dragged myself to my feet and faced him. To have backed down then would only have made matters worse for Georgie and me.

"Listen mate! Georgie is my friend. He won't do anything about the way you talk to him but I will," I snapped.

"How do we treat him, you little shit?"

"Calling him 'shit for brains' and 'retard'. How about I call you 'porky pig' or 'smelly'? You wouldn't like that would you?"

"Be careful young fella or . . . or," he answered; seemingly lost for words.

"Or . . . or . . . or . . . what?"

My spontaneous mimicry riled him and his face turned bright red.

"Easy! I'll deck you," he growled.

"You can try!"

I knew what his response would be. A youth, just out of school, would be another easy target.

"Okay, dipstick! Give me your best shot," he grunted and took up a fighting stance. He had a big, goofy grin plastered across his face as he turned to his mates watching.

He didn't know my dad had been a boxing champion and had taught me plenty of ring craft. I reasoned that this yob would be a brawler who would swing wildly, hoping to connect. All I had to do was box him.

"Are you sure you want to do this. If you apologise to Georgie I'll forget it," I grinned.

This infuriated him even further and he swung a wild right hand at me. I moved aside and he swung off balance. He charged at me again but I stopped him in his tracks with a snappy left hand that landed flush on his nose, followed by a right cross to his mouth. He wiped blood away from his lips and undeterred, walked forward continuing to swing aimlessly while I stepped away and peppered his face once again with a combination of lefts and rights. These punches jerked his head back and drew more blood. By this time, we were surrounded by a crowd of men, all of them shouting for my blood.

One of the men yelled out, "Come on Ken! He's only a kid. What's the matter with you?"

Another joined in. "Take him Ken!"

Ken responded by charging at me. I stood my ground and from close range unleashed an uppercut to the chin which set him on his backside. The onlookers became instantly silent as he lay motionless on the ground.

While I stood over him, one of his workmates grabbed me from behind and pinned my arms back. This was the signal for another friend to step forward and strike me but before he could, Georgie wrapped his arms around him in a bear hug. He used his colossal strength to force the man against the wall and bang his head repeatedly before throwing him to the ground like a rag doll. The man staggered to his feet and stumbled away, holding his head.

By this time I had managed to wrestle myself free from the man holding me. Georgie stepped forward in front of me and whacked him. There was a loud crack as the man's nosed caved in, blood spurting across his face. He cried in agony and slumped to his knees, holding his nose. The sight of Georgie unleashing his pent-up fury made the crowd wary and they all backed away quickly.

Momentarily I considered telling them where to go, but thought better of it. If I called them a pack of mongrel dogs, or words to that effect, they might gang up and thump the soul case out of me.

There were a few stifled rumblings from among the men but they retreated, taking Ken and the other two with them. As they left, one of the men turned and shouted, "You'll pay for this sonny!"

I ignored him and looked at Georgie.

"You okay?"

He nodded. This wasn't the end of our troubles because fifteen minutes later we were summoned to the deputy manager's office. I didn't care if I got the sack but Georgie didn't deserve to lose his job. Georgie was asked to remain outside while I was escorted into the office. The deputy manager was a thin, sour looking individual, with horn rimmed glasses perched precariously on the tip of his nose. He scowled at me as he sat behind his desk, drumming his fingers on the desk top.

"Well Harmon. Your first day on the job and you've been involved in a fight. What have you got to say for yourself?"

I explained to him about how the men treated Georgie and the taunts of Ken. He listened to my story quietly and then removed his glasses, polished them with a handkerchief and placed them back on his nose.

"The men might have teased Georgie but he only had to come to me or speak to the foreman and this would have stopped," he said in a soft voice.

This comment riled me. He was putting the blame on Georgie, not the men responsible for the string of cowardly taunts aimed at someone who was both incapable and unwilling to defend himself.

"The foreman was one of those calling Georgie names. You know full well that Georgie is not bright and you know he wouldn't come to you. He doesn't deserve to be treated the way he has been. He's a good worker and he keeps to himself. But I wasn't going to stand by and let those men call him 'retard' or 'shithead'. You don't have to worry about me causing any further trouble here because I quit. You're no different from those men. Fire me but don't fire Georgie. Give him another job away from those men. Look! Mr Mavrak works here. He's Georgie's neighbour. Let Georgie work with him. He can keep an eye on him," I said.

He scowled, his eyes widening behind his lenses. The glasses lifted slightly as he raised his eyebrows.

"I agree that you should quit. I don't think you could continue to work here after what just happened. As far as Georgie is concerned, he can't work with those men either, now. I don't condone their behaviour at all but these things do happen in a workplace."

His condescending attitude annoyed me but I didn't want Georgie sacked so I restrained myself and listened patiently.

"I will look at placing Georgie with someone like Nick Mavrak but if I can't I will have to let him go."

"Georgie deserves a chance, sir. I started the fight, not him," I pleaded; with as much conviction as I could muster.

"I know! On your way out tell Georgie to come in."

He dismissed me with a wave of his hand. Georgie was told to report the next day to the deputy manager and was assigned to work in the same section of the mill as Mr Mavrak. I lost my job but I knew that Ivan's dad would look after Georgie and that left me with a feeling of contentment.

CHAPTER 18

DECISIONS

My father, who understood why I quit my job at the sawmill, arranged for me to work at the local bike shop. He told me that I should relish the work because I loved tinkering with bikes. He was right of course and I loved the notion of becoming a mechanic. Receiving a wage and being satisfied in my job lifted me from the doldrums and I began to enjoy life. Georgie was happy at the mill and there had been no further incidents to disrupt our lives. Billy Jenkins left Roxborough for another large town, as did many of his friends. 'Good riddance to bad rubbish!' was all I could think.

In my spare time I painted. Painting was an escape for me as it helped me forget my troubles. Georgie usually accompanied me when I took my painting gear out into the bush. He would play with his dog and take walks in the surrounds while I painted. If the weather became too hot, I would pack away the painting gear, and we would have a swim. We talked about the good times we spent with Ivan, Sam and Amy. It was on one of these trips that I brought up the subject of Ben Parkinson.

"Do you still think about Ben Parkinson's death?" I asked.

"Yeah! Sometimes I have bad dreams. What about you?"

"I'm the same. It's not as bad now though."

"Same here. Do you ever think they'll find his body?" Georgie asked.

"Nah! Nobody's been asking about him and unless the mine is opened up I think it'll be okay. Just remember! Don't ever tell anyone what happened—not even you parents. It has to remain secret."

"I won't. It'll be our secret."

Despite his liking for local gossip and bragging about things he'd done, Georgie had kept his promise and told nobody our secret. At long last, the memory of that fateful night was growing dimmer.

Sam returned home two or three times during the year on a break from her studies. On one of these visits we took our relationship to the next level. It wasn't planned. Sam's parents had gone away for the weekend and she invited me over. One thing led to another and we made love for the first time. Afterwards I did feel guilty because I had always planned to be with Amy when I first made love.

I began to have serious doubts about my association with Amy when Sam declared her love for me and without thinking I had responded in kind.

In my next letter to Amy I informed her that I wanted to see her again. I wanted to sort out my feelings because I was leading both girls on with my actions. I wanted to have a friendly relationship with my conscience, as well as with both girls.

I hadn't visited Amy because I had no car and the nearest railway station was at Benton, some thirty miles away. It had been a frustrating three years since I had last seen Amy and I arranged to travel to her home one weekend in October. I was now the proud owner of a battered, secondhand car and my only concern was whether it would get me to Sheffield Plains, almost five hours' drive from home, without breaking down.

When I finally arrived in Sheffield Plains, I drove down a dirt road on the outskirts of town, until I reached Ruth's home. It was a small, white timber house, perched on a hilltop surrounded by wheat farms that stretched to the distant horizon.

It was an idyllic setting—quiet and peaceful. Large pepper trees shaded the western side of the house and in the front a small veranda overlooked a garden of colourful geraniums. I drove my car along the dirt road leading to the house and parked it in the driveway.

The scrunching of my shoes on the gravel path leading up to the house noisily heralded my arrival. Ruth appeared on the veranda, wiping her hands on her apron and brushing her hair back from her forehead. I was surprised by her appearance. She had grown very thin and haggard looking, dressed in a familiar long, cotton dress. It was obvious that the spectre of Ben Parkinson's demise still tormented her.

"Hello Ruth. Long time, no see!" I called out as I reached the steps to the veranda. She hugged and kissed me enthusiastically.

"My . . . it's great to see you again, Guy. You have changed. Let me look at you."

She stepped back and smiled as she gazed at me.

"You've grown into a handsome young man. How have you been?"

"Okay I guess. I've got a steady job now. I went through a bad patch for a while but things are looking up. How have you been?"

"Like you, I was down for quite a while. You can tell by looking at me, can't you? But it's getting better. Come inside!" she said, taking my arm gently.

She took me inside to the kitchen and put the kettle on before sitting opposite me at the kitchen table. The kitchen was homely and warm. A breeze moved the curtains on the open window, so that the sun streamed into the room, bathing it in its warm glow.

"Do you still think about it?" I asked.

Her eyes dimmed and she nervously fiddled with the top of her apron.

"Yes! For a couple of years the nerves got to me. It was terrible waiting—waiting for that knock on the door but now . . . cross my fingers . . . the anxiety attacks have disappeared. Still having nightmares?"

"Yeah! But luckily getting better. How's Amy coping?" I asked; my eyes scanning the room.

There was no sign of Amy. I couldn't wait to see her after three long years.

Ruth slapped her forehead and exclaimed, "I'm horrible. You're here to see Amy and wondering where she is. I'm so sorry Guy. She went to the supermarket but she should be back soon. She's coped better than I have but the incident with Billy has affected her more than I thought it would. She has a deep mistrust of young men—with the exception of you, of course. I'm glad you've come. Amy's so excited about seeing you again."

Ruth made sandwiches and a pot of tea and we moved into the lounge room. She poured the tea and as I nibbled on a sandwich I glanced around at several of her paintings on the walls.

"You're still painting. They're great."

"Yes! I'm lucky enough to sell some of my paintings in town. It helps pay the bills. Amy told me you were painting. How's it going?" she asked. She placed her cup on the table and leaned back in her chair.

"Fine! I've actually sold a few to locals."

"Good to hear . . . keep at it . . . sounds like Amy now."

There was a noise of a car travelling up the driveway, followed by the sound of a car door slamming. I heard the patter of footsteps running up onto the veranda and turned in my chair. Before I had the opportunity to stand, the front door burst open and the unmistakable figure of Amy dashed across the room and into my arms.

I could feel her heart pounding as she clutched me like a bear, squeezing for dear life. Slowly, she removed herself and sat on the coffee table, her eyes brimming with tears. Her face positively glowed as she looked me up and down. The promise of her mid-teens had been realised, for Amy had grown into a beautiful young woman.

Ruth had a huge smile on her face as she leant towards me.

"Guy's certainly grown up hasn't he? And he's so handsome."

"You look terrific!" Amy murmured.

"So do you!" I said.

We sat there staring at each other as Ruth cleaned the table and gathered the teapot and empty plates.

"I'll get out of your hair. You two need time together. It's good to see you, Guy," she said.

Amy took me to her room where we sat on her bed and had a brief gossip session. I was astounded to have forgotten how lovely she was. Sam was a striking beauty but Amy was even more so. She had an ethereal beauty—she could well have been an angel from heaven.

"I've missed you so much," Amy said, wrapping her arms around my neck and kissing me tenderly. I was completely under her control. My eyes closed and I had the sensation of floating—this was what I'd imagined heaven to be like. Finally we parted and returned to some semblance of reality.

"How's the modelling going?" I asked, holding her hand.

In one of her letters, Amy mentioned she had been asked to join a modelling agency.

She told me she had done some modelling for a photographer in Sheffield Plains but when he suggested she do lingerie shots, she realised he had hidden intentions, and so she quit. For a while she shied away from modelling but several friends persuaded her to continue.

"I went to Hambledon City for an interview at a modelling agency. They said they were interested in using me as a clothing catalogue model for large shopping firms. If I handle that, they said they might use me as a swimwear model as well."

"Swimwear model? I don't know about that. Why?"

"They said I wasn't tall enough to be a runway model but I had the body and looks to model swimwear. The money is good," she gushed enthusiastically.

"Yeah! But swimwear? I don't like the idea of men seeing you half naked."

"You're like Mum. I'd be wearing a swimsuit. It's no different from when I'm at the beach or the pool."

"Be careful! You know what happened with that other photographer," I warned.

"Don't worry! If I join the modelling agency, they will provide someone to be my agent and get jobs for me. They will look after me. It does mean I'll have to move to Hambledon to live."

"When?"

"They told me they would contact me within a week."

"Is it what you want?" I asked. I wasn't sure about Amy modelling.

"Well, I'm not doing anything at the moment and it's about time I got a decent job. I know I'll enjoy the work and I will be paid to do it. Don't you want me to do this?"

"No! Go for it! You'll make a terrific model. As long as the men look but don't touch I'll be happy."

Amy laughed and rained kisses all over my face and neck.

She whispered in my ear, "You're safe. The only man I want is you."

I stayed the weekend with Ruth and Amy catching up on all the news and re-kindling our friendship. No mention was made of either Billy Jenkins or Ben Parkinson.

I didn't forget why I was there—to see Amy and assess where we were in our relationship. Away from prying eyes we were able to get to know each other romantically but Amy was hesitant about going past the kissing stage. I was happy to move slowly and so I left it to her to make all the moves. Unlike Sam, she was an innocent, young woman. Although we didn't have the same interests, we shared a common bond—we had been brought together in that summer of '64. She thought of me as her hero and I derived a great deal of pleasure from that.

To some extent the weekend did resolve my conflict of interests. I loved Sam but Amy needed me more. She seemed so helpless and fragile—like a tiny, lost kitten. I didn't want her because I felt sorry for her but she was my first love and events of the weekend only reinforced this conviction.

Late on Sunday afternoon we were in her room snuggled up on the bed. These were our last few hours together before I returned to Roxborough. Amy looked up at me, dejected. Tears, like little diamonds, glistened as they collected at the corners of her eyes.

"Do you have to go? Stay a little longer . . . Please?" she pleaded.

"I have to go but I'll come back."

"Promise? I love you so much. You don't know how much."

"I love you too but I do have a job to go to," I answered.

"What if I go to Hambledon? I'll never see you. It's too far away for you to visit me on weekends."

She began to sob quietly as she lay in my arms. I didn't want her to go to the city but it was an opportunity for her to forge a career modelling—something that admirably suited her. What could I do? I had to support her. I kissed the tears away as I smothered her in my arms, feeling her soft warm body close to mine. My weekend visit to Sheffield Plains had ushered in as many new obstacles as it had removed.

We didn't speak for a minute or two, reflecting on being separated once more. I knew that she couldn't pass up the opportunity of a lifetime. It was then I had an inspirational idea. I sat up, a wide grin spreading across my face. Amy gave me a quizzical look and frowned.

"If you get a job in Hambledon, I'll quit my job and move there with you. It's perfect. I can get work and we can be together," I declared.

Amy sat there stunned but then her face lit up also.

"Are you sure?" she asked.

"Positive. What do you say?"

"It's the best news I've heard for ages. I've got to tell Mum."

She raced out of the room and returned, hanging on to an ecstatic Ruth. After years of doubt and anxiety she now had a reason to celebrate.

"That's fantastic news. You are the perfect couple so I couldn't be happier. Now look what you've done. You've made me cry," she smiled through tears.

Amy and I laughed and hugged her. It was decided. If Amy secured a modelling job in Hambledon I would join her.

On the journey back home I weighed up the pros and cons of my decision. Moving would mean leaving my family, Georgie and Sam. Telling Sam would be heartbreaking for both of us but only time would tell whether I had made the right decision. For the last three years I had moped around feeling sorry for myself. And now I was sure this was the right thing to do. I needed a fresh start.

I planned to continue writing to Sam, if she wanted me to and I would return to Roxborough on occasions to see Georgie and my family. How my parents would react to my leaving was another obstacle I had to overcome because I knew what my dad would say.

By the time I reached home I had convinced myself that moving to the city was the way to go and that Amy, not Sam, was my girlfriend,.

A week passed before I received a letter from Amy giving me the good news. She had been offered the modelling job in Hambledon. Once she had settled in the city she would write to me and I could join her. It would give me time to quit my job and say my farewells.

I wrote to Sam and explained what I was doing. Any considerate man would have spoken to her in person, but I found the task beyond me. I chickened out because I didn't want to face her. Writing a letter was the coward's way out. I tried to say that even though I loved her dearly, I loved Amy more. I wanted to remain best friends with her but if she didn't want to keep in touch, I would accept that decision. It was selfish, but I wanted both girls in my life.

Telling Mum and Dad of my decision was difficult because I had to face them. I picked a night when they were both at home and told them my news. They were sitting in the kitchen having a cup of tea when I approached them.

"Mum! Dad! I've got something to tell you. I'm going to move to Hambledon to be with Amy," I blurted out quickly.

They both looked up at me in utter surprise. Mum's face dropped and Dad placed his cup on the table and frowned. I knew what was coming.

"When did you decide this?" he asked. "I get you a good job at the bike shop and now you're leaving? Have you got a job in the city?"

"Well . . . No! Not yet . . . but I hope to get work in a bike shop, or something similar."

"Then why leave here? What's the point of going to the city when you don't have work there? Doesn't make sense. I mean . . . this girl of yours. You could visit her in Hambledon and still live here . . . Have you thought this out?" Dad snorted.

Mum interrupted. "It's to do with Amy isn't it? That trip to visit her . . . it was about this, isn't it?"

How is it that mothers seem to know exactly what their children are thinking? Mum understood why I was leaving.

"Yes! Amy's going to work in the city and I want to be with her. She needs me and I don't want to be away from her. If I stayed here I could only visit her once or twice a year. I wouldn't have to leave here if Hambledon was reasonably close but it isn't."

Dad grunted. "So . . . it's this girl . . . I should have known. So I suppose if it doesn't work out with her, you'll come home. The job in the bike shop won't be here if you do. Think about that."

As always, Dad was frustrated by my actions but I knew that Mum supported my pending move even if she didn't want me to go. She smiled.

"I thought you would settle down with Sam, but if Amy is the one then you have to do this," she said.

Dad continued to shake his head sadly but Mum moved forward and put her arms around me. Tears in her eyes, she kissed me on the cheek.

She wiped her tears and said, "You know we'll help you, no matter what."

"Thanks Mum! Thanks Dad! I've thought about this . . . a lot . . . and it's what I want to do."

Naturally, Georgie was upset at my leaving and the tears streamed down his face as he pleaded for me to stay. I suppose he thought that I would be one of those who were destined never to leave Roxborough. It was painful to see him so miserable. He was facing the prospect of losing contact with Amy and me and to make matters worse, Sam was at university so he would be alone.

"You can't go!" he cried.

"I've got to," I said. "Look! I'll come back when I can. We can still be friends and I'll write to you every week."

"You won't! You'll leave and I'll never see you or Amy again. Ivan's gone. Sam's gone—and now you. I've got no friends here."

"You'll be okay. You can spend time with Marty," I said. I tried to be positive about my leaving.

Georgie shook his head and turned to go. I clutched his arm and whispered, "Georgie! You know how much I love Amy. She's been through so much and I want to be with her in the city. I can't desert her now. It's not as though you and I will never see each other again."

"Cross your heart and hope to die?"

"Cross my heart and hope to die," I answered, solemnly.

I crossed my heart and spat on my hand and held it out. He spat on his hand and shook my hand. I wanted to say more but choked as Georgie trudged despondently back to his home, his head down and shoulders slumped.

CHAPTER 19

ANOTHER TWIST OF FATE

That very afternoon I received a phone call from Ruth. As I listened to her, my excitement at the prospect of joining Amy in Hambledon disappeared, replaced by ennui that was born of sheer panic and depression. I sat on my bed, devastated, as she continued.

Billy had witnessed the death of Ben Parkinson. So, his comments made after our fight actually contained some substance. Rather than tell the police he had decided to blackmail Ruth. Apparently, Ben Parkinson had told him that Ruth had inherited a sizeable amount of money. Ruth confirmed that this was true but didn't furnish any further details. Billy had contacted Ruth after getting her new address. Ruth said that he probably obtained it from a contact in the Post Office. Anyhow, he was quick to visit Ruth and Amy, laying it out plainly that he wanted money or he would go to the police and relate to them what he had witnessed at the cabin. Ruth paid. The blackmail had been going on almost from the day Ruth and Amy had departed Roxborough. She had kept all this from me for fear I might do something rash—even kill Billy. Immediately I was struck that this was an odd judgment. I might physically attack Billy but I knew I was no killer.

Why, then, was she telling me now? Ruth said that Billy had found out that Amy was going to Hambledon City to live with me and this had enflamed him. He completely lost control and shouted abuse at Ruth and warned her that if this happened, he would go to the police and tell them everything. Now I knew!

She went on to say that Billy was coming to see them on the weekend; she asked me to be present in case Billy's temper got the better of him once again. She worried that Billy might resort to violence and my support, she considered, would reassure both her and Amy as well as act as a deterrent to Mr Jenkins. Surely, Billy knew that Amy despised him for his loathsome actions towards her. So why would he expect her to change? Maybe it was his huge ego telling him that he could win her over or maybe he couldn't bear to see me with such a beautiful girl. I guessed that both reasons contributed to his sick outlook and appalling behaviour.

Billy was meeting with Ruth and Amy on Saturday. Once more Billy had entered my life and caused havoc. I flung myself down on the bed.

"What's the use?" I muttered, "Why me? Why me? Will it end—ever?"

I repeated this time and again as I smashed my fist into the pillow out of sheer frustration. Any hope I held of being able to live with Amy in peace and contentment had been crushed. I then made a vital connection with these events and the state of my life. Since I had met Ruth, I had stumbled from one catastrophe to the next. It was an unsavoury thought and I tried to tell myself that my overwrought emotional state was distorting reality. I clung to the hope that one day all would be well.

I drove to Ruth's home in Sheffield Plains on Saturday morning. During the trip I had time to consider what I might do when I confronted Billy Jenkins. As I drove up the driveway to the house I noticed a car parked nearby. I knew it was neither Amy's nor Ruth's, so I guessed it belonged to Billy.

Slowly I got out of my car and moved cautiously towards the front door. My breathing was shallow and laboured as I reached out to ring the doorbell. Suddenly, the door was flung open. My hands flew up to cover my mouth and muffle the scream trying to escape from within. I gasped and stepped back in horror. Ruth stood before me, hanging onto the doorframe. Her hands and clothes were spattered with blood and she uttered a whimpering cry of despair as the tears trickled down her face. I feared the worst. I surmised that Billy had arrived in a rage and attacked Ruth and Amy.

I rushed past Ruth, who had not spoken a word, and searched for Amy and Billy. I found them in Amy's bedroom. Billy lay face down on the floor, in a pool of blood. Amy was curled up on the bed, her body heaving as she sobbed uncontrollably. Her dress had been torn from her body. I sat alongside her and wrapped her in my arms in an instinctive attempt to calm her. There were no immediately discernible signs on her half-naked body to show that Billy had attacked her physically. Ruth entered the room and slumped in a chair.

"I was right about Billy," she said hoarsely." He arrived only an hour ago and not only demanded that Amy not see you again but wanted sexual favours from her. He grabbed her and despite her protests he ripped off her dress. She fled in here. He chased after her. That's when I took a kitchen knife and stabbed him in the back. Then you arrived."

"So it was really self-defence," I whispered.

"Yes! Once again I have killed someone who threatened my family. But will the police believe me?"

"Surely you won't tell them about Ben Parkinson?" I asked.

"I suppose you're right but we can't dispose this body like we did Ben's," said Ruth.

"Why not? We could put it in his car and drive it out of town and hide it. Who would know?"

"I hid a body once and that was horrible. I won't do it again. I'll tell the police and suffer the consequences."

Amy's sobs grew louder and I turned to comfort her. Ruth stood up and moved towards the doorway.

"I'm going to ring the police. I want you to stay with Amy. That knife I used is under the bed. Can you get it and place it somewhere near the body? The police will want to see it. Also, make sure that Amy doesn't get dressed. They'll need to see what he did to her. Okay?"

"Sure!"

I took the knife from under the bed and placed it near the body. My hands were covered in blood so I wiped them on a towel before returning to Amy. Her dress lay on the floor beside the bed and I took off my jacket and wrapped that around her. I held Amy close as I whispered soothing words. She nestled in my arms and ceased crying.

About ten minutes later, I looked up as two policemen appeared in the doorway with Ruth. Without speaking, they examined Billy's body and then left. I could hear muffled voices as they spoke to Ruth.

A few minutes later, one of them returned to the room, and placed the knife in a bag. He scanned the scene one more time and then wrote in his notebook. All this time I sat on the bed holding Amy in my arms. The second policeman entered and motioned to me. He was accompanied by a female officer, who moved towards the bed to comfort Amy.

"Sir! I'd like you to come out and tell me what happened," he said in a gruff voice.

I followed him into the lounge room and told him my story. What followed was to stun me.

"Sir! I'd like you to come with us to the police station to answer a few more questions."

Why did they want to question me? Ruth killed Billy so surely she'd have to go to the station.

"What about Ruth? Is she coming too?" I asked.

"We'll speak to her later sir. She has to look after her daughter now. I'm sure you understand."

"I suppose so, but I've already told you everything."

He took me out to the police car and by the time we arrived at the station, I was in panic mode. Something was not right!

My worst fears were realised when I entered the interview room. The senior constable sat opposite me at the table. He was in his forties, with close cropped hair. His unsmiling, grim face gave him the appearance of an army drill sergeant. If he wanted to unsettle me, he was doing a good job because I was shaking and sweating profusely. Of course, he noted my nervousness.

"You don't need to be nervous, sir. That's if you've done nothing wrong."

I answered with a tremor in my voice.

"I told you what happened. And I've done nothing wrong!"

The officer stood up and walked over to a water cooler and poured a drink. He placed the plastic container in front of me and I drank slowly, waiting for him to speak again. He slumped back into his chair and leaned forward. He spoke gruffly.

"We have a major problem. Your story differs from Mrs Parkinson's. She said that you arrived at her house and saw Billy enter her daughter's bedroom. You took a kitchen knife and followed him. When you saw him rip the dress off, you plunged the knife into his back three or four times, killing him."

My mouth open in disbelief, I stood up and faced him.

"You're joking! That's a lie! I arrived after she had killed Billy. She told me. Why don't you believe me?"

I was shattered. How could Ruth make such an accusation? Why had she done this? I tried to quell my rising anxiety but involuntary tears began to stream down my face and I brushed them away as I sat down.

The detective placed a cigarette in his mouth and lit it while I tried to settle my nerves. He offered me one but I shook my head. He continued his interrogation.

"She said that you and Billy had a fight. Is this true?" he asked.

"Yes. But that was a long . . ."

He interrupted, "Mrs Parkinson said that you were defending her daughter and I can understand that. She said that you loved her daughter and that you planned to go to Hambledon together. So . . . I can understand why you became so angry. I'd feel the same way, too but I would have grabbed him and called the police—not killed him."

"I did not kill him!"

"If your fingerprints are not on the knife and Mrs Parkinson's are, then you'll have no case to answer."

I grimaced and tapped my forehead repeatedly with my fist. I was so naive. So that's why Ruth asked me to pick up the knife.

"Ruth asked me to pick up the knife from under the bed so—without thinking—I did."

"Oh!" he said in a lowered voice. I knew he didn't believe me.

"Amy saw the whole thing. She'll tell you that I didn't kill Billy."

"Miss Parkinson did see everything but unfortunately for you sir, she confirmed her mother's version of events. She said that you did it."

A feeling of dread enveloped me. It was obvious that Ruth had planned this for some time. She had invited me so that she could later lay blame on me for a death she herself planned. Perhaps the death of Ben Parkinson had been planned too and Georgie and I had been duped into helping her. Amy was her accomplice on both occasions. I was stunned and sickened by this turn of events. I thought about telling the police about the death of Ben Parkinson but realised that with Billy dead I had no-one to back up my story. Georgie had stayed outside and had witnessed nothing of Ben's slaying. Ruth and Amy would collude and claim that I alone had killed Ben. That would plunge me into even more dire trouble so I opted to remain silent. I slumped forward onto the desk and closed my eyes.

The policeman stood up. He spoke clearly in measured tones, "Mr Harmon. With the evidence we have, you will now be taken to the police station watch house in Oldfield and formally charged with the manslaughter of Billy Jenkins. We don't believe it was premeditated. You were naturally upset and enraged by his attempt to rape Amy Parkinson. Do you understand the charges?"

I almost choked on my words but managed to utter, "Yes!"

"At Oldfield you will be fingerprinted and photographed. The police will probably release you on bail to the custody of your parents. The local court will hold a committal hearing to determine if you have a case to answer. If the magistrate finds that a prima facie case exists, then you will be committed to stand trial at a later date in the District Court in Hambledon. This might be months away. That will provide you with ample time to engage the services of a lawyer and prepare to defend the charges. Okay?"

"Yes, sir!" I whispered.

I had the feeling that I was part of a surreal nightmare because the circumstances I now found myself entwined in were so unbelievable. And it had all happened so blindingly quickly. One minute I was planning upon going to Hambledon with Amy, then a heartbeat later I was being charged by the police. I was in a daze.

I was allowed to phone my parents, who after the initial shock told me that everything would be okay. My father said that he would get a trial lawyer and we would defend the charges.

I was taken to Oldfield in a police car. I was fingerprinted, photographed and released on bail to my father. The police said that they would issue a summons and I would have to appear in Oldfield court for the hearing.

CHAPTER 20

THE TRIAL

My father engaged a well-regarded trial barrister to defend me and he accompanied me and my father to Oldfield several weeks later to appear before the committal hearing. After hearing the evidence the magistrate ruled that I had a case to answer. He committed me to stand trial at Hambledon District Court three months later. During this time I travelled every week to Hambledon to sit down and discuss the defence process with my lawyer.

Roxborough was a small community and it didn't take long for the residents to find out that I had been charged with Billy's death. With the gossipmongers enjoying a real Roman Holiday, I rarely ventured into town. I spent my time writing to Sam who was the source of my greatest support. Her letters kept me sane in this time of upheaval. Georgie regularly came around to my house when he finished work and we worked on my bike or walked his dog. On most days I travelled out into the countryside on my motorbike. This gave me an opportunity to relax and forget my troubles. Even so, I had plenty of time to mull over the events leading up to Billy's death and the subsequent bewildering actions of Ruth and Amy.

Sleep didn't come easy for me. Most nights for the first week I lay in bed thinking about the deaths of Billy and Ben Parkinson. Often I felt like crying but I discovered it was possible to 'cry oneself out'. There were no more tears. I think I was lucky I was young because I seemed to be able to absorb most problems but my parents, especially my mother, weren't coping very well at all. She began having headaches and also found it difficult to sleep at night. She was given medication but on several occasions when I couldn't sleep I ventured to the kitchen in the early hours of the morning, to find my mother clad in her dressing gown and sitting at the kitchen table, sipping a cup of tea. On these occasions I'd sit with her and we would chat. My mother was depressed because she wasn't able to help me. I could never forgive Ruth or Amy for the effects their actions had provoked in my family, and particularly in Mum.

After a discussion with my lawyer I agreed to tell my family the reason for Billy's death. With my parents, as well as Sam and Georgie present, I told the whole story—about the death of Ben Parkinson and the lies told by Ruth and Amy. They sat there, mouths open, ashen faced, as I told them about Billy's involvement.

"That Ruth is evil!" Sam murmured, "and her daughter is no better!"

"I can't tell the police about Ben's death because Ruth and Amy would say that I shot him and I would be tried for not one murder, but two. No matter what action I take, I can't win. Ruth has been too devious," I said, thumping my fist on the table.

My mother was too distraught to say anything as she slumped back in her chair.

"If Billy was alive he would be able to back you up but Ruth knew that. That's why she killed him. Surely someone from her past might be able to help us; you know . . . tell the court what she was like. Maybe she's done this before," my father argued.

"If we can get her name on the news or in the papers, someone who knew her might come forward. I think it's worth a try. Otherwise I will go to jail," I replied.

Sitting opposite me was my lawyer, Peter Johnson. He was in his mid-forties and neatly attired in a grey suit. His hair was turning grey, as was his moustache. What set him apart were his eyes. They were a brilliant blue—piercing, mesmerising. I knew that he would be a terrier in the courtroom and would defend me resolutely. My father said that he was a top trial barrister who had established a good reputation through years of practising law.

"I'll contact the TV station, the radio station and papers and tell them your story. I hope they'll inform the public about the trial—and Mrs Parkinson," he said.

He turned to my mother and rested his hand on her arm and spoke softly to her, "Mrs Harmon, Don't worry about Guy! I will do everything I can to ensure he is acquitted. He is innocent and he will be set free so don't be upset. Right now, Guy needs your love and support above everything else."

My mother fought back tears as Sam gave her a glass of water. She took a tablet from her purse and swallowed it down. Her expression was one of sadness and her eyes had lost their customary brightness, dimmed by a sorrow she kept inward. Looking at her right then, I tried yet again to fathom why my family and I were being punished.

"I'll see if I can get a good private investigator to delve into Ruth Parkinson's past. Maybe he can find something," Dad said.

After this visit I began to feel a little better. It was comforting to feel I had people who believed in my innocence. The newspapers had portrayed me as a jealous lover who, in a fit of unbridled rage, had killed an innocent young man. Hopefully, a more balanced version of events would emerge as the trial itself unfolded.

The trial date was fast approaching and despite their hard work my father and my lawyer had not discovered any new evidence that might be used to help prove my innocence. The newspapers and local television station had offered to present our side of the story. In doing so they made mention of Ruth and Amy; however, so far no-one from their past had come forward.

I was becoming resigned to the fact that I would most likely be languishing in prison until I was forty or perhaps even fifty years of age. However, one week before the trial, the private investigator unearthed some alarming facts about Ruth Parkinson. The investigator, Ken Taylor, was an ex-cop who was now in his sixties. He had many contacts within the police force and judicial system.

Ken Taylor invited us to his office to reveal the results of his investigation. He sat behind a large desk, covered in papers and folders and lit a cigarette. After two or three puffs he settled back in his chair and told us what he'd discovered. My father, Peter Johnson and I leaned forward in our chairs in anticipation.

"Ruth Parkinson's husband died from poisoning. He died before she came to Roxborough," he stated, flicking the ash from his cigarette onto the table.

This was a bombshell. We sat in stunned silence for a few seconds trying to comprehend what he was saying.

"Who was the man she shot at her home and we buried?" I asked. I looked at him uncertainly.

"That was her ex-lover, Jacob Wilson. Jacob Wilson was convicted of the murder of Ben Parkinson, but he told police that Ruth had poisoned her husband, in order to receive a life insurance sum of ten thousand pounds. He was convicted because it was he who bought the poison. He couldn't prove that Ruth poisoned her husband, even though she collected the life insurance money. The police claimed that she was probably an accomplice, but there was insufficient evidence for them to prove it. Ruth had stated that Jacob was very jealous and killed Ben because he wanted to marry her. The jury believed her—the grieving widow."

"Sounds familiar doesn't it?" remarked my father.

Ken Taylor continued. "I'm guessing that Ruth told Jacob Wilson that she would share the insurance money with him. When he got out of prison he went to see her to get his share and exact some form of revenge. That's when she shot him."

"That's how Billy found out about the money and that's why Ruth wouldn't tell me about Billy blackmailing her," I exclaimed.

"All this information is great but we might not be allowed to enter it as evidence because it has nothing to do with the killing of Billy," my lawyer interrupted.

"Why not?" I asked. "Surely it would help our case to show what kind of woman Ruth is?"

"But Ruth is not on trial, you are! The trial is about the murder of Billy Jenkins. What we need is concrete evidence that proves Ruth killed her ex-lover. Then the jury might be swayed."

These words deflated me. My resolve had just sustained a sledgehammer blow. My father saw my miserable face and tried to lift my spirits.

"It's a start Guy. We still have time. Maybe something else will turn up."

I muttered, "It's a pity Ruth didn't poison Billy like she did her husband."

The investigator said earnestly, "That's a great idea! If you get the autopsy report on Billy, it might show traces of poison in his body. That's if the coroner checked this out. If he hasn't you can ask that the body be exhumed for another examination and report. Billy had been visiting Ruth for months to get his payments. It would have been quite easy for Ruth to lace a drink with poison and give it to him."

My father intervened, "Why would she knife him if she had already poisoned him?"

"Perhaps she was in a hurry to get rid of him because he was asking for too much money or sexual favours. Perhaps she started by poisoning him and then stopped because she feared people would discover how her husband died. It's an area worth probing further;

I understand it's a remote possibility, but one worth looking into nonetheless," Ken Taylor explained.

"You're right of course," said my lawyer, "We have to explore every avenue. Also, if Billy had been a clever person, he would not have continued to blackmail Mrs Parkinson without confiding in someone, or, at the very least, writing down what happened to Ben Parkinson. That way, if something did happen to him, a rough brand of justice would be served."

"Billy was not stupid, I agree. I wouldn't be surprised if he wrote what happened in a book or a letter," I said. "Even a journal."

My father wrote in his own notebook and said, "I'll talk to Jim Jenkins and ask him to look for a letter or some such document."

"You can't mention the death of Ben Parkinson. All you can say is that Billy was blackmailing Ruth because he knew something about her past and he might have written it down somewhere. That's why Ruth Parkinson killed Billy," I said forcefully.

Knowing Jim Jenkins, I doubted if he would even bother to look and I was correct. He became very angry when my father told him about his son's foray into the world of the blackmailer. Jenkins Senior said that his son would not blackmail anyone and that he wouldn't even bother to look for a letter or note. That was the first blow.

The second came when the autopsy report showed no signs of poison—Ruth Parkinson had been too clever. All the avenues of investigation that might help clear my name had disappeared and unless someone came forward in the next few days, my cause was lost.

Billy's death had affected the townspeople of Roxborough. Most believed that I killed Billy because they couldn't believe that a gentle, quiet lady like Ruth could do such a thing. Conversely, the consensus believed I was an impetuous, jealous youth, eminently capable of killing a fellow human being. What exasperated me was that the townsfolk knew that Billy was a brute with a vicious, untrammelled temper. This, however, was no reason for him to be killed in violent circumstances. I had spent my whole life in Roxborough and still the majority of people refused to offer me even one fragment of support. Business at my father's store dropped significantly and my family members were snubbed at social events. As a result, my mother rarely went out. The upcoming trial was taking an unseen toll upon her delicate constitution. I hardened my resolve to win the case—as much for my family and friends as to clear my own name and resume living the life of Guy Harmon.

A few days prior to the trial, my lawyer schooled me in what to expect from the prosecution lawyers and how to answer questions. The trial, he claimed, might even be reduced to the simplest of all legal equations—it was going to be my word against Ruth's and Amy's. The major hurdle to overcome was my fingerprints on the knife; that, and the fact that I had threatened Billy.

CHAPTER 21

THE TRIAL BEGINS

The trial began on a Monday and I found myself in court seated alongside my lawyer, facing a judge and jury. The jury had already been selected. I didn't want my parents to attend the trial because it would be too much for them to handle. However, I did spot my father, seated with Georgie and Sam in the public gallery. I was happy my Mum was not with them. The jury had been sworn in and the offence was read out. I was asked to make a formal plea and I pled 'not guilty'.

The prosecution bought forward witnesses from my old school who testified that I had once threatened to kill Billy. They also called witnesses who testified about seeing my fight at the sawmill. Peter Johnson was able to cross-examine the prosecution witnesses and get them to admit that neither fight had been instigated by me. They admitted also, that both Billy and the man I fought at the mill deserved what they got. He did not want to put Georgie or myself on the stand to tell about Billy assaulting Amy. He reasoned that Amy would probably testify that Billy didn't assault her. Throughout these proceedings I sat quietly alongside Peter and listened to the evidence. At day's end I was taken to a cell that adjoined the courthouse.

On the third day, the prosecution put Ruth onto the stand. Not once did she look in my direction. She was dressed simply in her usual attire—long dress with her hair tied back neatly. She wore no makeup and she looked frail. No doubt the prosecution had some input into her appearance, mindful of how she should present to the jurors. My lawyer had warned me to say nothing so I sat with my head in my hands as I listened to her lies. This was a woman I had befriended. This was a woman who received my help when Amy was assaulted and, when she shot her ex-lover, I helped her in disposing of the body. Ruth Parkinson had certainly duped me.

When the prosecutor sat down, Peter approached Ruth to begin his cross-examination.

"Mrs Parkinson! Why did you ask Guy Harmon to come hundreds of miles to your place when you knew Billy Jenkins would be there?" he asked.

"I needed his support." Her reply was steady, unhurried.

"Why was Billy Jenkins a regular visitor to your home when it has been established that Guy Harmon and your daughter were planning to live together in Hambledon and were in love?"

"Billy was in love with Amy, too," she answered simply.

"So you thought it was okay for your daughter to see both of them. That's not fair to either of these young men, is it?"

"I suppose not."

"That doesn't sound logical to me at all. I put it to you that the only reason Billy Jenkins came to see you was to blackmail you."

"That's not true! Why would he blackmail me? It doesn't make sense," Ruth said abruptly.

"I agree. It doesn't make sense at all. Just as it doesn't make sense that you would allow Billy Jenkins to visit your daughter when you knew full well that she loved Guy Harmon and planned to go to Hambledon City with him. What makes even less sense is why you would want Guy at your home when you knew Billy would be there. What do you say to that?"

"I've already explained," she answered tersely.

"I find your explanation rather puzzling, as, I'm sure, does the jury. Now Mrs Parkinson, I understand that your husband, Ben Parkinson, died several years ago from poisoning. Is this correct?"

I glanced in her direction to gauge her response but the question didn't faze her at all. She betrayed no emotion, not guilt, not triumph, not remorse.

"Yes, that is so."

"And you collected a tidy sum of ten thousand pounds in life insurance after he died. Is this correct?"

"Yes!"

The prosecutor objected, saying that these events were not connected with the death of Billy Jenkins; however, Peter said that he wanted the jury to know what kind of woman Ruth Parkinson was. The judge, although apprehensive, allowed Peter to continue.

"Is it true that your ex-lover, Jacob Wilson, went to jail for the murder of your husband," Peter asked; turning to face the jury.

"Yes!"

"Jacob Wilson claimed, under oath, that you planned the death of your husband and asked him to buy poison. He was convicted because it was proven he had obtained this poison and you testified that he did it because he was jealous of your husband and wanted him out of the way."

"I did not kill my husband. Jacob Wilson wanted my husband dead so he killed him and he was punished. I was not charged," she said emphatically, looking at the jury.

"Sounds all-too-familiar doesn't it? Jacob Wilson takes the rap for a crime he says you executed and years later Guy Harmon takes the rap for a crime he says you executed."

The prosecution objected to this so my lawyer was forced to withdraw the remark. In my peripheral vision I noticed that several jurors seemed to be swayed by Peter's remarks even though Ruth had remained cool under pressure of the focus her testimony had generated. She was so calm and collected but I believed that a seed of doubt had been planted in the jury's collective psyche, even if that seed was exceedingly small.

How I wished we could reveal the circumstances of the death of Jacob Wilson and thereby reveal the reason why Billy had been blackmailing Ruth. It was a real misfortune we didn't have some physical evidence to corroborate what I had told everyone, the police, my parents, my lawyer, even Georgie.

The prosecution called on Amy to testify. In contrast to her mother, she was very nervous and pale. She confirmed her mother's story about the death of Billy. All the time she made no effort to look in my direction. To me she was a Judas. If she really loved me she would have told the truth, fearless of the consequences. However, as the saying goes, 'blood is thicker than water'. Peter had no intention of being verbally severe towards her because he didn't want her to gain sympathy from the jury. He adopted a 'softly, softly' approach.

"Amy! Would you rather I call you Amy or Miss Parkinson?"

"Amy is fine."

"Amy! Do you love Guy Harmon?"

"Yes!"

"Do you love him a little or very much?"

"Very much."

"You were planning to go to live in Hambledon City with him, weren't you?"

"Yes!"

"Did you love Billy Jenkins?"

"No!"

"Did you tell him that?"

"Yes! Many times!"

"Yet he still continued to visit you over many months. Is this true?"

"Yes!"

"It seems strange that he did this even when he knew that you didn't love him and you planned to go away with Guy Harmon. Why would Billy Jenkins do this?"

"I don't know!"

"Why didn't you tell your mother to instruct Billy not to come?"

Amy's lips began to tremble. I understood her nervousness. It couldn't have been easy to tell blatant lies. I hoped that Peter would persist with his line of questioning because of the tell-tale flaws that were beginning to appear in her demeanor.

Peter asked, "Would you like a glass of water?"

Amy nodded and tried to regather her composure as she sipped the water.

"I gather your mother knew that you didn't love Billy. Is this so?"

"Yes!"

"Did she ask Billy to stay away from you?"

"I don't think so."

"If I were in your mother's position I would certainly have told Billy not to come. Any responsible, caring parent would have done so—at a minimum."

Once again the prosecution objected. Peter was instructed and told to withdraw his remark. The jurors' faces indicated that they believed him, so his manoeuvre was worth the risk he had undertaken, since it had scored a telling point.

"Amy! Was Billy Jenkins blackmailing your mother?"

"Not as far as I know! No!"

"Did your mother kill Billy Jenkins?"

"No!"

"Amy! Do you still love Guy Harmon?"

"Yes!"

"His friends have visited him and written to him many times in the months leading up to this trial. Have you visited him or written to him?"

"No!"

"I see. That's also very strange considering you planned to live in the city with him because of your so called love. I would think that if someone protected you from a scoundrel such as Billy Jenkins that would strengthen your love for your defender. Maybe you have a guilty conscience—or you don't really love Guy. Sorry! I withdraw those remarks, your honour."

The judge admonished Peter and told him that if persisted with his remarks he would be held in contempt of court. It didn't matter because he was slowly undermining the credibility of Ruth's and Amy's testimonies.

"I have no further questions," Peter said and sat down.

He leaned in towards me and murmured softly, "I think that the jury is having some doubts about the Parkinson women's stories."

The prosecutor asked if he could approach Amy to ask her a question. He stood before her but faced the jury. He spoke slowly and loudly so that everyone would hear him.

"Amy! Did the prosecution ask you not to see Guy Harmon or write to him because it might influence the evidence at this trial?"

"Yes!"

The prosecutor had no further questions and Amy was excused. She left the courtroom without looking in my direction. I'd clung onto the tiny fragment of hope that Amy loved me but her evidence and behaviour finally convinced me that I meant nothing to her. I was angry at myself for being so easily duped by Amy and her mother.

Before the trial continued into its fourth day, Peter Johnson sat down with me and told me what to expect from the prosecution when I was put onto the stand. No matter how much they badgered me and tried to discredit me, he insisted I had to remain calm. If I lost my temper or became aggressive towards them I would be playing directly into their hands because their aim would be to expose me as an extremely jealous, angry man who was capable of committing murder.

Peter put me on the stand and proceeded to ask me about the death of Billy and my relationship with Ruth and Amy.

"Guy! You were good friends with Ruth Parkinson and her daughter when they lived in Roxborough. Is that correct?"

"Yes!" I answered.

I felt all eyes in the courtroom were focused on me as I answered. My hands trembled and I tried to conceal them from view by placing them in my lap. I took a couple of deep breaths and a sip of water to steady my nerves. As I sipped the water I glanced around the courtroom and noticed Jim Jenkins seated in the public gallery. He wasn't in uniform. There was no soft light in his eyes—they were inscrutable, cold and dark. He had a mask-like countenance that gazed upon me with utter contempt. His lips curled in anger. My eyes promptly shifted from him, searching for a supportive friend. I spotted Sam. She smiled a brief, wan smile and I lifted my hand in acknowledgement. She was seated alongside Georgie and my father. I placed the glass on the bench and turned to face Peter. He continued his questioning.

"Guy! You and Amy fell in love and you planned to live with her in Hambledon. Is this true?"

"Yes!"

"Would you consider yourself a jealous person when other men looked at Amy or spoke to her? She is a beautiful girl so I'm sure lots of men noticed her."

"No! Not at all! Having other men trying to earn her attention didn't really bother me."

"Would you please tell the court what happened on the day Billy Jenkins was killed."

I re-told what happened in detail, speaking steadily and taking my time as Peter had suggested. He wanted my version of the events to be clearly understood by the jury. Following my explanation, he continued.

"What did Ruth Parkinson say to you about the visits from Billy Jenkins to her home in Sheffield Plains over many months?"

"She told me over the phone that Billy had been blackmailing her. She didn't say why but, with the benefit of knowing what happened later, I think it was to do with either Jacob Wilson or her husband."

I looked directly at Jim Jenkins in the gallery and said loudly, "I had hoped that Billy had left a letter or note explaining why he was blackmailing Ruth Parkinson but nothing has turned up so far. If there was a letter, or some other documentation, I'm sure it would explain everything."

"Guy! Did you kill Billy Jenkins?"

"No. I did not!"

"Do you know who did kill him?"

"Ruth said that she stabbed him to protect her daughter."

Peter turned to the jury and uttered, "Thank you Guy. I have no further questions."

The prosecutor stepped forward and leaned against the rail of the jury box. He looked at the jurors intently and took a handkerchief from the top pocket of his jacket and mopped his brow. As he turned to face me, he slowly folded the handkerchief and placed it back in his pocket. I knew that these were mere ploys and that he was trying to unnerve me—and it was working.

I glanced at Peter and he gave me a reassuring smile. The prosecutor had a loud, overbearing manner and emphasised his questions with dramatic, flamboyant gestures. He cleared his throat before speaking.

"Mr Harmon! You say that Ruth Parkinson killed Billy Jenkins, yet it was your fingerprints that were on the knife, not hers. You explained how this happened but it seems abnormal that you would handle a murder weapon, knowing full well it would be checked for fingerprints. Don't you think that most people wouldn't touch any evidence till the police arrived?"

"I didn't have time to think. And right then, I did not think of the knife as a murder weapon. She asked me to put the knife near the body because it was under the bed. Without thinking I did as I was told," I said emphatically.

"Or maybe your fingerprints were on the knife because you were the only one to have handled it. Isn't that so?"

"No! I did not stab Billy Jenkins with a knife."

He turned back to the jury and unbuttoned the jacket of his suit revealing a paunch that swelled out over his belt. His ruddy cheeks; a large red nose on a rather plump face, and thinning grey hair completed the picture. He hitched up his trousers, scratched his stomach and turned back to face me.

His eyes narrowed suddenly and from within their depths a mere spark seemed to ignite an inferno. He pointed his finger at me threateningly.

"Well now, I put it to you that you saw Billy with Amy and you became enraged. So enraged that you took a kitchen knife and plunged it into his back four times, killing him."

"No! I did not kill Billy Jenkins!"

I said this loudly and distinctly but remained calm. Peter Johnson had alerted me to expect an attack of this nature, so I was prepared.

"Furthermore, you knew that he loved Amy Parkinson. You had a fight with him over her and stated in front of witnesses that if you saw him anywhere near her you would kill him. That isn't the action of a boyfriend who's not the jealous or angry type—rather, it's the opposite."

"When I said I would kill him it was just a figure of speech. It was in the heat of the moment. I didn't really mean that. It was years ago and I said it just to scare him off," I answered; looking in the direction of the jury.

My heart started to flutter and my mind raced as I struggled to remain in control of my emotions. The prosecutor turned back to face the jury and gallery. He moved towards the jury and then swivelled and repeated his accusation in a louder voice, full of unbridled scorn.

"I find what you are saying hard to believe. Again I put it to you that you killed Billy Jenkins in a fit of anger and then blamed Ruth Parkinson for his death because she allowed Billy to visit Amy."

"No! No! That's not true! Billy was blackmailing Ruth in connection with the death of her husband and she wanted him out of the way. She planned to use me as a scapegoat. That's the truth."

The prosecutor let out a rather contrived loud sigh and turning to the judge said,

"I have no further questions for this person."

I stepped down and resumed my seat alongside Peter. He whispered, "Well done!"

With no more witnesses scheduled, the judge informed the court that he would hear closing arguments the next day. The court was adjourned. Even though Peter had made sizeable dents in the prosecution's case I still sensed that the jury still believed that I was guilty. I was sure that the fingerprints on the murder weapon and my one-time threat to kill Billy were uppermost in most jurors' minds. Tomorrow would mark the last opportunity my defence lawyer would have to change their minds.

CHAPTER 22

NEW EVIDENCE

When I was escorted into the courtroom on the final day of the trial I was met by an enthusiastic, smiling Peter Johnson.

"Guy! Great news! Jim Jenkins came to see me last night. After your testimony yesterday he went to his house and searched Billy's old room for a letter or note. He found nothing but he remembered that Billy had asked him to place an envelope in the police station safe. When Jim opened the letter, he found it was addressed to him and it explained the reason for Billy's blackmail. He said that he would be willing to testify today if asked. I shall appeal to the judge to admit the letter as exculpatory evidence and allow Mr Jenkins to read the letter to the jury as part of his testimony."

I was overcome with emotion and put my head in my hands on the table. I brushed away tears as I sat up.

Peter patted me on the back and whispered, "Hang in there! This might be the answer to our prayers."

When the judge entered the chambers, he stood up and asked, "Your honour! May I approach the bench?"

The judge motioned both Peter and the counsel for the prosecution to the bench. Peter handed the letter to the judge who commenced to read it.

Peter said, "Your honour. I've only just received this letter from Mr James Jenkins, the father of Billy. It has a great bearing on this case as you will undoubtedly see. It will explain why Billy Jenkins was killed and why Guy Harmon should be acquitted of all charges. I would like to enter it into evidence and put Mr Jenkins on the stand."

The judge handed the letter to the prosecutor who read it before handing it back. He voiced his strong objection but the judge ruled in favour of Peter and allowed the letter to be admitted as evidence. Jim Jenkins was sworn in and waited patiently for Peter to begin.

"Your name is James Jenkins, more widely known as Jim Jenkins, and you are the father of the deceased Billy Jenkins. Is this correct?"

Jim Jenkins answered, "That is correct."

"Could you please tell the court why you came to see me last night?"

"Last night, I found a letter written by Billy. It was addressed to me and was dated the day before he went to see Ruth Parkinson."

"Is this the letter?"

Peter held up the letter and Jim Jenkins nodded and replied that it was.

"Your honour, I'd like to enter this letter as exhibit A for the defence. Would you please read the letter, Mr Jenkins?"

Jim Jenkins took a pair of glasses from his top pocket and put them on. He picked up the letter and quietly read it to a stunned courtroom. The letter revealed the circumstances surrounding the death of Jacob Wilson at the hands of Ruth. Billy had witnessed his killing through a side window of Ruth's house and had begun to use his knowledge to blackmail Ruth. The courtroom remained eerily silent as the remaining contents of the letter were read. Many onlookers and several of the jury panel placed their hands over their mouths in shock and disbelief. Then, a murmur ran around the room, gathering momentum until the judge ordered silence.

When Jim Jenkins had finished, Peter asked him, "Mr Jenkins. When this trial began you firmly believed that Guy Harmon had killed your son. Is this correct?"

"Yes!"

"In light of this evidence, do you still believe this to be true?"

"No!"

The prosecution interrupted, claiming that it was Mr Jenkins' opinion only, and should be stricken from the trial transcript. The judge agreed and ordered the jury to disregard it. However, once more Peter had scored a telling blow for my acquittal.

After Jim Jenkins left the witness box, Peter recalled Ruth Parkinson to the stand. As she entered, the people in the gallery arched their necks forward to catch a glimpse of her. A buzz of excitement spread throughout the courtroom. At long last I believed Ruth would be revealed for what she really was—not the quiet, demure woman they had observed as she told lie after abysmal lie, but a scheming, calculating woman who was eminently capable of killing another human being.

She was trembling as she entered the witness box, her face devoid of colour. Peter waited for the hum to abate before he began his new questioning.

"Mrs Parkinson. You have heard the contents of the letter. Would you agree that this explanation of the death of Jacob Wilson is true?" he asked.

"Yes!" Ruth whispered.

"Could you please speak up Mrs Parkinson?" Peter asked. He wanted everyone to hear her answers.

"Was Billy Jenkins blackmailing you?"

"Yes!" she replied in a clear voice.

"So you lied before about this?"

"Yes!"

"Did you also lie about the death of Billy Jenkins?"

I expected Ruth to own up to this and admit to killing Billy but she straightened up and looked Peter in the eye.

"No! I didn't kill Billy. Guy Harmon did," she said firmly.

"How can we believe you when you lied about Billy Jenkins blackmailing you? What kind of woman is prepared to lie and continue to lie . . . even if it means sending an innocent young man to jail? You cannot be trusted to tell the truth," Peter yelled angrily.

She knew that she was cornered but she wasn't going to capitulate and admit anything. She remained steadfast in her resolve to see me go to prison.

Peter raised his voice again and snapped at her, "Who had the most to gain from the murder of Ben Parkinson? You did. In the order of ten thousand pounds. Who had the most to gain from the death of Jacob Wilson You did, because you weren't prepared to pay him any money and you didn't want him around any longer. Who had the most to gain from the death of Billy Jenkins? You did, because he was blackmailing you for money. Dead, he couldn't testify about the death of Jacob Wilson. I put it to you that you didn't ask Guy Harmon to come to your house that Saturday to protect you. You wanted him there so you could blame him for Billy's killing, a killing you contrived to commit. You had your daughter Amy lure Billy into her bedroom and you followed him. You stabbed him to death and then ripped Amy's dress to make it appear that he had attacked her. When Guy arrived, you asked him to pick up the knife. Now, did you kill Billy Jenkins?"

"No," she answered but her voice wavered and her face betrayed her words.

The prosecutor declined to cross-examine, so Ruth Parkinson left the stand and the courtroom. As she left, my father called out to her, "You are a lying, evil woman. I hope you rot in hell."

She rushed out the door, brushing past reporters, as the judge called for order. Peter recalled me to the stand.

"Guy! Why didn't you tell the court about the death of Jacob Wilson?"

"I thought that if I told about Ruth shooting him she would take the stand and blame me for his death. The only people in the room when he was shot were Amy, Ruth and me. I didn't know that Billy had witnessed it."

"Thank you Guy. I have no further questions."

The prosecution had nothing to add so the judge adjourned the trial for the day. I hoped that the jury would be swayed by this new evidence.

Peter was emphatic that this new evidence, especially since it had been volunteered by the father of the victim, would work in favour of my acquittal. It was obvious that so, too, did my friends and my father. They smiled and waved as I was led back to my cell after this breakthrough day. As I crawled between the sheets, a new spirit—one of hope—enveloped me. Somehow life was now seemingly full of possibilities. After many sleepless nights I was at peace, as I lay my head on the pillow. However, the trial was not over yet and I knew that anything could happen, so I was still far from confident about the outcome. I did manage a couple of hours sleep, though.

It was the final day of the trial and both counsel were prepared to deliver their closing arguments. The courtroom was packed as I was escorted to my chair. The constant ripple of noise abated when the judge entered and took his seat. The prosecution presented their arguments first, focusing, as expected, on Ruth's steadfast denial and my fingerprints on the murder weapon. Following these closing arguments, Peter smiled at me and stood to address the jury.

"Ladies and gentlemen of the jury! If you have a reasonable doubt in your minds concerning the death of Billy Jenkins, then you must acquit Guy Harmon of the crime. Only if you are absolutely sure that he killed Billy, can you bring down a verdict of guilty."

He paused before continuing.

"The evidence you have heard during this trial points overwhelmingly to the fact that Ruth Parkinson killed Billy Jenkins, not to protect her daughter as she has resolutely claimed, but to rid her life of the man who had been blackmailing her over the death of Jacob Wilson, one of her former lovers."

Peter turned and pointed at the prosecutor.

"The prosecution has tried to prove that Guy Harmon killed Billy Jenkins in a jealous rage, but the undeniable truth is that Ruth Parkinson invited Guy to her house on that fateful Saturday, so she could frame him for the murder. Her husband was murdered by poisoning. If Jacob Wilson murdered Ben Parkinson because he was a jealous lover, then why did he visit Mrs Parkinson that night in Roxborough? Certainly, it could not have been because he still loved her. The evidence from Billy Jenkins' letter to his father affirmed that Jacob Wilson was an angry man who was violent, on many occasions, towards Ruth Parkinson. Wilson was angry with her because her testimony put him in jail and because he wanted his share of the insurance money."

He fixed his eyes on the jurors and continued.

"Mrs Parkinson shot Jacob Wilson. On that basis it becomes quite conceivable that she could kill Billy Jenkins too. Guy Harmon is an innocent young man caught up in events orchestrated by Ruth Parkinson. How can we believe her version of events when she lied about the blackmail? Amy Parkinson, like Guy, was merely another pawn in her mother's premeditated conspiracy. I have no doubt Miss Parkinson lied about the death of Billy Jenkins because she loved her mother and didn't want her to go to prison."

"Every scintilla of evidence points to the guilt of Ruth Parkinson and your only course of action is to acquit Guy Harmon of all charges. You must return a verdict of not guilty. Thank you!"

It was brief and concise. The jury was asked by the judge to leave the courtroom and consider the evidence presented and try to reach a verdict. Peter informed me that it might take hours or even days for them to agree on a verdict. The trial was adjourned and I was taken back to my cell.

I sat on the bunk with my head in my hands and waited. At the end of the day a verdict had not been reached. I woke up in the middle of the night. Checking my watch I saw it was after one in the morning. I lay in bed and I re-lived the trial. I endeavoured to reason that the longer the jury remained out, the more they might have doubts regarding my guilt.

In the morning Peter relayed to me the news that a verdict had been reached. It had seemed an eternity but in essence it was only half a day after the closing arguments when I was escorted back into the court. The courtroom was hushed as the jury slowly filed in and took their seats. Their looks of unbending neutrality gave no hint of whether they deemed me guilty or innocent.

The judge punctured the silence.

"Ladies and gentlemen of the jury. Have you reached a verdict?" he asked in an imperious tone.

The foreman of the jury stood up and replied, "We have."

"Will the prisoner please rise for the verdict!" he ordered.

Peter motioned me to stand up and face the judge. I buckled at the knees and took his arm for support. I was trembling, feeling sick to my stomach. If they had found me guilty my life was effectively over.

"What is your verdict on the death of Billy Jenkins?" asked the judge.

"We find the defendant, Guy Harmon, not guilty of the manslaughter of Billy Jenkins," stated the foreman clearly.

At the sound of those words, I was overcome with emotion and collapsed into Peter's arms. I wanted to cry but the tears did not come. I covered my face with my hands, trying not to make a sound as my body shook. Taking several deep breaths, I lifted my head, straightened up and stood alongside Peter, as the judge continued.

"Guy Harmon you have been found not guilty of the manslaughter of Billy Jenkins by a jury of your peers. You are discharged."

The crowd in the gallery erupted with rapturous applause. The jury was dismissed and I found myself surrounded by my father, Sam and Georgie. They hugged and kissed me as the tears flowed freely. My mother was not present but my father said Georgie's father, who had been at the trial, had gone to a public phone to relay the good news.

As I celebrated my release I was approached by two police officers who informed me that Ruth Parkinson would be charged with the manslaughter of both Billy Jenkins and Jacob Wilson.

They went on to say that Georgie, Amy and I were accessories in that we helped Ruth dispose of Jacob Wilson's body and we would be required to appear at a committal hearing to determine if we should stand trial as well. The hearing was set down for the following week but the police asked that Georgie and I show them the location of Jacob

Wilson's body the next day. Peter intervened to say that he would represent us at the hearing. This new police intervention quickly flattened everyone's high spirits, but Peter eased our worries and brought some optimism back to the group by telling us he felt there was a good chance that we would not have to face any charges at all.

I returned home to a hero's welcome from my mother and a few close friends. She hugged and kissed me and the tears flowed once more. She stayed by my side all night, not wanting to share me with anyone else.

CHAPTER 23

A NEW BEGINNING

T he next day, two police cars, a police van and a coroner's van pulled up outside our house. Two plain clothes policeman knocked on the door and escorted, Georgie, my lawyer and me to one of the cars. This police presence had been kept a well-guarded secret so there were no reporters or inquisitive onlookers.

We travelled out to the abandoned gold mine where Georgie and I revealed to them the gravesite of Jacob Wilson. We were escorted from the mine while several burly policemen, with shovels in hand, dug up the remains. While this was going on, we travelled in the police van up to the waterfall and showed them the burnt-out shell of the car. When we returned, we took the detectives into the house and demonstrated by re-enactment what had taken place on that fateful night.

By this time the body had been exhumed and taken away in the coroner's van. Before they left, the detectives told us that we would be issued with summons to appear as witnesses at the committal hearing to decide whether Ruth should be tried for the manslaughter of Jacob Wilson, and disposing of his body and for the manslaughter of Billy Jenkins. When I asked if Georgie and I would be charged with burying Jacob Wilson's body and not telling the police, I was informed that this would be decided at the hearing. It seemed that, at long last, the end of this sorry saga was in sight.

At the hearing, the evidence was presented and Ruth was committed to stand trial. Most of the evidence against Ruth was circumstantial but the prosecution believed they had enough information to prove their case. Georgie, Amy and I were not charged but we were issued with an official warning.

At the trial, Georgie, Amy and I gave evidence and told our side of the story. Ruth was found not guilty of the manslaughter of Jacob Wilson because she was defending her daughter and me. However, she was found guilty of disposing of his body.

The prosecution argued that even though Georgie, Amy and I helped her bury the body, we were only sixteen at the time and Ruth as the adult was the person responsible.

On the charge of killing Billy Jenkins, she was convicted of manslaughter but her sentence was reduced because it could not be proven that Billy had not attacked Amy.

Amy would not testify against her mother and Ruth's defence counsel argued that Billy had attempted to rape Amy. After the verdicts were handed down, the judge said that he would sentence Ruth at a date to be determined. Peter told me that she might get a sentence of five to fifteen years or, with an extreme measure of good fortune, a suspended sentence. It could go either way. Irrespective of the outcome, she and Amy would no longer be a part of my life.

After the trial I had time to reflect on the behaviour and actions of Ruth and Amy. I concluded that Ruth had planned to kill her husband Ben Parkinson, but that the death of Jacob Wilson was a totally spontaneous happening—not planned. She had been trying to protect me from being shot. However, she did plan to kill Billy and implicate me. I believed that Amy did love me but not enough to put her mother in prison by telling the truth at the trial. Now it was over, I could begin a new chapter—hopefully one without the anguish and stress and, more relevant, one without the presence of either Ruth or Amy.

Ruth was sentenced to six months jail for the disposal of Jacob Wilson's body and implicating minors in her actions. For the death of Billy Jenkins she was given a sentence of ten years but this was reduced to five years because although the jury considered she had planned to kill Billy, they also considered that there were mitigating circumstances. She paid a lowly price for her direct involvement in two deaths; and that was not taking into consideration a third killing, the poisoning of her husband.

Even though the townspeople of Roxborough had, by and large, welcomed me back I found it impossible to forgive the many who had snubbed my parents and spread malicious rumours about me and my family. I decided that I would go to Hambledon to live and work in relative anonymity and without the overhanging stigma that accompanied the unfortunate deaths of two men, one of them a sometime friend. My family understood my reaction and agreed that it was the best course of action. For me to remain in my home town would mean dwelling forever beneath the clouds of embarrassment that lingered long after the trial, even though my innocence had been proved conclusively.

Two days later I departed for Hambledon with my meagre possessions. Of course, Mum had packed sheets, pillows, blankets, towels and even food. I'm sure she would have come with me to help me settle in but I assured her I could cope. Over time I had come to expect gestures such as these from her but I was taken aback when dad placed an envelope of money in my hand.

"Until you find a job you'll need money to pay the bills," he said gruffly.

"Thanks Dad!"

As we said goodbye outside my home, Georgie arrived. He stood to one side, head lowered, trying to conceal tears. I walked over to him and held out my hand.

"See you buddy!"

His bottom lip trembled as he shook my hand. I kissed Mum, shook Dad's hand and gave my little sister Jan a hug. I was about to hug Marty when he shoved out his hand.

As we shook hands I whispered in his ear, "Look after Georgie! He needs a friend."

He nodded. I waved goodbye as I slowly drove down the street.

After arriving and settling in at Hambledon, I spent a week trudging the streets looking for work. I soon found out that finding a job in the city was not an easy assignment and that sitting in my room every night after a fruitless day was depressing. I was truly thankful for the money Dad had given me.

I persevered and, for once, good fortune lined up on my side, because on the Wednesday of my second week in the city, I secured work in a motorcycle shop. As in Roxborough, my main task was to repair and detail motorcycles. I celebrated by dining out at a local Chinese restaurant on the Friday night. After the meal, I walked along the footpath back to my room, gazing at the city lights and the never-ending line of vehicles passing by.

The city was so different from Roxborough in so many ways—the constant noise of cars and machinery, the kaleidoscope of coloured lights and the variety of smells wafting on the night air. These smells, emanating from restaurants nearby, mixed with the car exhaust fumes overpowered my senses. Life in the city was a totally new experience for a country boy.

I paused and gazed up at the night sky through the sooty haze.

"Right at this moment someone in Roxborough is looking at those stars too," I told myself.

I laughed out loud.

"They'd be staring at a beautiful, clear night sky," I laughed again.

I continued strolling along the path. As I reached my apartment block, the wind swept along the path, flapping the collar of my jacket. Papers and rubbish swirled like tiny cyclones as dark clouds concealed the reassuring bright yellow face of the moon. Rain looked imminent, so I scampered into the building.

As I entered my one-room apartment my eyes swept the room. At one end was a tired, tattered, old sofa bed. I walked across to the far corner of the room where there was a kitchen sink alongside a stove and small refrigerator. I put the kettle on in preparation of making a cup of tea. I reached up to a cupboard above the sink for crockery and utensils. While the kettle boiled I put my jacket in the wardrobe and moved to the only window in my apartment. I peered out at the rain tumbling from the sky, on to the cheerless, gloomy building next door. Raindrops smacked rhythmically against the window pane, creating silvery patterns. I turned and surveyed the remainder of my apartment. A long time ago, the walls of the room had been white but were now grey with age and in dire need of a revitalising coat of paint. In many places, the paint was cracked and peeling and the ugly brown carpet on the floor was threadbare and stained. I was fortunate that at the far end of the room, there was a separate toilet and shower area. It was a depressing sight but for the moment it was all I could afford.

"It's not home or a palace but it'll do for now," I told myself.

I pulled out the sofa bed and placed a stack of records on my record player. I listened to the records with the sound turned down low. After a reviving cup of hot tea I lay on the sofa listening to the rain drumming on the window pane. I closed my eyes and drifted back to the summer of '64, so far gone now, but so close in my living memory. It was midnight when I finally fell asleep. I slept soundly—no nightmares, no lonely thoughts.

For the rest of the year, I worked during the week and spent most weekends travelling down to the coast or riding my bike along country roads. Mum wrote to me every month to enquire how I was getting on and kept me up-to-date with the gossip from Roxborough. Although Georgie didn't visit our house very often my mother continued to make the effort to ask him into the house for a drink and biscuits or cake whenever he passed by.

I still wrote to Sam. She wrote back but the tone of her letters had changed from girl who had declared her love for me to more like those of a friend. It didn't matter because I was happy to have her as a mate.

On three or four occasions I made the effort to return to Roxborough to visit my family and friends, especially Georgie. Life was full and rewarding and Mum and Dad were delighted that I was enjoying my time in Hambledon.

I spent Christmas and the New Year with my family. In the New Year, I took up painting again. I entered a few pieces in local art shows and although I didn't win any major prizes, I sold quite a number of my works, which was most satisfying. It was during this year that the letters from Sam began to lessen. Only rarely did she respond to any of my letters. On one of my visits to Roxborough, Georgie told me that she was in a serious relationship with a businessman. I was happy for her.

CHAPTER 24
MEMORIES

It had been ten years since the death of Ben Parkinson and I was sitting on the steps of my parents' house in Roxborough in company with Georgie. It was Saturday 28 December, 1974 and as we sat talking, my brother Marty and my sister Jan, came up the driveway in Marty's car. After school, Marty had joined the Air Force as a trainee mechanic. I only saw him at Christmas or on other family occasions. Even then, we didn't have much to say to each other. He had his own circle of friends. As with Marty, I only saw Jan on a few special occasions. She was at College studying to be a kindergarten teacher. They each grabbed a handful of parcels and bags from the car and approached Georgie and me.

"What's with you? Nothing to do?" smiled Jan.

"Hi Jan, Marty," said Georgie as they shook his hand.

"Georgie! You still hanging out with my horrible brother," Marty said with a huge grin.

"Yep!"

"Where you two been?" I asked, ignoring Marty's remarks.

"We've been shopping and catching up with old friends. We've come home to get our swimmers to go to the pool," answered Jan, putting her parcels down on the steps.

Marty, Jan and their friends never swam at the Waterhole. Most of them didn't have bikes to ride and it was easier to go to the local pool.

On a whim, Georgie and I decided to visit Ruth's old place, not to reminisce, but to see if the demons that had haunted each of us still wielded any power. I was worried about how I would react after all these years. I slowly drove up to the house. We had been informed by townsfolk that no-one had lived there since the departure of Ruth and Amy. Even from a distance we could see that it was in urgent need of repairing. The roof was missing several sheets of iron, the paint on the walls had almost disappeared and the railing on the veranda was threatening to topple into the garden bed directly below. The path and the house surrounds were overgrown with grass and weeds. We stood in front of the house, the miserable scene before us re-kindling a kaleidoscope of conflicting emotions.

"It has changed, hasn't it?" I said huskily.

We ploughed our way through the undergrowth and stepped onto the veranda.

"Be careful!" I warned, "Some of the floor boards are missing."

We peered in through the dirty, broken windows that were obscured by dust and cobwebs; however, neither of us wanted to venture inside.

"Do you want to go up to the mine?" I asked. "We can stay in the car."

"No! There's nothing I want to see there," Georgie answered, "unless you want to go."

"Nah!"

I was surprised at how calm I had remained in visiting the scene of that horrific crime. More surprising was that not once did I think of Ruth and Amy. Hopefully, time would wreak its own conspiracy to dim all memories of that incident.

I woke with the morning light flooding the room and after a leisurely breakfast, walked down the street to ask Georgie if he wanted to go swimming with Sam and me at the Waterhole. Sam was home for Christmas and had come over to see me. It was another steaming hot day—far too hot to be sitting around at home and sweltering. I found Georgie playing with his dog in the backyard. He still lived with his parents and still worked at the sawmill. I felt sorry for him because although he had some close friends, he didn't have a girlfriend. I felt this was a genuine pity, because he was such a kind and generous person.

"Hey, Georgie! Wanna come out to the Waterhole with Sam and me?"

"Yeah! Can I bring Troy?"

"No worries," I replied.

As Georgie walked his bike to my home, Sam told me that she was now a veterinarian working in Benton, a large town to the west of Roxborough. She was to be married in the New Year but neither Georgie nor I had been invited to the wedding. Sam said that it was going to be a small, intimate wedding at Benton with only family present.

"I hope you understand, Guy," she said, "I don't want you to be upset about not being invited. You are still my dearest and closest friend."

"That's fine, Sam," I said. Considering her feelings towards me and the fact we had once been lovers I had not expected an invitation.

It had been many years since the three of us had been to the Waterhole together and we remained unsure as to what may await us upon our return. Maybe the trail was blocked or the Waterhole had dried up. Nonetheless, it had been an integral part of our lives as youngsters and the curiosity factor alone made it a worthwhile journey. With Sam on my bike and Georgie on his, we roared up the dirt track to the swimming hole. Troy sat precariously on Georgie's lap as we rode along the track which was rougher and narrower than I had remembered. Odd, I thought, that my perception of the past had played a trick on my memory—or so it seemed.

The Waterhole was fenced off so we parked our bikes and completed our trek on foot.

"It hasn't changed," exclaimed Sam in delight when we reached it.

Georgie and I stripped down to our shorts while Sam peeled off her top and shorts to reveal a blue bikini. Both Georgie and I whistled in appreciation. Sam, ever the little girl, giggled at our responses.

"Last one in is a rotten egg," she yelled as we raced to the water's edge and plunged in.

Troy didn't want to miss out on all the fun so he jumped up and down on the bank, yapping loudly. Georgie pulled him into the water and he dog paddled for a while before dragging himself out. He shook himself violently and then proceeded to race up and down the bank. Georgie played with Troy while Sam and I swam and cavorted in the water. It was though, fleetingly, we were sixteen again—happy, full of fun and with not a solitary care in the world.

We lounged under a tree after our swim and recalled our times at the Waterhole. I didn't mention Billy but I did reminisce about happier times.

"Georgie! Do you remember the times we drank your father's beer and smoked my father's cigarettes?"

Georgie laughed, then scrambled to his feet and went to his bag. Triumphantly, he held up a bottle of beer. We laughed. We took it in turns in having a swig but we didn't drink much because the beer was lukewarm.

"Do you remember the time you thrashed Hank Jones?" he asked with a huge grin.

"Yeah! Whatever happened to him?" I asked. I'd almost forgotten about 'Hank the Tank'.

"He was killed in a bar room fight in Shackleton. He said something disrespectful to a woman and her boyfriend pulled a knife and stabbed him," Georgie said.

"He just never learned to keep his mouth shut, did he?"

"Nope!"

For a while we sat staring into the water. I thought about Ivan and the great times we had all enjoyed way back in 1964.

"Have you heard from Ivan?" I asked, as we stretched out on the grass. I had not seen Ivan since he left school.

"All I know is that he became one of those people who go to court to help others."

"A lawyer?"

"Yeah! I heard that he has a wife and three kids."

"I'm happy for him," I said. "He was a good mate!"

We sat and chatted for a lengthy time, perhaps two hours, recalling those enchanted times we'd had together when we were young. I glanced up at the sky and remarked, "We'd better get going. The sun's setting and I don't want to be riding in the dark on this track."

I helped Sam to her feet and we took one last look at the Waterhole. A warm, soft breeze had replaced the heat of the day as we slowly made our way home. The shadows had lengthened and I could smell the scent of eucalyptus blossoms drifting on the evening air. To me this was the best time of the day—the earthy smells of the dry grass and leaves, the breeze caressing the body and the quiet stillness of the forest, interrupted occasionally by the call of native birds. It was a lullaby soothing the tired body. Spending time in the country re-energised me and as always, I had a heavy heart when I had to leave Roxborough and return to the city.

CHAPTER 25

GEORGIE'S NEW LOVE

When I returned to Hambledon I moved into a new apartment to begin the next chapter of my life. For a time I did consider moving back to Roxborough but I wanted to paint and Hambledon gave me more opportunities to display and sell my art. I began painting in earnest and I channelled all my free time and energy into it.

Over time, art became my primary focus and at a solo exhibition where I sold most of my paintings, I met Chris, who became my manager. My career as an artist thrived and Chris gradually persuaded me to make it my full-time profession. With Chris as my manager I soon became well known in art circles and made a host of new friends, both personal and professional.

I often visited my parents but when Dad retired and sold his store, they moved to the coast to live. After they moved I only went back to Roxborough about once a year, primarily to see Georgie.

Georgie wrote to me about his new girlfriend, Susan—his only girlfriend. She was a recent divorcée and had moved to Roxborough with her young daughter. I was happy for Georgie. At long last he had a companion to share his life. Letters that followed were full of news of their relationship and how thrilled he was. He even mentioned the possibility of marriage. Strangely though, his last letter to me didn't mention Susan at all.

Shortly after, Georgie's mother wrote to me and her letter completed a more rounded picture of Susan Brown. Apparently, Susan regarded Georgie as a means to an end. Susie, as Georgie always called her, arrived in town with her ten-year-old daughter and set up residence at the local caravan park. She discovered that Georgie lived with his parents and had a permanent job at the sawmill. Even though Georgie wasn't paid a huge wage he was a diligent saver and over time managed to establish a healthy bank balance. He had a battered old car, rarely took a vacation and still lived with his mum and dad. Virtually the only money he did spend was either on his parents or his pets.

Upon learning this information Susie had ensured that she and Georgie became acquainted. At first, he took her out for evenings and bought her small gifts but gradually she began to take advantage of his trusting nature, asking for and receiving larger and more expensive gifts.

She told Georgie that she wanted to rent a small house but didn't have the money to pay the weekly rate because she couldn't find a job. Poor Georgie, ever-willing to help another human being, set her up in the house and paid her weekly rent. As he became more involved and attached to her, Georgie spent more and more of his hard-earned money catering for her needs. Pat Henderson said that she and her husband Tom didn't intervene because Georgie was so happy and he truly loved Susie.

Tom became suspicious when he overheard townspeople talking about Susie and how she was ripping this guy off and taking his money. He went around to her house and found that Susie was not the only one living in the place. Another couple lived there as well. None of them had jobs and Tom soon realised that Susie had made no effort to find employment. Mrs Henderson told me that she and her husband were always puzzled why an attractive young woman would take an interest in Georgie—unless, of course, she had a hidden motive. They were prepared to give Susan the benefit of the doubt but to allay any fears Mr Henderson went to the local bank and asked the manager, a friend of his, to inform him if and when Georgie tried to withdraw any large sums of money.

Matters came to a head when Susie told Georgie that her mother needed an operation that would cost three thousand dollars and she didn't have the money. She told Georgie that if her mother didn't have the operation she was in grave danger of being left crippled and she would have to move in with her mother and care for her. That meant leaving Roxborough—and him. Of course Georgie didn't want her to leave so he went to the bank to withdraw three thousand dollars from his account.

The bank manager told Georgie that he would have to wait until the next day for such a large amount. This gave the manager time to relay the news to Tom Henderson. When Tom explained to Georgie that he knew of his intention to withdraw three thousand dollars, he asked Georgie why he needed such a large sum.

Georgie repeated to his parents the story that Susie had fabricated. Georgie said that she was a wreck—sobbing and hysterical—and he wanted to help her. Tom Henderson quietly visited Susan Brown that night without Georgie's knowledge. He gave her two choices: she could repay Georgie and leave the town, or he, Tom Henderson, would report her scheme to the police. When she claimed that she truly loved Georgie, Tom challenged her to prove it by refusing to accept any further money and gifts from him.

She packed up and left in the middle of the night, leaving Georgie heartbroken and out of pocket. The police were later to reveal Susan Brown as a scam artist who travelled from town to town, preying on naïve, gullible men.

I visited Georgie to help him recover from his heartbreak. He really didn't care about the money but Susie was his first and probably last 'girlfriend'. This unfortunate experience was to have far-reaching consequences, both for Georgie and all members of the Henderson family. Mrs Henderson told me of her concerns for Georgie when I visited.

"I worry about Georgie," she said. "What might happen to him when Tom and I die? Who will look after him? I know his brothers and sister would but they are married and have their own families to care for."

"I'm sure they'll step forward to make sure he'll be okay," I answered.

"I know, but my concern is how he will react when we pass away. Tom and I are the main supports of his life and I hope that when that time comes he won't do anything drastic. You know . . . have a breakdown or even worse. It bothers me."

"Mrs Henderson . . . ," I said, holding her hand gently.

"Call me Pat . . ."

"Okay! Pat! I will always be around to look after Georgie so you really don't have to worry. Okay?" I tried to assure her because I understood how she felt.

"Thank you Guy. That makes me feel better."

Georgie was never vindictive towards Susan but neither was he the same man after she departed Roxborough. He never mentioned her name or made any attempt to get to know other women. His parents became his life's focus.

On one of my yearly pilgrimages to Roxborough, Georgie informed me that Sam was no longer married and was planning to return to the town as a vet. There was a horse stud near town where she had been offered a job. That meant that Sam could renew her friendship with Georgie and after the episode with Susan, he was never more in need of a close friend. I never, ever considered renewing my emotional relationship with Sam. She was a friend and that was that.

CHAPTER 26

THE PRESENT—1984

I n 1984, twenty years after the summer of 1964 I was a thirty-six-year-old artist, unattached and still residing in Hambledon. There are occasions when fate intervenes in our daily lives, setting in motion a sequence of events whose outcome we could never have foreseen. These events were branded indelibly in my memory, and I was destined to re-live them frequently over the next two decades. However, it is true that time heals all wounds.

I sat up with a start. The silence of the night was disturbed by my heart pounding against my rib cage. After waking in the darkness, I fumbled for the bedside lamp. I switched it on and squinted at the clock face. It was a blur so I rubbed the sleep from my eyes and tried again. It was three in the morning.

I let out a silent curse and struggled out of bed, looked at the time again and decided instantly that sleep was no longer an option. I made a pot of coffee and sat on the edge of the bed, pondering another sleep-deprived night. Even though time had healed most of the wounds that had been inflicted on me, there were occasions when I couldn't sleep and this was one of those times.

I'd had been involved in many relationships with women over the years but because of Amy I had remained distrustful and wary. As a result, all my attempts at romantic liaisons were, at best, half-hearted and all had eventually failed.

I looked at my appearance in the bathroom mirror. Despite my unkempt hair and sleepy appearance I considered myself 'not bad' for a man in his mid-thirties. Sure, I had developed a slight paunch and I had put on a few extra kilos but most people thought I was only twenty-nine or thirty. My hair was receding a little but overall, despite the adversities in my life, I had weathered well. I didn't bother with a shave but had a quick shower before dressing.

Fifteen minutes later I was on my motorbike, roaring along the expressway out of the city. The rush of the cold morning air against my face as I leaned forward on the bike, helped shake the cobwebs. I had taken this trip many times over the years. As the sun rose above the distant horizon to greet me, I turned and, reluctantly, headed back in the general direction of the city lights.

Back in my apartment I was able to go back to bed for a few hours of much needed sleep, before preparing for the day ahead.

In the early afternoon light I gazed silently at the sprawling metropolis below the large window of my apartment—dirty streets, an endless stream of cars and tall, grotesque buildings enveloped in the summer heat haze and the sooty, smoky pollution of a city. Glaring down from a cloudless sky, a savage, brutal sun, struggled desperately to extinguish the forest of air-conditioned blocks of steel and glass. To me, cities were arrogant—they insinuated themselves on the environment and stamped their authority without regard for anyone or anything. They provided a haven for a sprawling jungle of hustlers with their illegitimate egos, and a never-ending throng of busy people always on the move. To some, cities were lonely, unemotional places. There were times when I retreated happily to the quiet surroundings of the countryside simply to escape the urban maze and allow myself time to gather my thoughts.

"A penny for your thoughts."

I turned to face a delightful young woman holding a glass of champagne in an outstretched hand. I took it and smiled wistfully at her.

"Sorry Emma!" I said, glancing briefly around the room.

Emma and a small group of my friends faced me, champagne glasses in hand. I had been so preoccupied with my thoughts I had completely forgotten their presence.

"A toast!" she exclaimed. "A toast to Guy's exhibition tonight. May he sell lots of paintings."

"And make lots of money," added my manager, Chris.

They all laughed as they raised their glasses and drank while I watched in amusement. I gulped down my drink and joined them.

"Look at him," cried Mandy, an artist friend. "He's good looking, he's successful but he hasn't settled down with a woman. Why not Guy? You're thirty-six years-old. You need to find a girl and marry and have a family."

Andrew, a close friend, shushed her and gave her an icy stare.

"It's a decision Guy will make when he's ready, Mandy, so leave him alone."

Before I could answer, John, another artist, interrupted.

"Guy lives in the past. He plays sixties music and watches those old movies . . . you know . . . the good old days."

"He's a romantic," Chris murmured, "and there's nothing wrong with that."

She smiled and I grinned back at her and made a face. I shook my head.

"I hadn't really given much thought to a permanent relationship. Maybe in time I will."

Emma grabbed my arm, stared into my eyes and fluttered her eyelashes.

"What about poor, little, old me?" she winked suggestively.

Andrew laughed. "You'd eat him alive. Leave him alone. You're embarrassing him."

"Yeah! Leave me alone," I said. "Let's get off this subject. Who would like another drink?"

I covered my awkwardness with a fake grin and moved to the bar. The group laughed and I quickly refilled their glasses. The conversation shifted to idle chit-chat about the usual mundane things.

As I composed myself I observed closely my circle of friends. In the centre of the group was a picture of elegance, a slim body encased in a smooth, silky, cocktail dress, her long dark hair neatly framing a tanned face.

This was Chris, my manager, who also happened to be Andrew's manager. She was always on the move . . . talking on the phone or racing around the city looking after her list of clients. She dressed like a business executive and sometimes sounded like a pretentious, upmarket person but really, after I got to know her, I discovered she was the exact opposite. Chris was down-to-earth and very understanding. I liked her because she was supportive of me at all times. Perhaps if she had not been married, I might have been interested.

She turned and noticed I was detached from the group, looking vague and distant. She understood me perfectly and knew I needed time by myself.

She announced in an assertive voice, "Time to go friends. Guy needs his beauty sleep before the exhibition . . . Up! Up! Let's go!"

She motioned to the group and herded them towards the door. They were still engrossed in conversation and barely had time to turn and say goodbye as they left. Chris was the last to leave and blew a kiss as she closed the door behind her.

I smiled and acknowledged the group with a nonchalant wave before moving across to the entertainment system. The sounds of sixties music filtered through the room as I gathered the glasses and bottles and tidied up. Finally I grabbed the handful of letters from the desktop and slumped in my favourite chair. I thumbed my way through the bills and other miscellaneous paraphernalia until I spotted a small envelope, handwritten and addressed to me. I recognised her neat compact hand. The letter was from Sam. I ripped open the envelope and took out what appeared to be a newspaper clipping and a letter.

It read:

> *'Dear Guy,*
> *I'm sorry to be a bearer of tragic news. I think it best if I pass on some sad information to you in person, rather than in a letter. I believe it will be easier for both of us if we were to meet in person. I shall be at your exhibition on the sixteenth and I will explain the newspaper clipping and the bad news.*
> *Love,*
> *Sam.'*

She was going to be at the exhibition tonight. I picked up the clipping but as I read it, my hands began to tremble and the clipping slipped through my fingers onto the floor.

Tentatively I picked it up and tried once more to read it. My heart felt like a live grenade, ready to explode, as I focused on the headlines . . . "HUMAN REMAINS FOUND IN MINE SHAFT".

I put my hand to my temple in a helpless gesture. Another body in the mine, but who could it be? Sam would not have sent the note to me unless she thought it held some significance for me. Surely it wasn't Georgie! True, I hadn't heard from him in two months, but no, it couldn't be him because his parents would have contacted me.

I was trembling, so I went to the table and poured myself a good sized glass of whisky. My hands shook as I downed it in two swallows. I sat down and continued reading. I had difficulty reading the words but managed to read on. The article said that the skeleton of a male person had been found in an abandoned mine tunnel near the town. There was evidence of foul play and police were treating the case as a homicide. Fear pricked me again.

I dropped the clipping onto the table and poured another drink. I collapsed back in the chair, slowly sipping the alcohol as I tried to compose myself. I wanted to know the tragic news. The music had stopped. I gazed at the portrait on the wall of my apartment. It was of Sam as a teenager, a labour of love that I had painted from a small black and white photo she had given me. There was another portrait of her in my new exhibition. I glanced at my watch.

"Oh shit!" I said, "I'd better get going."

The opening of any art exhibition of mine was always a pleasure for me but there was also an element of pain. I was expected to mingle with the critics and art-loving public and talk about my work enthusiastically. I wanted people to enjoy my work but I really didn't want to talk about it. I shunned large crowds and, as a boy with country roots, I loved peace and quiet.

However, I knew that to sell my art I had to endure these functions. The exhibition was a qualified success and it was well received by the critics and the patrons, much to Chris' delight.

"Congratulations, Guy. It's a huge success!" she gushed, kissing me enthusiastically on the cheek.

I managed a half-hearted smile that wasn't very convincing.

"You don't look too happy. Anything wrong?" she asked.

"Nah! I've got a few things on my mind . . . It's personal but I'm fine . . . really I'm fine . . . Thanks for your help with the exhibition, Chris. Much appreciated."

"Can I do anything for you?"

"Nah! Look I'm okay! Don't concern yourself. Enjoy the night. It's no big deal."

When Chris realised that I wasn't going to divulge the cause of my touchiness, she excused herself and moved away to engage a patron in animated discussion. I moved to the back of the room to be by myself. On the back wall, in a corner, well away from the other paintings was my latest portrait of Sam. It was not for sale—at any price.

As I approached, I noticed a woman standing in front of it, her back to me so I couldn't see her face. She was slim, with long, blonde hair tumbling down her shoulders and as I moved closer, she heard my footsteps and turned to face me. My heart stopped for a brief moment. It was Sam, my dear childhood friend. She was still the second most beautiful girl I had ever met. The years had been good to her. Her features were not flawed; she was almost wrinkle-free and with a skin that remained unblemished. She had the body of a twenty-year-old.

We stood stock-still, as if frozen, each unable to move or say anything, mentally turning back the hands of time. After she had married I hadn't seen her for many years, nor had I even heard from her except for the occasional Christmas card. Sam uttered a heart-wrenching sob as we embraced. The memories of our time together came flooding back as we held each other, completely unaware of the onlookers who had gathered around us.

Realising we had attracted a curious audience; I took Sam's hand and led her out on to a balcony.

"It's so good to see you, Guy," she said warmly, wrapping her arms around me once again and kissing me on the cheek.

"I can't believe it! After all these years . . . Sam! I don't know what to say. I still can't believe my eyes," I stuttered, my voice choking.

We sat down, trying to ignore the clamour of the city in the background—the incessant, harsh din of car horns mingling with the constant growling and complaining engine noises, and the dazzling, flickering lights. I tried to settle my nerves by gazing up at the tranquil, moonlit sky. I had so many questions to ask.

"I suppose you're wondering what I have to say about the newspaper clipping," Sam said.

She gently squeezed my hand and tears pricked the corners of her eyes. I prepared myself for the bad news.

"Guy! You see . . . the body they found in the mine behind Ruth's place was Jim Jenkins."

This was a shock. I was stunned. There was an awkward silence as I came to grips with this totally unexpected news. This was a genuine bombshell . . . Jim Jenkins. But why? Who killed him and why was he placed in that mine? Jim was a hot head who had a violent temper and over the years he would have made plenty of enemies but was it a co-incidence he was placed in the same mine as Jacob Wilson? I glanced at Sam.

She brushed away a tear, paused and took a deep breath.

"Guy! The bad news is that he was killed by Georgie."

I was speechless. I couldn't comprehend this news at all. Georgie was a gentle giant who was incapable of hurting anyone. How could this have happened? If Georgie killed him, Jim Jenkins must have done something terrible to Georgie.

"What happened?" I asked, fearing the worst.

"About three years ago, Jim retired. He was renowned as a drunk and a womaniser. Since Billy's death he had continued drinking in a big way. It got so out of control that he was forced into an early retirement from the police force. Georgie told his parents that he was driving home one night when a person stumbled onto the road in front of his car. It was Jim Jenkins, intoxicated as usual. He was hit by Georgie's car. Jim died on the roadway. When Georgie recognised Jim, he panicked and took his body out to the mine and buried him in the tunnel," Sam explained hesitantly.

It was easy to understand why Georgie panicked. Jim was an ex-policeman and Georgie had a history of enmity with his son Billy that stretched back more than eighteen years. It would be a simple matter for the police to claim that Georgie deliberately ran Jim down, to exact revenge after all this time.

That's how Georgie would have looked at it. It was an accident and Georgie was not the type of person to seek revenge. To have this happen to such a harmless, sweet person was not bloody fair. I was sure the burial of Jacob Wilson in the mine influenced Georgie to hide Jim's body there as well, for it was the only point of reference Georgie had to guide his actions. Sam continued her story.

"Two teenage boys discovered the remains of Jim's body while poking around in the mine. Georgie had placed it there a year ago. It must have been a living hell for Georgie, knowing he had killed someone and trying to keep it a secret. He told no-one, not even you, me or his parents. Jim Jenkins lived alone and when he disappeared the local police simply concluded that he had left town on a whim. There was no evidence or reason for them to think otherwise. Jenkins had no close friends and being the town drunk he wasn't really missed by anyone."

"What did the police do when they found the body?" I asked.

"Evidence indicated that he had been killed elsewhere and then taken and hidden in the mine. They started interviewing all those who might have had a reason to harm Jim. Georgie was one of the first they interviewed—or interrogated—because some person or persons informed the police about the incident with Billy from all that time ago. Naturally, poor Georgie cracked under the pressure and told them what had happened and they arrested him for murder."

"Surely if it was an accident they wouldn't arrest him for murder. He might be in trouble for burying the body, but not murder."

Sam continued. "The police didn't want to believe him. Even though they had no real evidence they were determined to charge Georgie with murder. The fact that he was a little slow intellectually was also a contributing factor."

I was fuming. This was so typical. The police had forged a mistrust in Georgie back in 1964 by refusing to believe him and they had rekindled that mistrust nearly twenty years later, again by refusing to believe him.

I said angrily, "They had no case. They had to know that Georgie was just a child in a man's body. Georgie should have been set free. Poor Georgie. He would have been 'out of his mind'; and what about his parents? Their worst nightmare comes true. It stinks!"

I stood and leaned over the balcony railing with my head slumped on my chest, trying to come to terms with this dreadful news. Sam joined me and put an arm around my shoulder. She lowered her voice to a hoarse whisper.

"They kept Georgie in jail overnight. When his parents visited him, he was a broken man, shattered. The police had convinced Georgie he was guilty. They told him he was going to a prison where the inmates would make his life hell. Tom Henderson told Georgie not to worry because he had not meant to kill Jim Jenkins; but Georgie believed what the police had already told him."

"Bastards! I hope those cops rot in hell!" I spat.

At this point, Sam broke down and bowed her head, sobbing, as I tried to comfort her. She steadied herself and faced me, tears flowing freely down her cheeks.

"It was all too much for Georgie, Guy. That night he used his belt to hang himself in his cell."

It was though I had been hit by a lightning bolt—I was numb with shock. I felt a despairing scream rising from deep inside me, rushing to the surface as I leaned over the railing. I stared up at the sky, clenched my fists and cried, "No! No! No!" as I pounded the railing. It was so unjust. One of my dearest childhood friends was dead. This was the worst news possible. I was devastated. I sobbed—great wracking sobs that came from deep within, shaking my shoulders and making me gasp for breath.

"His parents didn't want to tell you over the phone so I said that I would come and tell you face-to-face. I am so sorry."

Sam put her arms around me and held me close as we stood on the balcony, grieving for a friend who had been a carefree companion as well as my staunchest ally in that fateful summer of 1964. Georgie's death was as unnecessary as it was tragic. There was no doubt—bad luck had followed us since that ominous meeting with Ruth and Amy. It was as if their entry into our lives had unleashed a diabolical curse.

CHAPTER 27

JUST A MATTER OF TIME

S am and I travelled back to Roxborough together to attend Georgie's funeral. It was a poignant, melancholy journey to lay to rest a dear friend and spend some time with his grieving parents. Memories flooded back as Sam stopped her car on the summit of the mountain and we looked down onto the town.

In all the years I had been making the trip back home, Roxborough had changed very little. The town square, the church steeple and the Karinya River winding its way through the valley were easily recognisable guides in the landscape. I could see the track leading up to the Waterhole, the sawmill where Georgie had worked and the main street of the town. We stood beside the car, recalling our teenage years. Sam's arm was around my shoulders and she rested her head against mine.

I felt a bittersweet mix of emotions as we made our way down to the township and drove along the main street to the town square. Before attending the funeral we strolled once more along the sundrenched streets. We stopped at the café for a drink. It hadn't altered much over the years. Sadly though, my father's general store had been replaced by a supermarket. With the heaviest of hearts we drove to the church for the service as dark, storm clouds drifted in from the north, accompanied by a cool breeze. As we entered the church the heavens opened up, mirroring our own feelings of sadness and grief.

Sam and I sat near Georgie's family, a few friends and my family, to bid our sad farewells on this wet, windy, summer's afternoon. Ivan did not attend. His absence was disappointing because he had been another of Georgie's closest friends all those years ago. I would have welcomed his presence too, since I hadn't seen or heard from him since he left school. In many ways I felt Ivan was lucky he had not been involved in the tragic events of 1964 because his upbringing and faith would have produced in him an ongoing struggle to come to terms with what happened.

Inside the church, I choked back a sob as I sat down next to Sam. I closed my eyes and felt the indescribable pain of losing a dear friend. In my mind's eye I could hear Georgie's inimitable laughter and see his smiling face as I sat, clutching Sam's hand. Consumed by these thoughts I eventually opened my eyes but tears clouded my vision. For a moment everything looked as though it was shrouded in a mist. Slowly the mist faded and objects in the church became visible. Sam squeezed my hand again.

Sam and I spent a couple of hours with Pat and Tom Henderson after Georgie had been put to rest. We reminisced about the good times as well as discussing some of the newsworthy events that had occurred in Roxborough over the past twenty years. Georgie had doted on his parents and looked after them over the years. He had been a true friend and a wonderful son.

Georgie's mother told us that the property Ruth and Amy had called home had been sold to the local timber company for logging purposes. This was good news because it meant the mine would not be re-opened. After the discovery of Jim Jenkins' body, the company had used explosives to block the entrance to the mine. The mine's closure could be interpreted as a divine signal from the universe. Now we were free at last and could get on with our lives.

After leaving the Hendersons, Sam and I returned to her home where I was staying for the duration of my visit. Before we turned in for the night we chatted about life after Roxborough. Sam opened up and talked about her marriage. Her ex-husband was a wealthy businessman, who worked his way to the top by being mean-spirited and aggressive. Just like an adult version of Billy Jenkins, he could lay on the charm or just as easily lose his temper when he didn't get his own way. As he became more successful, he changed into a contemptible and narrow-minded human being. Vulnerable, Sam had fallen prey to his charming manner and he had swept her off her feet. However, after they were married, she swiftly came to realise she was little more to him than a pawn in his ambitious plans—someone he could place on public display and use to his advantage in his business dealings. The charm and sparkle quickly became tarnished and the marriage ended in a nasty divorce after Sam discovered that her husband was having an affair. After this experience she had shied away from long-term relationships with men.

Sam and I had always been the best of friends. We had been very close and I always felt that if I hadn't fallen in love with Amy I would have married her. Losing Amy broke my heart but now I needed to acknowledge the healing process and get on with my life. Meeting Sam again reinforced my love for her and I decided that I wanted to spend the rest of my life with her. I spent time with Sam over the next few weeks and, thankfully, she felt as I did.

When I finally asked her to marry me we were standing on the veranda of her home. I squeezed her hand tightly and looked uneasily into her eyes as I popped the question. I need not have worried because she clapped her hands enthusiastically and smiled happily before answering, "Yes!"

Looking up into my eyes she grinned mischievously and said, "I've been in love with you since I was a little girl."

She embraced me and I kissed her tenderly on the cheek. Arm in arm, we went outside into the garden and gazed up at a cloudless sky, bathing in the soft glow of the moon smiling down from the heavens. As we stood side by side, my eyes drank in the beauty of the night sky and the smiling, radiant face of the young woman by my side.

The soft fragrance of timber burning on the warm night air tickled my senses and revived pleasant memories of my time in Roxborough.

The storm clouds had disappeared, taking with them the burdens and troubles of the past twenty years.

I had come to realise during this time, that the most difficult journey in life is the one that leads to truth. My life had resembled a roller coaster ride with many ups and downs. However, standing in this idyllic garden setting and with Sam in my embrace, I understood that I was now ready for another embrace—that of a new beginning. I turned and cupped her face gently in my hands. Gazing into her eyes, I kissed her again and again.

She smiled and murmured softly, "I always knew it would be just a matter of time."